Praise f

"Full of action, this is a compelling, realistic, and exciting thriller."

—*Kirkus Reviews*

"Determinedly multi-ethnic [and] fast-paced ... the book will draw reluctant readers who enjoy action and adventure."

—*Booklist*

"The writing is edgy and filled with descriptions of futuristic technology and a world spinning out of control ... entertaining, credible, scary, and memorable."

—*VOYA*

"Shocking and unrelenting—Kinch delivers a blistering, no-holds-barred tale of a dystopian future that feels all too real."

—Arthur Slade, winner of the
Governor General Award for
The Hunchback Assignments

THE FIRES OF
NEW
SUN

THE FIRES OF

NEW SUN

A Blending Time Novel

MICHAEL KINCH

flux™

Woodbury, Minnesota

First Edition
First Printing, 2012

Book format by Bob Gaul
Cover design by Kevin R. Brown
Cover art: Sword © iStockphoto.com/sunexpo
Editing by Ed Day

Flux, an imprint of Llewellyn Worldwide Ltd.

Library of Congress Cataloging-in-Publication Data
Kinch, Michael P.
   The fires of New SUN: a Blending time novel/Michael Kinch.—1st ed.
      p. cm.—(Blending time ; [2])
   Summary: Although the Nswibe refugees find safe haven at a New SUN outpost, infighting and treachery make them ill-equipped to fight off a 'gade attack and Jaym, Reya, and D'Shay must work to reunite the factions before mounting a daring counterattack.
   ISBN 978-0-7387-3076-9
[1. Science fiction. 2. Violence—Fiction. 3. Survival—Fiction. 4. Friendship—Fiction. 5. Africa—Fiction.] I. Title.
PZ7.K56532Fir 2012
[Fic]--dc23

                                                        2011035527

                                          Flux
                            Llewellyn Worldwide Ltd.
                             2143 Wooddale Drive
                            Woodbury, MN 55125-2989
                                www.fluxnow.com

                    Printed in the United States of America

For Margie

SUN BLENDING PROGRAM

The Blending concept was conceived by a Global Alliance think-tank called SUN (Society to Unify Nationalities). SUN's goal was to aid the people of Africa who had been devastated by several disasters: the Monkey Pox-III epidemic of 2049; the famines and resulting Pan-Af wars of the 2050s; and finally the Great Solar Flare of 2058. Africa took the brunt of the Flare. The resulting bombardment of gamma rays damaged Africans' chromosome-11. This caused aborted and malformed fetuses, often referred to as "scramblers." Scientists predicted African populations could become extinct within a century. But in 2062, Alliance geneticists discovered the C-11 damage was a recessive trait. Therefore a non-African paired with an African could produce viable offspring. The Global Alliance funded SUN's Blending Program in 2067, and non-African youth were immediately recruited for the African experiment. The program continues despite reduced funding and continuing strife in Africa.

—*GlobaPedia: fltt.GlobPed.sunprog.swz*

THE PEOPLE

Jaym: S'teener from the NorthAm Corridor / Race: Caucasian / Assigned: Africa for SUN Colonist Program / MOS: Blender/Skill: Hydro-Tech.

Reya: MexiCal s'teener immigrant from NorthAm Corridor Refugee Camp / Race: Hispanic / Assigned: Africa for SUN Colonist Program / MOS: Blender / Skill: Med-Tech.

D'Shay: S'teener from the NorthAm Corridor / Race: Af-Am / Assigned: Africa for SUN Colonist Program / MOS: Blender / Skill: Carpentry.

Lingana: Blender match for Jaym / Age 17 / Resident of Nswibe, Chewena, Africa / Race: African / MOS: C-11 Damaged Blender Candidate.

Giambo: Older brother of Lingana from Nswibe / Occupation: Quarryman / Leader of Nswibe refugees.

Nakhoza: African girlfriend of D'Shay / Former SUN lieutenant / Base: Wananelu, Chewena, Africa / Status: AWOL / Fled with D'Shay from Wananelu.

Bettina: SUN scout / Volunteer from SouthAm / Base: Mozambique, Africa / Status: MIA / Last assignment: North Highland forest villages / May have joined New SUN rebel forces.

Annja: A pioneer of SUN's Blending Program / Birthplace: The former Netherlands / The leader of the New SUN rebels in the Blue Mountains of Chewena.

Tarkin: Blender from Australia / Defected to New SUN / Annja Van Eijk's second-in-command at Outpost-1 in the Blue Mountains.

Daku: Blender from the Warlpiri Group of Indigenous Australians / Friend of Tarkin.

Xian: Blender from China / Electronics expert at New SUN Post-1.

THE PLACES

NorthAm Confederation: The area of the former United States north of MexiCal and south of Canada. NorthAm is a confederation of independent regions, or *Sectors*.

The Corridor: Also known as the *Seattle Sector* of NorthAm.

MexiCal: Old Mexico and the southwest regions of the former United States. Sparsely populated due to desertification since the 2030s.

Chewena: Country in S.E. Africa. Capital City is Wananelu.

Wananelu (wun-AHN-uh-loo): Capital city of Chewena.

Nswibe (n-SWIB-uh): Home village of Lingana and Giambo in Chewena.

Ezondwei (ez-OND-way): A major village near the New SUN headquarters in the foothills of Chewena's Blue Mountains.

1

THE CROSSING

The Zomba Savannah

The plateau from Wananelu, on the east, to the Kings
Range (the so-called "Blue Mountains"), to the west,
is a vast savannah of approximately 150,000 square
kilometers. At an altitude of 1,000 meters, the daytime
temperatures soar while the nights bring killing frosts.
Lack of water has kept the plateau uninhabitable, and
those attempting to cross it can only do so on treacherous
unpaved tracks. A plan to lay tarmac for an east-west
highway crossing the savannah was terminated by savage
battles of the Pan-Af Wars.

—*A. E. and R. S. Smit. "The Topography of Southeast
Africa." (Cape Town, 2061)*

Jaym mopped sweat from his forehead and glanced at
Lingana limping beside him. Her face was drawn, tight
with pain. His guts cramped to see her like this. Here they
were beneath a blazing sun, trekking across this endless plain.
They had no shelter and there was no time to tend to the
wounded. But even now the able-bodied were dragging, but
they had to keep moving. They had fled from the burned ruins
of Lingana's village because they knew the 'gades would return

in force. Their only chance of survival had been to head for the Blue Mountains in hopes of finding a New SUN outpost.

The wounded had been triaged and tended to as best as possible, but many villagers refused to leave until relatives were given a proper burial. When they finally left, those who couldn't walk were carried on makeshift stretchers. Jaym knew some of the wounded would die on the road, but they couldn't leave them in the smoldering ruins of Nswibe with vultures already circling.

In the chaos of leaving, Lingana had tried to console crying children, wailing mourners, and did her best to tend to the wounded. But she forgot about the thorn traps they had set to slow the 'gades. The vicious thorns had punched through her sandal, stabbing deep into her heel. The pain of the poisonous acacia barbs was agonizing.

Jaym forced a shaky smile. "How you doing?" he asked Lingana. Her face was twisted from pain. *Damn,* he thought. After a week on this savannah trail, her wound had festered and spidery red veins snaked up her leg. If that continued... *No. They'd fix her up at the outpost. They had to.* He grit his teeth and shifted the weight of her arm around his aching neck.

He glanced back to see his Blender buddy, D'Shay, with Nakhoza. She'd taken a 'gade bullet to the shoulder, and now leaned on D'Shay as they trod the dirt road leading to the blue-gray mountains on the horizon. As they trudged under the African sun they carted their few belongings, shouldered the wounded, and paused daily to bury and mourn villagers who had not survived 'gade bullets.

Jaym discovered that burial out here was not easy. No one had a shovel, and the red savannah dirt was dry and hard as adobe. Thank God Giambo brought his quarry pick to break through the hardpan. Jaym and others tried to help with machetes, knives, and even pointed sticks to hack out shallow graves. Then, those who were able helped gather heavy rocks to pile up cairns. Prowling hyenas would not get their loved ones.

When they started from Nswibe, Jaym guessed the Blue Mountains would be a two- or three-day walk. The sharp, clear African air made them appear only twenty or thirty kilometers across the plains. But after seven days of hauling wagons and the wounded, the mountains still seemed distant. Unlike Lingana's home in the lush Nswibe valley, this vast savannah had no water, just cracked earth, dust, and withered grassland. *God,* thought Jaym. This must be like what Reya and her family had to do during their exodus from the smothering dustbowl and dunes that had been MexiCal. But this landscape was littered with the detritus of some forgotten skirmish of the Pan-Af Wars. Burnt-out shells of trucks, armored rovers, and half-tracks lay like blackened carcasses. As they walked past the carnage, villagers steered clear of the wreckage. "Ghosts," said Lingana, her voice weak. "My people sense the spirits of the soldiers trapped inside forever."

Jaym tried to keep his eyes on the dusty path, but couldn't help but glance at a charred chopper—a giant twin-bladed Russian model. It looked like an RPG had sheared off the rear of the craft. The remains of the pilot sat in the cockpit, his charcoal-stick arms raised as if reaching for the sky.

"Hey, Jaymster," said D'Shay. "All this remind you of anything?"

Jaym nodded. "Yeah, the Old Seattle Sector." He tried to concentrate on Lingana hobbling at his side, but the burnt ruins they were passing stirred up memories of his life in the Corridor.

—————————

The hood in his own sector hadn't been hit as hard as the old business sector during the Riots and Troubles. His "home" had been a one-bedroom unit cobbled from a long-abandoned office complex. Mom had tried to pretty up the plywood walls that divided the units. She actually concocted some "paint" by mixing beet juice with dish soap and covered a couple of walls. If their daysleepers objected to the color of the beet room, they didn't say anything. They must have figured purple-red walls were better than naked plywood. Jaym rarely saw the day-sleepers who shared their flat, except for a few times when he scrambled out late to tech school, or had to do shit-work for the landlord: trapping rats; dusting poison for cockroaches; unclogging toilets. His hood was no paradise, but nothing like some of the places in the South Corridor—such as SeaTac, where D'Shay grew up.

In Jaym's grandparents' time, the Corridor had been called the Seattle-Tacoma Corridor—really just two sprawls grown into one. Then came the Changes. The Melting, the sea rise, and the subsequent changes in Pacific currents. Then the weather shifts followed. The Pacific storms and life-giving rains that always drenched the Corridor in the winters now moved north to British Columbia.

Mom said when she was a girl they'd still get a couple of good rains in December or January—enough to fill some of the reservoirs. But then the water rationing began and the governor asked for help from the feds, but the federal government was facing food riots on the East Coast. Some of the states in the Midwest and the Deep South formed Confederations, cultivating their own militias and hoarding dwindling food stocks. The Corridor was cut off from interstate suppliers, so food rationing and hunger set in.

Jaym heard there used to be fat people throughout the Corridor, but that sounded like an urban myth. How could there be fat people when Mom's collarbones stuck out and her arms and legs were like broom handles? Jaym wasn't as skinny because Mom always gave him half her dinner. "No, Jaym," she'd say, "I'm stuffed. Really." In his teens he realized she was starving herself for him. He dreaded becoming a s'teener—but at least he'd be assigned by the Alliance and sent beyond the Corridor and Mom wouldn't keep starving herself. Maybe by now she was actually putting meat on her bones.

Jaym first met D'Shay at the Blending Training Center located in Old Seattle, the Corridor sector that looked like a war zone. The center was a concrete building behind the razor-wire that kept people out of the ruins. Getting off the Alliance bus at the center was the first time Jaym got a look at the once-thriving area. High-rise office buildings had been turned into concrete and steel shells blackened by the fires and pocked by shelling during the anti-corporate riots. The Space Needle across the seawater inlet leaned like a broken statue. The gigantic disk at the top had been blown in half by anti-corp terrorists, and the tower itself was bent when intense fires melted the steel supports. And the area was littered with National Guard choppers shot down during the height of the riots. They were blackened ruins with their rotors shattered and pilots cremated within—like the fallen choppers Jaym was passing now.

He looked away from the battle ruins they skirted and shifted his arm to ease more weight off of Lingana's injured foot. Up front, Lingana's brother, Giambo, took the lead, his limp seeming to get worse by the day. Jaym had become so used to Giambo's leg that he didn't even notice it—until now. Jaym recalled the day Giambo told him how 'gades had clubbed and shattered his leg bone and dragged away his bride-to-be. He wondered if that memory was plaguing Giambo as the pain of his limp grew worse.

Giambo suddenly stopped and held up his arm. He pointed to the north where a plume of dust arose—maybe four or five klicks away. Jaym had seen dozens of dust devils dancing across the savannah like mini-tornadoes, but this plume was different. Had to be a caravan of vehicles.

"Jay-em," said Lingana. "You think they be 'gades?"

"I don't know. From all that dust there must be a half-dozen rigs. But ... maybe they're not 'gades." *But who else would they be?* Not GlobeTran military forces. They should be out here protecting the Blending Program, but they'd withdrawn to the safety of the capital. Except for scattered groups of New SUN guerilla fighters, the 'gades had free rein of the countryside.

"Dust coming closer," said Giambo.

"Take cover!" shouted Nakhoza. Then she yelled in Chewan to the villagers.

Jaym took Lingana by the arm. "Whatever happens, follow Nakhoza's orders. We can't panic." Lingana nodded, wide-eyed. Jaym squeezed her arm. In a stand against a 'gade attack, he trusted Nakhoza more than anyone in their group. Without Nakhoza's SUN training, the 'gades would have massacred everyone in the battle at Nswibe. Yes, the village had been lost, but thanks to her defensive strategems they managed to defeat the 'gades.

"Carts and wagons together!" shouted Nakhoza. "Mothers keep children silent. Warriors, spread out in the bush with weapons." She ran to one of the wagons. "Camouflage sheets out, quickly."

Jaym and D'Shay ran to help spread the sheets across the carts. Nakhoza hadn't had much to work with, but before they left, she had the Nswibe women dye two-dozen sheets and blankets in patchy patterns of earthen tones. Thrown over the carts, the sharp edges and corners softened in the savannah background. From a distance, Nakhoza had said, the effect could resemble a grove of scrub in the grassland. And with all the metal carnage scattered across the plain, they should be less noticeable.

"Good," she said. "Warriors take positions. Women, children, and the wounded stay low behind carts. Yes. Okay, make prayer and we wait. If we must fight, do not fire until I shout the command." Jaym and the others with weapons scattered to take cover behind clumps of brush.

As Jaym lay in the grass, he felt his heart pounding against the warm earth. He checked his rifle. It was an old Chinese semiautomatic with a cracked plastic stock. He could have chosen one of the high-tech models taken off 'gades, but this was simple. Just jam in a clip and pull the trigger. No confusing LEDs or buttons to fiddle with.

Beneath the dust plume Jaym could now see vehicles. Two

armored half-tracks in the lead followed by half-a-dozen rovers and trucks. They were approaching at a tangent, now no more than a klick away. The leading vehicles had .50-caliber machine guns mounted in turrets. The best the Nswibe fighters might do is to hold them off for a few minutes while the women and children scattered. A few might make it. God, would Lingana have any chance with her injured foot? Only if she could find cover behind brush. But brush was scarce out here, mostly knee-high grass with a few islands of scrub. But maybe she could crawl under one of the metal hulks.

Jaym's gut tightened. This was it. The 'gade convoy rumbled closer. It was beginning to cross the faint trail they were following.

But the column didn't slow. It rumbled by in a haze of dust, only a few hundred meters away. The rover at the rear of the column was an old pickup truck with a machine gun mounted in back with a single gunner.

Jaym saw a sudden movement from the corner of his eye. *Oh, shit!* It was one of the Nswibe men. He'd leaped from cover, and was now running and shouting in Chewan.

"No!" shouted Nakhoza, but the man was now screaming, chasing the pickup and spraying bullets at the convoy. The 'gade in the pickup jumped to his machine gun and fired. The Nswibe warrior was thrown backward in a spray of red.

NEW SUN
BASE CAMP

To: Global Alliance Hdqrs in Geneva
From: African Subcommittee
Investigating the Blending Program.
Re: The "New SUN" Movement in Africa

At this time we know little about the activities of
the so-called New SUN movement, which seems to
have originated in Chewena, Southeast Africa. This
subcommittee has received conflicting information
from our African posts as to the status of the Blending
Program. As you know, the SUN was created by a
Quaker organization in the former Netherlands. SUN
was dedicated to helping the people of Africa survive the
effects of the Great Solar Flare and warlords ravaging
rural populations. But when the operations of SUN
were taken over by GlobeTran, Ltd., we have heard little
regarding the status of the Blending Program. This
so-called New SUN movement may be an attempt to
revive SUN's original mission. We know next to nothing
about the locations or leadership of New SUN.

At this point we urge Alliance Headquarters to pressure the commanders of GlobeTran, Ltd. to release data relating to the current progress of the Blending Program.

—*Classified Internal Memo, 23 Jan 2070*

Reya leaned against a warm canyon wall and looked out across the morning haze hanging over the savannah. She was a few hundred meters down the canyon, just trying to find some solitude from the bustle of the New SUN camp. Since she was still recuperating from her gunshot wound, she felt useless. She hated that feeling. She was used to work and being valued for her strength and courage—not seen as an in-the-way invalid.

Reya had now been at the New SUN mountain sanctuary for two weeks. She was alive only because a SUN scout, Bettina, found her wounded in the highland forest in Mozambique. Reya's arm had been torn open by a 'gade bullet when she and the other women held captive made their break from the 'gade camp. Most survived the daring escape, but as Reya tried to save her wounded friend, Mai-Lin, she took the bullet in her upper arm. She'd almost bled to death as she pushed her way through the forest underbrush to make it to the edge of a tiny village in the middle of the night. Thank God a village woman had heard her weak cries for help. They carried her into a hut where Bettina and the medicine woman worked to keep Reya alive.

Ten days later, Bettina had to report back to the New SUN base in the Blue Mountains. She had to leave, and said the villagers would help Reya recuperate for a few more weeks. Reya insisted on going with Bettina. Bettina finally relented, and somehow prodded and half-dragged Reya across the barren savannah under blazing sun to this refuge.

Bettina was at home here because she knew most of these New SUN people, at least her former SUN colleagues who'd been replaced by GlobeTran Ltd. Rumors were that much of the policing in Wananelu, once performed by SUN personnel, had been given over to former 'gade mercenaries who showed little compassion for the struggling locals.

Annja van Eijk, the matriarch of this group, headed the New SUN post. Although Reya heard occasional grumbling about her leadership, Annja was gutsy and one of the original founders of SUN. She told Reya she was determined to head this disparate group of recruits toward the same goal—to defeat the 'gades and corrupt GlobeTran authorities keeping this country mired in poverty and fear. The 'gades were actively trying to crush the Blending Program in the countryside, yet GlobeTran did nothing. As long as the 'gades left GlobeTran alone, Globe-Tran simply looked the other way.

Annja's second-in-command was a good-looking boy named Tarkin, but Reya discovered he was a real dick. Bettina told Reya to just ignore his irritating glances and comments about "intrusive newcomers." Tarkin tried to relegate her to a shelter at the edge of camp, but Annja said Reya needed to become a part of camp, and must be integrated into camp life, even if she was unable to work or train until her wound was better. Until then, she was to observe and learn.

Observe, thought Reya. Watch and learn. See how they planned scouting missions, how they trained with new weapons, how they set up better communications. *Just don't get in the way* was the unsaid message. But being on the sidelines brought back the old feelings of being a MexiCal refugee back in the NorthAm 'gee camp. It brought back the memories of razor-wire fences and the fear of getting knifed by one of the camp gangs. Many MexiCal 'gee kids had lost their families during their flight north to escape the dust storms and creeping dunes engulfing ranches, farms, and entire cities to the south. Too often 'gee-camp gangs took the place of family.

Like the thousands of other 'gees, Reya had come north with her family on foot, hoping for the Promised Land of the Seattle Corridor. There they would find rain, get a piece of land, and raise a garden that didn't wither in the drought and hot wind that tore the soil into storms of brown dust. Her father had fought the wind and the dust while most neighbors packed to go north.

Her *papá* fought by digging a well by hand. Reya, her mother and sister did their best to keep the dust out of the house. They tried to seal the window casing with tape and stuffed rags under doors. But within hours Reya would be mopping and wiping dust from floors and tables. They all wore dust masks or damp kerchiefs around their mouths and noses, but still blew out muddy snot.

Her mother pleaded with *Papá* to give up the dry well. He and Uncle Ramos had dug so deep that they had to strap three long ladders together to bring out the dirt. But he couldn't keep his mask on as he dug. And at night Reya cringed at the sound of him hacking up muddy phlegm. Dust pneumonia, some called it. He actually began to run a fever, but he wouldn't stop until Uncle Ramos screamed for help that day in June. They lowered ropes to bring him up. *Papá's* mouth was covered with frothy, muddy blood.

After a week of gasping and coughing, he was gone. The doctor said five of his ribs had broken and his heart burst from the coughing. After they buried him, the family packed and started north along the rubble of old I-5, a roadway that once carried petrol cars. There were still cars—those rusted hulks on the shoulders, and sometimes burned-out cars in the middle of melted asphalt. That all happened before Reya was born— the rationing, the riots, neighbors killing neighbors for food, or even stealing petrol to escape.

But that terrible time was prehistory to her. In the 'gee camp, Reya had been relieved when she finally turned seventeen and became a s'teener, the time for Alliance placement. And to get placed as a Blender was such a stroke of luck for a MexiCal girl. Most in the 'gee camp were sent south to dig on the Canal—a make-work project to bring water to the south. What a joke. Everyone knew there'd never be enough water to wet the canal. It was said hundreds, maybe thousands, working on the canal died of the heat, the cave-ins, and dust pneumonia.

But here she was, finally safe in the Blue Mountain sanctuary. So after all the crap she'd gone through, she could put up with Tarkin's bullshit.

During the days, Reya exercised and stretched the muscles in her healing arm. She also wandered around camp, watching, observing the New SUN fighters and workers. About half were blenders, and half Chewans. A few Chewans had been part of the old SUN organization and still wore SUN-issued khaki tee shirts, shorts, and light hiking boots. Others were natives who'd survived raids on their villages. Most of the villager women did much of the cooking, and had families to care for. But one tall Chewan girl, about Reya's age, stood apart. She was an archer named Maykego. Regal and strong, she always gave Reya a little nod and said, *Moni*, if she passed near. As far as Reya could tell, Maykego was the only female of the half-dozen archers in camp. Most New SUN fighters, Chewans and blenders, carried rifles slung over their shoulders and packed 9mm pistols on their hips.

With her wounded arm still in a sling, there was no way Reya could handle a rifle. Her upper arm muscles were so chewed up she might never be able to raise a rifle. But she could learn to use a pistol and be of some use if the 'gades ever raided this place.

She'd never seen anyone actually shoot with a bow and arrow. Somehow it seemed like such an outdated weapon, something natives only used before they got their hands on guns. But Maykego carried her bow and quiver with such pride.

One day, Reya followed Maykego to watch her practice at the range downslope. From a distance, her motions were almost Zenlike. Drawing an arrow from the quiver to the bowstring in a quick, fluid motion. The ease of her stance. The assured draw of the bowstring. The steady release and follow-through as the arrow hissed into the straw target. She wanted to talk to Maykego—to find out about this aloof young woman and why she became an archer. Maybe they could be friends. Maykego seemed like a loner, and Reya had no friends in camp except Bettina, who was always busy scurrying for Annja.

Friends, she thought. On the ship over she made two guy friends, Jaym and D'Shay. Where could they be now? They had to be living with their African families. Funny, she thought, how Jaym had been so nervous about meeting his bride-to-be, but D'Shay was eager to meet his "chocolate honey," as he referred to his blending match. Be so nice to see them again. They'd declared themselves *The Three Musketeers* aboard the transport ship. Each of the three was so different, yet during the Atlantic crossing, Jaym and D'Shay were the closest thing she had to a family.

She missed her own family with such a deep ache. She prayed each night to the Holy Mother to keep her mother and little sister, Leeta, alive and from harm back in the Corridor 'gee camp. Her mother, she knew, would try to stay alive long enough to see Leeta become a s'teener. If the Holy Mother answered Reya's prayers, Leeta would one day be selected as a Blender. If she did come to Africa, Reya was going to find her—no matter what, no matter how.

Reya had had such hopes that the African boy she was assigned to would have a family that would welcome her, and they would care for each other. They'd have kids and a future. They might live in a village and she'd probably learn the language, but it would be worth it all.

But it was time to quit feeling sorry for herself. She needed to become part of this family of New SUN people—if ever she could find a purpose.

3

MOUSE VS. LION

The Rover X-37

The predecessor of the Rover X-37 was the *Nyla* RG-31, a multipurpose mine-protected armored personnel carrier (APC) manufactured in South Africa. The original prototype was based on the *Mamba* APC of TFM Industries. The X-37 is built from an all-steel welded armor hull and features high suspension, typical of South African mine-protected vehicles, providing excellent small-arms and mine-blast protection. The vehicle is designed to resist a blast equivalent to two TM-3 antipersonnel mines detonating simultaneously. Its 452-N Mercedes engine has been modified to run on syn-petrol power, and the fuel tanks allow a 1,000 km range. Slanted bulletproof glass and a turret-mounted .50 caliber machine gun make the Rover X-37 a swift, formidable military vehicle for all-terrain fighting. Although production ceased following the Pan-Af Wars, dozens survive in the hands of warlords in several African nations.

—Michuriu, James. "Military Vehicles of the Pan-Af Wars." Alliance War Department Information Memo #413 (May 2067)

For the sake of God!" shouted Nakhoza, "everyone stay flat to the ground!"

The pickup truck gunner raked the savannah brush where D'Shay, Jaym, and the others lay. D'Shay heard a woman scream. Bullets hacked into grass and brush like a sickle.

D'Shay pressed his face to the dirt. Damn, this was *not* what he'd signed up for. Not this suicidal-warrior shit. Back in the Corridor, in that seedy hacker's apartment, he'd paid big money to get his assignment switched to the Blending Program. Hell, then he didn't even know what a Blender was. He just knew it wasn't the death sentence of Canal duty where no one ever returned. The other choice had been "military," where he was sure to get his ass shot up in some country he never heard of. Well, here he was, fighting for his life in a country he'd never heard of. Hell, he just wanted to be with Nakhoza. Wasn't that the Blender idea? Just find a sweet African honey and settle down in a quiet village.

"Riflemen!" yelled Nakhoza, "Take out the machine-gunner!"

D'Shay aimed and squeezed. Nothing. *Shit,* still on safety. He flipped the safety and lifted off his belly enough to take aim. He squeezed off bursts as gunfire chattered from all sides. Still the machine-gunner continued to rake their positions. The 'gade shooter was protected by a steel plate with a view-slit. Sparks flared off the plate as the machine gun chattered. D'Shay heard the hiss of bullets just overhead and saw dirt spattering too close.

"Sharpshooters!" commanded Nakhoza. "Fire at the vision slit in the armor plate."

D'Shay was no sharpshooter, but he held his breath, took

aim and fired. Rounds were sparking so close to the slit. Suddenly the barrel of the machine gun lurched up, firing a final burst into the sky. A 'gade jumped from the pickup cab and ran back to man the machine gun. D'Shay fired with the others. The 'gade spun and went down. The driver of the pickup spun the pickup around and sped to the other end of the column.

Those around D'Shay whooped and whistled.

The other 'gade rigs began to swing around. "Those are armored rover APCs," shouted Nakhoza. "Aim at the driver windshield! Do not fire in bursts or they will spot you. Take aim carefully. One shot at a time!"

A half-track APC rumbled toward them. D'Shay couldn't see the driver, only the reflection of sunlight on a dusty windshield.

"All you Blenders!" shouted Nakhoza. "These vehicles have right-hand drive."

D'Shay shifted his rifle to the driver's windshield and fired. Bullets pocked the glass, but the steel monster kept coming. *Bulletproof windows.* Should have known. Damn, the thing was gonna just run over them; crush them under its wide tires and grinding rear tracks. It was only fifty meters away, bucking over the rocks and gullies of open savannah. Behind it, other rigs were turning, heading this way.

The oncoming rover stopped maybe twenty meters away. The turret gun up top spit fire as it raked the brush. *Damn.* The only way to stop it was for some of them to rush the rover and take out the gunner.

Someone behind D'Shay screamed.

That scream jolted through him like a bolt of electricity.

God, he thought. That could have been Nakhoza. Will be if that gunner keeps firing. Okay, he thought. There's no way out.

"Jaym! Giambo!" he shouted. "Run with me! To the rover doors! Nakhoza. Cover us! Keep the turret gunner busy!"

"You heard!" shouted Nakhoza. "Open fire at the turret."

Okay, thought D'Shay. *Hero time.* "Jaym, Giambo. Now!"

D'Shay ran low, dodging and weaving as bullets kicked up dirt around him. Out of the corner of his eye he saw Jaym sprinting to the right. D'Shay glanced back in time to see Giambo go down. *Shit, not Giambo!*

It only took D'Shay seconds to reach the driver's door. The driver's eyes were wide as he struggled to put the Rover in reverse. D'Shay grabbed the door handle.

Locked! The glass would be bulletproof. But how bullet-proof? He slammed the muzzle of his rifle against the window. Squinted, then fired. The driver jerked like a gut-shot rabbit. Yes! Not bulletproof at point-blank range.

The passenger leaped from the other door. D'Shay heard the shots of a .45, and then saw ... Nakhoza. She jumped inside and reached over to unlock the driver's door.

D'Shay pulled the driver out and climbed onto the bloody seat. He gawked at Nakhoza. "What the hell are we—?"

"Not now! Can you drive this?"

"But ... where's Jaym? Is Giambo—"

Then he saw Jaym, scrambling up the hood of the Rover, up to the turret with his 9mm pistol. He couldn't hear Jaym's shots over the machine gun up top, but there was sudden silence. No one shooting now. The shadow of a body tumbled from the turret.

"D'Shay!" snapped Nakhoza. *"Can you drive this thing?"*

"Yeah, yeah..." I think." D'Shay looked at the gearshift. Good, almost exactly like the controls in one of the black-market vid-games back in the Corridor. The same right-hand joystick for steering; the left for acceleration. The rover's engine was still rumbling.

"Hurry," said Nakhoza. "Turn 'round and kill next rover. Ram it." She popped a new clip in her 9mm. "Giambo is okay. He cannot run so good with his crooked leg. He just trip and fell. I am taking his place."

D'Shay worked the sticks and swiveled the Rover a hundred-and-eighty degrees on its tracks. He now faced another rover firing at him. The bullets pocked the windshield, but it held.

"Fast as you can now," said Nakhoza.

D'Shay pushed the accelerator to full throttle. *Shit, shit!* he thought. This is gonna be suicide.

Overhead, Jaym had opened up with the turret machine gun.

Only ten meters to the next APC. He wanted to grab Nakhoza's hand before they hit, but he had to keep his hands on the knobs. He held his breath and braced for the collision.

But, yes! At the last second the oncoming rig swerved left and tilted. It ran into a deep wash and flipped. Its tracks spun helplessly in the air. Jaym fired at its underbelly. Sparks shot off the undercarriage, then the rover exploded in flames.

"Petrol tank," said Nakhoza. She grinned.

"Goddamn," said D'Shay. "We're alive. But there're three more trucks and..."

The lead truck's wheels threw dust as it spun around and headed up the road. The others followed suit.

"We actually did it," whispered D'Shay.

Nakhoza nodded. "Even a mouse is gonna fight for life when he is trapped by a lion. We just beat the lion."

———

Jaym climbed down from the gun turret and stared at the burning rover in utter disbelief. D'Shay and Nakhoza climbed out to stand with him. One by one, the others in the savannah grass began to stand. Nakhoza shouted, "All is clear!"

Lingana hobbled over to Jaym. She was shaking when he hugged her. Nearby, D'Shay wrapped his arm around Nakhoza's waist and said with a serious expression, "As our Defense Goddess, please don't let the 'gades come so close next time. Just a few klicks farther away, okay?"

Nakhoza grinned and poked him in the shoulder. "Yes sir, Mister Du-Shay. Ten kilometers good 'nough for you?"

"We'd appreciate that, ma'am."

———

They walked on under the burning sun. Jaym tried to carry Lingana piggyback, but after a couple of hours, his legs burned and his ankles shot electric pain with each step. When he was at a point of collapse, he was forced to let Lingana walk beside him, grimacing as she hop-stepped. But he couldn't stand to see the gentle profile of her face so wracked by pain. After only minutes he said, "Okay, Lingana, it's time for me—"

"No, Jay-em. No more. Look how the others show their courage. Many are sick and wounded, but still they walk. I am my father's daughter. He would want me to walk with my people. To give them courage as he would do." Her lips pinched tight as she held her trembling chin high and pushed on beside him.

"Nakhoza?" Jaym rasped. "Any idea how much farther to those mountains?" Her left sleeve was torn from her shoulder wound. The bandage had been linen white, but was now the color of the road's red dust; her blood still oozing.

Nakhoza shook her head, then coughed and licked her cracked lips. "I cannot say, Jay-em. But I think we must now rest the wounded and the elders."

"Giambo!" yelled Jaym. "We gotta take a break. Let's stop for our water ration at those trees." He pointed to a grove of struggling trees throwing patches of thin shade. But any shade was welcome out here.

Giambo nodded. Although he was the strongest in the caravan, his shoulders seemed to slump as he shuffled forward.

Jaym helped Lingana limp toward the grove.

"Lingana," asked Nakhoza. "Do we have enough water for another ration today?"

"I do not think so. Maybe a half-ration."

Nakhoza clapped for attention. "Come, everyone. Take rest under the trees and we shall have a little water." The villagers trudged forward to collapse in the sparse shade of the scrub oaks.

"Let's get you in the shade," said Jaym.

"Yes, but first I must talk to that woman by the cart." Lingana limped over to the Chewan woman leaning against the water-barrel cart and nodded to her. "Enough for a half-ration, yes?"

The woman shrugged. "Yes, but I think we have 'nough for one more day only."

"We must take the chance," said Lingana. "Else more will die before sundown."

The woman shouted in Chewan, then English. "Half water ration for all." As people filed by, she dipped water from the 30-liter plastic jug; one-third liter per person. Some were too weak to line up, so family and neighbors took drinking cups to the cracked lips of the wounded and bony elders.

Jaym looked beyond the grove of trees and wondered if he'd ever get used to the African heat. The afternoon air shimmered over the savannah making the tall grass seem as if it was being blown by hot wind, yet there was not the slightest breeze. The leaves of the oaks that sheltered them hung motionless. Cicadas chirred in the heat and locusts buzzed in the stubble of the plain as Nswibe parents shooed flies from the weary faces of their children.

Jaym thought about the lack of real leadership in this struggling band of survivors. The battle with the 'gades had killed most of Nswibe's leaders: Mr. Zingali, five of his best warriors, and a half-dozen village men and women. Mr. Zingali had been Nswibe's chief, so the burden now fell on his son's shoulders—Giambo. Back in Nswibe, Giambo had been sullen and reclusive, spending most of his waking time mining in his jade quarry. His father had made all the village decisions.

Giambo moved alongside Jaym and Lingana. "Lingana," he said. "I must talk alone with you."

She shook her head. "What you say to me, you say to Jay-em also."

"What's going on?" asked Jaym.

She gave him a gentle poke in the ribs.

Giambo said, "No! I want talk to you as family. Jay-em is not blood."

Not blood, thought Jaym. *Jesus. He'd fought alongside Giambo, and Lingana's my blending match. Did he still see me as a worthless mzungu?*

Jaym got up to leave but Lingana grabbed his sleeve. "No! Jay-em will come too," she said firmly in English. "Jay-em's blood gonna be in my children. He will be 'blood' through your nieces and nephews. Yes?"

Giambo glared at Jaym. "Then you gonna keep what I say quiet to three of us? Like family would? Else I lose face and fail as Nswibe people chief."

"Of course," said Jaym. "I swear."

Giambo nodded, then the three moved to the back of the scrub grove and sat in the dry grass.

Giambo looked aside, his face a mask of worry. He spoke softly, avoiding Jaym's eyes. "Sister, I cannot take place of our father. God did not make me like him."

She put her hand on his muscled forearm. "Giambo, you fought like a mighty warrior against the 'gades. Father's spirit is proud of you. You will make a fine chief."

He hesitated, fists clenched. "A warrior, yes, but not a true chief. I cannot … see ahead like father. Not like you—or Jay-em. Even Nakhoza and DuShay have clever spirits. I only see and act at the moment time."

"Giambo," said Jaym. "I respect you as our leader. Believe me, we all do."

Giambo read Jaym's expression, then gave a little nod. "*Zikomo,* Jay-em."

"You're welcome."

Lingana smiled. "Maybe you do not need to be chief alone, Brother. Jay-em, Nakhoza, DuShay, and I can share your burden."

Giambo cocked his head. "But there can only be one chief."

"But even a chief needs a council. We will be yours. Yes?"

"I will lose face with villagers," said Giambo.

"No. We will honor *you* as chief. We work and plan together, but you make final word."

"Yeah," said Jaym. "I'll stand by you, and I know D'Shay and Nakhoza will, too." He grinned. "After all, you're gonna be my brother-in-law."

Giambo took a moment before he nodded. "You will not tell village people of this talk?"

Lingana shook her head. "No. This is sacred talk between brother and sister—and Jay-em. Come. Jay-em and I will gather your council."

Minutes later, Lingana, D'Shay, Nakhoza, and Jaym squatted at the edge of the grove. Giambo's sun-red eyes stared at grass stubble he poked with a stick. He spoke slowly, without the usual fire and hostility Jaym sensed back in Nswibe.

Giambo said, "I must honor tradition of our village, and my father. I will be Nswibe chief. But I ... need you wise words to help plan and do best for my village peoples." He looked at them one by one as he spoke. "You, Lingana. If I be killed you be village head. Already you show courage. 'Sides, you gonna make strong Zingali babies with Jay-em."

Lingana blushed.

"Yes, yes. You not bride yet, but I be pleased that Jay-em be with you. He show much, much courage 'gainst 'gade killers in our battles. I think he be like a Nswibe man now."

Jaym's eyes widened. *Good God,* he thought. *One minute I'm an unworthy mzungu, the next I'm family.*

Giambo nodded toward D'Shay. "And DuShay, I now see you more than just a brown blender boy. I think you be almost clever as Lingana."

"Brave too, right?" said D'Shay. Nakhoza grinned and poked him in the shoulder.

"And you, Nakhoza. You be a warrior girl—no, a warrior woman. And you be trained in ways of SUN and know much for us." He paused, and looked at each in turn. "I speak as chief, but we be leaders together, yes?"

D'Shay lifted an eyebrow. "You mean you want us to take turns leading?"

"No. We gonna work together. You gonna be my..." His mouth twisted as he struggled for the word.

Lingana leaned forward. "I think my brother wants us all to be advisors—his council."

"Yes," said Giambo. "My council."

Lingana held her chin high. "Giambo, I am proud to be your sister. This is what a wise man would do. To use the strength of each other."

Giambo held out his palm. Jaym placed his palm against Giambo's rough skin. Light against dark. Lingana covered his hand with hers, giving him a slight squeeze and smile. His heart jumped like a rabbit. Finally Nakhoza and D'Shay followed. "We be one forever, yes?" said Giambo.

"Forever," they said in unison.

Giambo nodded and stood. "Nakhoza. How far, you think to Blue Mountain camp?"

She puffed her cheeks. "Cannot be much farther, twenty kilometers at most."

"So, 'nother full day," said Giambo. He glanced ahead at the heat-scorched savannah. "No water, no shade. Many of our people may die."

"What if we stay here until night?" asked Jaym. "Most people are worn out and really need more rest. Here we've got a little shade. I know the big cats come out after dark, but if we travel at night we wouldn't need as much water, and the wounded and elders will travel easier."

"I think it is worth the risk," said Nakhoza. "We might even make it by daybreak."

Lingana nodded. "I agree. The moon is bright and we can use torches to scare cats and hyenas."

"Good," said Giambo. "We must take chance. We let people rest, then leave after sun go down. If we walk close together I think we be safe 'nough from big cats." He grinned and slapped his knee. "Yes. I like this council way."

4

ARRIVAL

Cultural History of the Blue Mountains Area
Permian in age, the Dwanian Uplife of western
Chewena consists of a mixture of soft limestone
and volcanic tuff riddled by natural caves and an
intricate maze of human-made tunnels that deserve
further exploration. Some of these latter features show
sophisticated evidence of occupation and continued
expansion from Neolithic times to a few hundred
years ago. Tree ring data indicate the region suffered a
25-year drought in the 1600s, the time when the area
was likely abandoned.

—*G. N. Sølberg. "Prehistory of Southeast Africa,"*
(Harare, 2047)

Lingana and the others walked all night, shouting and thrusting torches when cat or hyena eyes shined too close. Jaym carried her piggyback, but by midnight he staggered from exhaustion. One of the women gave Lingana a makeshift walking stick—her slain husband's spear. Between the support of Jaym's arm and the spear, she was able to take much of the weight from her inflamed foot.

Jaym knew that if they didn't get Lingana's infection taken

care of soon, she could lose her foot. God, even if someone at the New SUN camp knew how to amputate, would they have sterile instruments and antibiotics? They would be in the mountains, maybe with only a first-aid kit. He shivered. Then she'd die.

No. They'd have to have the medical supplies. They would be treating wounded and must have med-techs and equipment. She'd live. She had to.

———

At the hint of dawn, Jaym and the others saw the silhouette of the foothills just a few hundred meters away. The column stopped. The people leaned against the carts like rag dolls.

Jaym still had his arm around Lingana's shoulders. He felt her quiver from pain and exhaustion. He had tried to say words of reassurance during the night, but his mouth was so dry and his lips swollen that his words must have been little more than mumbles.

The first rays of sun began to strike the hills that rose steep from the savannah floor. Jaym saw no sign of a trail or anything hinting of the New SUN outpost. Only rocky outcrops, cliffs, and house-size boulders. Had they missed the camp? Could it be many kilometers to the north or south?

Giambo, D'Shay, and Nakhoza stood beside Jaym and Lingana. "This should be it," said Nakhoza, her voice weak. "These are the nearest foothills of the Blue Mountains. The intel maps I saw at my old SUN post showed this to be the place. We could be a kilometer or two north or south, but the camp can't—"

Dirt spattered only meters in front of them. Within a split-second, the crack and echo of the gunshot rumbled across the plain. A flock of scarlet firefinches cried as they burst from a tangle of nearby brush.

Giambo scanned the hillside and pointed. "They shoot from there. To the right of twisted tree by the cliff." He raised his rifle.

"No, Giambo," shouted Jaym. "Don't!"

Lingana took hold of Giambo's wrist. "Brother, please. I think it is only a warning. A test."

"Yes," said Nakhoza. "There was only one shot. Besides, from that distance a sniper could put a bullet through your forehead."

Giambo lifted his chin defiantly, but slowly lowered his gun.

Jaym stripped off his dusty white tee shirt and waved it overhead.

"Jay-em, what you doing?" asked Lingana.

"Flag of truce," he said. "Shows them we mean no harm."

A male voice boomed from the hillside. "Stack your weapons twenty paces toward our position. This means *all* weapons—guns, spears, and knives of any sort. If you do this, you will receive water and aid. If you do not, we must consider you enemies."

Giambo hesitated. "If we give up weapons," he said, "they could slaughter us like sheep."

"We don't have much choice," said Jaym. "Besides, they could have mowed us all down if they wanted. And we're as good as dead if they don't give us water."

"Brother," said Lingana, "our people cannot survive

another day without water and shelter. We must do what they say."

Giambo turned to the villagers. "People! We must lay down weapons. *All* weapons: spears, knives, guns. Come and put them with mine." He stepped twenty paces toward the hillside and laid his rifle and machete in withered weeds. One by one anxious-faced villagers filed forward to do the same.

Jaym slipped on his shirt as he carried his rifle and Lingana's walking-stick spear to the pile of arms.

They waited. Finally six men and two women started down the hillside, most with automatic rifles raised. Lingana squeezed Jaym's arm tighter.

"Get behind me, Lingana," said Jaym. She moved behind him and placed her hand on his sweat-soaked tee shirt.

A tall, tan, older white woman was in the lead, the only one without a rifle. In fact she had no sidearm or even a knife. She and her companions paused to glance at the pile of weapons, and then continued toward Giambo.

Giambo took a step toward the woman.

"Are you the headman?" she asked. Her voice was even and confident. The woman's English was flawless, but Jaym detected an accent he couldn't place. Some of her words rolled more from her throat than her tongue. Her long face was as weathered as a leather purse, and a shock of gray hair poked from her billed cap. Jaym figured she had to be older than his own mother, but was as tall as him, and her sky blue eyes shone with confidence—and kindness.

"I am Annja van Eijk, head of this camp." She motioned to a young white man beside her. "This is Tarkin, our second-in-command." Jaym watched Tarkin scan the villagers, warily, almost as if he was looking for a target. He did not have Annja van Eijk's look of kindness. His steel-gray eyes were narrowed as he looked from face to face. He was dark from the African sun, but he had dirty blond hair cropped like a shorn goat. He wasn't as tall as Jaym, but was solidly built and wore a sleeveless muscle shirt. He wondered if this Tarkin was a blender or former military. The haircut and cocky attitude said military.

Another guy stepped forward. "This is Daku," said Annja. "He is a weapons expert and works with Tarkin on tactical logistics. And here," she said, "is Xian. Our communications expert." Annja smiled at Xian. "Give Xian a few wires and he seems to come up with receivers and most devices that seem impossible to create out here."

Xian made a little bow and grinned. "What Annja say is true. I am boy genius."

Giambo nodded to Annja van Eijk. "I be Giambo Zingali, chief of the Nswibe Village people." He swept his arm at those near him. "These all be my council."

Jaym noticed Tarkin's smirk. He was glad Giambo ignored Tarkin. To Annja van Eijk, Giambo asked, "Then this be the main New SUN camp?"

"It is, and welcome." She looked at the ragged and wounded villagers. "Please tell your people not to be alarmed, but we are going to fire three shots in the air—only a signal to bring assistance."

Giambo shouted the warning to the villagers. She nodded to Tarkin who fired the signal. Within moments a dozen people appeared from the rocky hillside and descended with carts.

Lingana clutched Jaym tighter. "You and I, Jay-em. We are going to *live!*"

He kissed her forehead. "Damn right we are."

REUNION

"Hold a true friend with both hands."

—*African proverb*

———————————

Reya watched New SUN personnel help these newcomers navigate the rocky trail up to the outpost. 'Gades must have forced them from their village. Some were bandaged or had arms in slings; others limped and held onto someone's shoulder. She saw only one white face in the group and near him a light-skinned African who—

"Sweet Mother of God!" she hollered. Reya ran down the trail shouting, "D'Shay?"

"Reya!" he laughed. "I don't believe it."

She ran over and gave D'Shay a hug. "Who would've thought? My God, it's nice to see a friendly face."

He cocked an eyebrow. "These people not the friendly type?"

"No, most are great. It's just that I'm new, so I feel like I'm in their way. I haven't been assigned any duties because of this." She held out her bandaged arm. "Gunshot. Until I'm healed, I'm supposed to stay on the sidelines while everybody runs around like ants."

Reya grinned at Nakhoza. "You gotta be D'Shay's blender bride. Am I right?"

D'Shay winced. "Reya! Be a little subtle, girl. We're not officially, uh…"

"Come off it, D'Shay. I can see you two are a pair." She held out her hand. "Hi, I'm Reya. D'Shay and I came over on the same transport ship."

Nakhoza smiled as they shook hands. "I am Nakhoza, a former SUN officer."

"Your shoulder," said Reya. "You take a 'gade bullet?"

"Yes, in battle at Nswibe Village."

Reya rubbed her own bandaged arm. "I took one lower. It tore up my triceps."

A voice nearby shouted, "Reya? Is that *the* Reya Delacruz?"

Reya glanced over to see Jaym helping a native girl walk. She ran over and gave Jaym a hug. "Damn, you and D'Shay made it here together."

"Yeah. Well, had to keep our shipboard pact. We all promised to meet up somehow."

Lingana laid her head against Jaym's shoulder, her eyes barely open.

"This is Lingana, Reya. We're blending partners."

"Jackpot, Jaymster. She's gorgeous." Reya saw the pain on Lingana's face. "You don't look so good, *chica*. You been hurt?"

"It's her foot," said Jaym.

Reya kneeled down to look. "Damn. That a snakebite?"

"No," said Jaym. "She stepped on a thorn trap when we fled her village."

Reya gently laid her hand on the swollen foot. "It's hot and full of pus. She's got an infection going." Reya stood and took Lingana's free arm. "Here, Hon, loop your arm around my neck. Yes, good. You ready, Jaym?"

"Yeah. You think she's gonna be okay?"

"Let's just worry about getting her up the trail. We've got a small infirmary at the post."

Giambo stepped in front of them. "White girl. Where you takin' my sister?"

Reya glared at him. *This big rude guy is her brother?* "To the infirmary, if that's okay with you, big brother."

"Is 'infirmary' a hospital? She needs hospital and doctor."

Reya felt her face burn red with anger, but kept her voice steady. "The infirmary has medicine. There's no doctor here, but I'm a med-tech and—"

"No! I want a doctor. Where gonna be closest doctor?"

"Look, fella, I'm the closest thing you're gonna find to a doctor out here. This isn't the big city. Now, get out of the way and let us help your sister."

Giambo narrowed his eyes at Reya, but then nodded. "I gonna carry Lingana. You show the way, yes?"

"Fine," said Reya. "Follow me, and watch your step. The trail is rough till we get to the post entrance."

Giambo swept Lingana in his arms, cradling her like a child. He glanced at Jaym. "You stay. You are not family yet."

"Wait a minute," said Jaym. "I want to—"

Nakhoza touched Jaym's arm. "I think it is best you stay with us, Jay-em. He wants to be with his sister alone. He acts rude, but I know Chewan men. I see the fear in Giambo's eyes. I think he very scared for Lingana and maybe does not want you to see his fear."

Jaym watched Reya and Giambo head up the trail.

"It's okay, man," said D'Shay. "Reya's gonna patch up Lingana just fine. Just let Giambo be with her alone till Reya's done."

————

As the Nswibe refugees were helped up the trail to the outpost, Xian stopped to watch the big Chewan take the girl from the white boy and go towards the outpost with Reya. The white boy looked stricken as his two friends tried to comfort him. Xian knew it was time for a little distraction.

He walked over to the trio and made a slight bow. "Greetings. I am Xian Tsiu, and, as the best tour guide in east Chewena, I gonna lead you up to post, and long the way point out highlights." He grinned. "No tips required."

"Uh, sure," said D'Shay. "I'm D'Shay, this is Nakhoza, and he's Jaym."

"Yes, Jaym. I see your blender girl going with Reya. I think Reya do very good, so do not worry about them. You see them soon." He motioned to follow. "Come, lady and gentlemen, to the amazing cavern outpost we go."

Two-hundred meters up the trail loomed the dark cavern entrance. "Impressive, yes?" said Xian. "Twenty meters high in center, and fifty meters wide. And look all 'round you. We in box canyon with cliffs hundred meters tall, and no exits. Least none you can see."

"A perfect fortress," said Nakhoza.

"Come inside and enjoy coolness with other refugees."

"Praise the Lord," said D'Shay. "Must be thirty degrees cooler in here."

The cavern floor was flat with rows of tents. The Nswibe refugees had gathered to one side where they were being served bowls of chamba stew and water. Cots had been brought out for the sick and elderly.

"Where's the infirmary?" asked Jaym.

"Is in the back of cavern," said Xian. "But I think you just let Reya do her job, Jay-em."

"The floor is so flat," said Nakhoza. "It is like a giant hand has moved the rocks and smoothed it with hard earth. Did you New SUN people create this?"

Xian shook his head. "Annja say other people did this hundreds of years ago. You gonna be surprised when you see all the hidden places. But I think tour is over for now. Please, join the others and get food and water. They will also assign you a sleeping cot and tent."

"When can I see Lingana?" asked Jaym.

Xian sighed. "Old Chinese proverb say, 'Patient man receive best outcome.' That was Confucius, I think. Or maybe from fortune cookie."

WOMAN'S 'TUITION

"Courage is fire, and bullying is smoke."
—*Benjamin Disraeli*

A week after they arrived, Jaym and Lingana sat on a sun-warmed slab of white limestone a few hundred meters beyond the cavern. By now the cliffs across the canyon had thrown a merciful shadow over the area. They sat quietly and looked at the golden light slanting over the vast savannah plain. Flocks of blue-green swifts swooped overhead snapping up mosquitoes. Jaym felt the hint of slightly cooler air sliding in for the evening.

He laid his hand on the silky skin of Lingana's bare knee. He was glad to see her smile without the grimace of pain. She could also walk without much of a limp. "How's the heel?" he asked.

She lifted her gauze-wrapped foot. "Reya changes the bandage every day, and she says it heals very well."

Jaym laid his hand on her knee. "I was so freaked out," he said. "Did you know that after Reya treated your foot your fever seemed to burn you up? I slept by your cot, and that first night you were talking and shouting in your sleep—in Chewan. Thought I ... might lose you."

She took his hand. "I do not remember so much, but I am glad you were with me." She kissed the back of his hand. "Did I tell you that Reya was very good with the knife? She tell she learned first-aid training at her MexiCal school. She made the blade sterile in a flame before she cut." Lingana hunched her shoulders and winced. "Giambo was there, but, oh, Jay-em. I wish you could have held my hand when she pushed the knife into my heel. I only remember the pain. She said I fainted then."

"Yeah. You slept for two days. Reya squeezed about a liter of pus from your foot. We weren't sure if her outdated antibiotics would work."

"I thank God they did," said Lingana. She smiled. "Reya and Giambo had a fight before she treated me. Giambo questioned her skill and they were soon yelling at each other. Don't remember their words, but both have a temper. I think they have made a truce since."

"Reya may be feisty," said Jaym, "but you can trust her with your life." He rubbed his hand over her thigh as the first stars appeared in the eastern horizon.

"I felt good enough to walk around and explore the cavern today," she said. "I think it is very clever and took much work to make it. Reya says it's a natural cavern and long ago people dug chambers and passages into the hillside. The top half of the cliff is hard rock. I doubt that even Giambo and his pick could make a dent in it. But the bottom cave layer is softer. Annja van Eijk said there must have been hundreds of people here to dig the rooms and passageways. She thinks it's an ancient city fortress, maybe hundreds of years old. But she says it's been occupied and modified more recently—maybe as a stronghold during the Pan-Af wars."

Lingana rubbed her thumb on the back of his hand, her expression sober. "Jay-em, I think it be good if you have a talk with Reya."

"Sure, but Reya and I have plenty of time to catch up."

"No. You must talk soon, and private. I do not know what is the bother with her, but I sense something is wrong. I notice when she tended to my foot that Reya became quiet and did not smile whenever Tarkin or his guards came near—she seemed maybe frightened."

"That's not like Reya," said Jaym. "I've never seen anyone intimidate her." Jaym looked at the Milky Way beginning to glow overhead. Maybe, he thought, Tarkin was intimidated by Reya's grit. Would he try to bully it out of her? But maybe he just suspected everyone outside his own tight circle. He might figure the New SUN compound was a place 'gades would try to infiltrate. They could pose like blenders in a group of villagers seeking refuge—a Trojan-horse ploy.

Jaym squeezed Lingana's knee. "I think Tarkin's just a bit like Giambo. Maybe it just takes time for him to trust people. He's a leader here, and a lot of leaders have to watch their backs."

Lingana raised an eyebrow.

"Um—like watching behind for wild animals when you walk through the bush."

"Yes, perhaps it is just caution that causes Tarkin to act the way he does. But, still, please talk to Reya. Maybe it is woman's 'tuition, but I think there is something Reya fears."

Jaym smiled and nodded. "Sure, I'll talk to Reya—in private."

———————

The New SUN people and Nswibe villagers had set up rows of makeshift tents across the compound's vast floor for all the newcomers. Jaym walked past lantern-lit tents, some with a sick or wounded family member, and many with kids, all pre-Flare children, of course. He wandered through aisles of tents until he finally heard Reya's voice. She was talking with another girl in Spanish, their conversation low, their voices intense.

He stood outside the tent, waiting for a pause. "Knock, knock," he said softly.

Reya pulled back a torn sheet. "Jaymster! *Buenas noches, Señor. Mi casa es su casa.* Come on in."

"You sure? Sounds like you two were in the middle of something."

The girls glanced at each other. "Nothing that can't wait," said Reya. It's so good to see a friendly face."

Jaym stepped inside and dropped the flap in place.

"You've met Bettina, right?" asked Reya.

He nodded to Bettina. "Hi, I've seen you around."

She smiled. Bettina was shorter than Reya, but had Reya's dark hair and eyes. Their skin was also that same golden brown.

"It's good to see you, Jaymo," said Reya. "I never thought we Three Musketeers would really ever get back together again." She glanced at Bettina. "Jaym and I got stuck with each other in 'Culture Awareness' class back in the Corridor."

Jaym nodded. "Reya knew more than any of us and was

kick-ass ready for the Blending Program. I was clueless and feeling sorry for myself, so I just drifted through training without trying. Reya was the one who got me to realize that this whole Blending thing was serious." He grinned at her. "Man, you had an attitude."

"And, as I recall, you didn't. There I was, so stoked that I was actually out of the 'gee camp and wasn't heading for Canal duty. I was finally free of the camp's razor wire and grab-ass guards. No more rationing and gang threats. And all you were was, 'poor me, I gotta go to Africa and maybe hook up with some brown babe and be free from all the Corridor crap.'"

"Guilty as charged," said Jaym. "Clueless, naïve, and a bit screwed up. I'm sooo glad I got out. And Lingana is more than I could ever hope for. I gotta admit, it wasn't all magic sparks and love at first sight. I sure didn't impress Lingana, or her family. I was still feeling sorry for myself. And talk about culture shock."

"You did get a babe," said Reya grinning. "It just ain't right that you stumbled into the Blending Program and hit paydirt. I knew D'Shay was gonna be alright. He was up to anything, and he lucked out. Nakhoza seems to be a sweetheart; and nobody to mess with." She grinned. "So, damn. When do I get my chance?"

"You mean a guy?"

"No, dummy. A tree stump. Hell yes, a guy!"

Bettina chuckled. "You are a very good-looking and smart girl, Reya. I think you get a chance at many good-lookin' *hombres*, yes?"

Reya shrugged. "So far it's not been that good. Did I tell you about my debut as a blender in Africa?"

"Not really. I guess your logger guy in Mozambique didn't work out."

Reya put her face in her hands. She shook her head. "Never made it. I was kidnapped, raped, and made a slave in a 'gade camp. Some of the women had been kept there for years. A couple committed suicide attempting to escape. The camp's pitbulls always chased them down. Thank God I escaped. But we blasted the 'gades to pieces on our way out." Reya looked aside and hugged herself. "Shit. Let's talk about something else."

Jaym hesitated. "Yeah, I really came to ask you about something that's bothering Lingana." He glanced at Bettina, then back to Reya. "Maybe I should catch you alone tomorrow."

"Hey, no. Whatever you want to say you can say it in front of Bettina. Reya patted the dirt floor beside her. "Sit down. What's on Lingana's mind?"

Jaym settled cross-legged. He spoke softly. "It's just that—well, Lingana says you don't seem to be yourself around Tarkin and his guards. Thinks something's going on that you aren't talking about. She says it's her 'woman's intuition.'"

Reya and Bettina exchanged looks. Bettina touched Reya's arm and said something in Spanish. Jaym had no idea of her words, but her voice and expression were tense.

"No, Bettina," said Reya. "It's okay. Speak English. I trust Jaym as much as you."

Bettina bit her lip, but nodded.

Reya twisted her fingers as she spoke. "Okay, here it is. Since we arrived a couple of weeks ago, Tarkin and I have had some run-ins. When Bettina and I got here, we got the same kind of 'welcome' your group received. A gunshot warning, then a grilling by Tarkin and his buddies. Annja was visiting village leaders at the time, so Tarkin got to play big-man leader. I should have kept my mouth shut, but I couldn't take his crap."

Jaym smiled. "I'm stunned."

Reya waved her hands. " I mean, here we were, fried in the heat, my bandaged arm still seeping blood, and Bettina on her last legs to get me that far. Did we look like big bad 'gades?"

Jaym sighed. "I don't know a thing about Tarkin except he's not real friendly—and he has that strange accent. Where's he from?"

"He said 'Down Under,' whatever that means."

"Australia," said Jaym. "I hear it's duned over as bad as MexiCal."

Reya shrugged. "Even if he went through the same crap as I did, he doesn't need to act like an asshole and bully people."

"So, why did Annja choose him as her lieutenant? They don't seem a match."

Reya shook her head and massaged her wounded arm. "He's acts the good, obedient second-in-command when she's around. Maybe she figures they balance each other's skills—some kind of weird yin and yang. Annja's a pacifist—well, as much as she can be in these times—while Tarkin's anything but. Annja puts up with Tarkin because he's a natural when it comes to fighting 'gades. She realizes that if we *don't* defend the local villages and ourselves, the 'gades will happily cut down anyone in their path. She must accept Tarkin as a necessary evil. He and his handpicked goons are just blenders like us, but they strut around like minor deities." She lowered her voice. "If it wasn't for Annja, Tarkin and his storm troopers would—"

The tent flap swept open. Reya's eyes widened.

"Hark!" said Tarkin. "Did I hear my name mentioned in vain? Aha! I see one of our new guests is getting to know the ladies. You are James, yeh?"

"It's Jaym. Hey, do you always stick your head in a tent without warning?"

Tarkin grinned. "Or, the question could be: Why are you in the tent of two single girls? Aren't you already matched with that petite native girl?"

Jaym saw two of Tarkin's guards in shadow behind him. "Look, Tarkin. Reya and I came over on the ship together. We were catching up on—"

"Catching up. Great!" Tarkin squatted in the tent entrance, his face unreadable. "Don't let me stop you."

Reya's expression hardened. "Come on Tarkin, give us some privacy."

"They were just talking about their troubles with the 'gades," said Bettina. "They both have been through much and simply—"

Tarkin held up his hands. "Of course, you newcomers deserve a little time alone. Oh, hey—on my way by your tent, James, should I tell your village girl you're just chatting with a couple of friends? I wouldn't want any camp gossips to misinterpret your visit to these charming girls."

Jaym stood, his face flushed. "Thoughtful of you, but maybe you'd better butt out of our private lives."

"Of course. Your private lives are nobody's business—unless it interferes with New SUN's mission." He winked. "Good night James, good night ladies." The flap closed.

Jaym balled his fists.

"Asshole," muttered Reya.

"Yeah," said Jaym. "And a devious asshole."

AFRICANS ALL

van Eijk, Annja (b. 2018, Tijerdam, The Netherlands)
Annja van Eijk received her PhD in Social Anthropology
at the University of Bern in Switzerland. After The
Melting flooded her homeland, she took a position at
Geneva's Academy of Global Studies. Dr. van Eijk is
primarily known for her role as one of the founders
of SUN. She also launched the African Blending
experiment in order to negate the C-11 damage caused by
the Great Flare. Her SUN organization recruited youth
from countries unaffected by the Flare to help resurrect
decimated African populations. It is believed that she
may be somewhere in East Africa assisting with the
Blending Program.

—*Global Dictionary of Biography: fltt.Globdictbiog.sz*

———————

'Shay had just finished his usual breakfast of spicy cornmeal mush and was rinsing his wooden bowl in the wash
barrels—one with soap, the other with clear water (well, sort of
clear). By now he was getting immune to the peppered mush.
When he first arrived in Nswibe the stuff seemed to sear off his
taste buds, but now he could probably eat the mouth-flaming
peppers Reya described from her childhood in MexiCal.

He was wiping his bowl with a ragged dish towel when Reya hollered, "Come on, D'Shay. Annja wants a meeting to talk to us newcomers."

D'Shay followed her from the cavern to the flat overlook out front. He'd snatched bits and pieces of conversations that hinted a mission might be in the works, and the Nswibe survivors were going to be part of it.

Nakhoza caught up with him and gave his hand a little squeeze. "Morning Mr. DuShay."

"Morning, Gorgeous." As they walked, he thought how her touch was such a grateful surprise. It somehow made him feel stronger. Gave him a sense of ... what? Fulfillment? Maybe that was it. Well, maybe even love. Hell, he didn't know. Back in NorthAm he'd had girlfriends, but all that was about making out and then getting as far away as he could. Sure, he loved to rub his hands over Nakhoza's sweet curves. She was so damn hot. Some other girls had been as steamy, but since he first saw Nakhoza it was more than testosterone. He wanted to protect her. Even take a bullet for her.

But there was that itch of worry he just couldn't shake. Worried that she'd find some stud who'd recite poetry and say the stuff that turned a girl's brains into helpless, romantic putty. But so far it was good. If only it could stay that way.

Outside, he and Nakhoza settled near Jaym, Lingana, and Reya, all squatting on their haunches, African style. Annja wore khaki shorts, shirt, and a dusty ball cap—all about the same tone as her tanned skin. D'Shay figured she could camouflage into the bush as easily as a gazelle—well, a tall gazelle. With her were Tarkin, of course, and four other New SUN people older than any of the blenders—maybe in their late twenties. Probably former SUN personnel.

"I thought this was newcomers only," D'Shay whispered to Nakhoza.

Reya overheard and leaned close. "Me too. God, I hope we're not gonna play some kind of getting-to-know-and-trust-you game. Be just my luck to get Tarkin as my trust buddy."

"Please," said Annja. "Let's not talk now." She smiled at each of them.

Her face was lined by age and weather, but her expression was one of complete ease. Almost saintlike. But how could she act so mellow? D'Shay had heard how Annja had been through so much shit. The ocean had swallowed her homeland, and rumors were she'd lost all her family in one of the Euro-plagues.

Tarkin, standing beside her, cracked his knuckles as he looked at the newcomers with narrowed eyes.

"Welcome, Africans," said Annja.

Nakhoza raised her chin. "Amai Annja, but some are not—"

Annja held up a palm. "Nakhoza. We are now all Africans in heart and spirit. Your children will be a new generation of Africans—a wonderful brew of light and dark, spiced with the traditions of many cultures."

Nakhoza's hand moved against D'Shay's on the warm earth.

Annja let her words sink in as she smiled at each of them in turn. "You each will play a critical role in New SUN's struggle to carry out the goals established by the founders of SUN. As you know, births in Africa were normal until about six months after the Great Flare." Annja held her arms. "Thus you are here. You blenders are Africa's hope. Humans arose from this continent, and from it they will blossom anew. A blending of humanity can be positive in so many ways. Besides procreation, perhaps your blending will help break down ethnic and tribal barriers. You, my young friends, are embarking on one of humankind's greatest experiments."

"But we can't forget," said Tarkin, "there are barriers. We have 'gades and government corruption to overcome."

Annja's expression turned weary. "Tarkin is right. As a Quaker, I thought this noble movement would be peaceful because we had the support and protection of the Global Alliance."

"But then came along GlobeTran," said Tarkin.

Annja nodded. "Yes, that was a grave miscalculation. I'm not certain the Alliance Command is aware of the consequences of outsourcing to GlobeTran."

"Politics and greed," muttered Tarkin.

"Whatever the reason," said Annja, "we now have little support but our own. And as you have discovered, there are many in the land who would do us harm. These so-called 'gades are lawless groups lead mostly by white thugs who want the Blending experiment to fail. If it did, Africa and its resources would be all theirs."

"Is this outpost the only resistance?" asked D'Shay. "No offense, Ms. Annja, but if they discover this place ... "

"We are not alone. There are two other pockets of New SUN in these mountains—both groups smaller than this base, but they are embers of hope. We remain separate so if one group is overwhelmed, the others might survive."

"But we have to be cautious," said Tarkin. "Sometimes the New SUN movement has been compromised from within. It is not difficult for a new refugee to sell us out to the 'gades for a few gold pieces."

Giambo stood, his face tight. "You think we Nswibe people gonna tell 'gades? That why you keep our weapons? Do you insult the honor of my people? We already fight 'gades and many of us die."

"Take it easy, mate," said Tarkin, "I'm just saying that—"

Annja stood and waved them quiet. "Enough, gentlemen! We *must* trust one another. We *will* stand together, starting now. Tarkin will return your weapons today."

Tarkin looked aside, his expression unreadable.

"We have talked enough," said Annja. "We will soon *act together!* I have intelligence from our northern camp that 'gades are moving on villages in the foothills only thirty kilometers from here. We need to send a reconnaissance team within a few days to determine 'gade activity. We have little time for formal training, so I'm going to integrate you new arrivals with our own working teams."

Tarkin frowned.

"I will interview each of you newcomers and assign you to teams best suited to the needs of this outpost. We face many dangers ahead, and must face them together. As of now, there are no newcomers. We are all New SUN. Understood?" She glanced at Tarkin and Giambo.

"Yes, Amai Annja," said Giambo.

Tarkin smiled and nodded. "Of course, Annja."

DRILL

To: Drone Control Ctr.

From: GlobeTran Headquarters, Chewena

Message from a New SUN outpost #1 reports the location of a 'gade complex commanded by a rogue warlord. This is the same group that has chosen not to cooperate with us. They must be eliminated. Arm drone and set to strike reported coordinates of 1454C and 8832J.

—*Msg intercept by GlobeTran Stn, CHW-12.*

That afternoon Reya was the first to be interviewed by Annja.

"It's lovely today," said Annja, "let's meet outside."

Reya chewed her lip as they walked toward the cavern entrance. She knew Annja was going to assess the strengths and weaknesses of each newcomer. But with her useless arm, what could she contribute to this outpost? She was an on-call med-tech, but the post had two other med-techs with more experience. She'd rather be a fighter, but she'd take anything but kitchen duty. She had enough of that as a 'gade camp slave.

Before they reached the entrance, six metallic clangs rang out. People scrambled inside and ran past them toward the rear of the cavern. Annja sighed. "Sorry, Reya, but we'll need to postpone our talk for a bit. We have to take cover in the back. Another drill."

Reya jogged with Annja and others to the back of the cavern. "Think it's a false alarm?"

"A routine precaution," said Annja. "Six rings means a drone flyover. There are often two or three a week. It's always better to stay out of sight—just in case."

Reya glanced over to see D'Shay and Nakhoza trying to suppress laughter. D'Shay was something else—even making jokes during an air raid. Nearby, Jaym and Lingana crouched, talking softly. When Jaym spotted Reya, he gave her a thumbs-up.

But Reya now heard the subsonic hum of the drone—something that vibrated in her gut. She suddenly felt dizzy and began to pant. She had to kneel on the stone floor to keep from passing out. Her vision blurred as she was hit by flashes of her captivity in the 'gade camp. Images of Mai-Lin and the other enslaved women whirled; the sound of the drone's engines as it came to take out the camp. Then the crushing panic as she and the women fled—sprinting to gain enough distance from the camp before the Alliance drone blasted the camp, and a hundred meters of surrounding forest, to fragments.

Get a grip, she told herself. The GlobeTran controllers here would know this was a New SUN post. She hugged herself and tried to slow her panting. Her lips quivered as she forced out her words. "W-why should we worry about a G-A drone? I mean, they're only after 'gades, right?"

Annja touched her shoulder. "You look ill. Are you feeling alright, Reya?"

Reya nodded, and pressed her forehead to her knees. No, she would not barf. Not here. Not in front of Annja.

"The drones are aging weapons," said Annja. "We've had a couple of 'friendly fire' incidents where drones hit New SUN scouting teams. The video feeds on the drones are weak and replacement parts are nearly impossible to get now. So those monitoring the drone vid feed sometimes can't distinguish a friendly from a 'gade."

Reya sat silent with the others, waiting, listening. That sickening low-pitched hum grew closer and closer. She felt chilled and the hair on her arms prickled.

"It's overhead," said Annja. "The all-clear ring is three chimes on the alarm. That should come—"

A blinding flash lit up the cavern. The explosion threw Reya and others to the ground.

"*Godverdomme!*" shouted Annja.

Screams of women and children.

Slabs of rock thundered from the cavern ceiling.

"Stay down!" shouted Annja. "There could be—"

Another explosion, higher on the hillside. The cavern rocked. More debris fell to the floor.

Annja and Reya lay shoulder to shoulder, waiting. After a minute they sat up, dust still settling from the explosions. Annja stood. "I think it is over. Ring the all-clear signal!" she shouted.

Three metallic clangs echoed through the cavern.

"Any casualties?"

People stood and shook off dust and grit. "None here," shouted Jaym.

"Nor here," said Tarkin. "Just crushed some empty tents."

Reya looked to the cavern entrance. House-size slabs of rock now blocked much of the opening.

Annja stood dazed for a moment, then snapped orders. "Tarkin, Giambo! See to your people. Xian, come with me. We've got to contact Drone Control."

That evening Annja gathered Giambo's and Tarkin's key people. Reya was surprised that Giambo wanted her to be part of the group. "With my useless arm?" she had said. Giambo had nodded. "Lingana say you be a smart girl. Jaym and DuShay want you there too."

So here she was with the others, sitting at the rough wood meeting table in one of the cavern chambers. A kerosene lantern threw their shadows against the stark white of the stone walls. Annja looked from face to face as she spoke. Her expression was grim. "Xian has thoroughly checked traces of our outgoing communications. I deeply regret to report that someone at our post has compromised our location."

"But, who would do that?" asked Reya. "And why?"

"I'm guessing it's a newcomer," said Tarkin. "We know our own people are trustworthy. What better way to find the location of a New SUN post than by infiltrating as a refugee."

"What you be saying?" said Giambo. "Do not insult us. We not be traitors!"

"Gentlemen, *please!*" said Annja. "It is too early to speculate. Xian says it is possible this was just an oversight. Perhaps someone sent a message to another New SUN post and failed to cloak it. From now on, anyone using the comm room will need to sign in and out with the guard on duty. Remind those with comm room clearances that every message *must* be cloaked. Understood?"

Reya and the others nodded.

"We must move past this incident," said Annja. "We have much to do, starting by giving our new arrivals assignments within this post. We need them trained and integrated quickly because it is time that we go on the offensive. To begin, I want to send a team of envoys to the main village a few kilometers to the northeast. It is called Ezondwei. Its people are the survivors of several villages savaged by the Pan-Af Wars. We have never made contact with the village, and we don't necessarily expect a warm welcome, but we must try. Ezondwei is in a position to observe movements on the savannah and in the foothills. They are our best chance to gather information on any 'gade movements overlooked by our comm intercepts. Not all 'gade squads carry comm gear, so they often go undetected. We cannot afford any surprises."

"Dropping in on this village unannounced sounds a little risky," said Reya.

Annja nodded. "Perhaps, but we must ally with them and seek intel. Besides, they are our neighbors. It's about time to show them we mean them no harm; explain to them that we need each other in these times."

"I'll take a team of my people to the village," said Tarkin.

"You will also include Giambo and his choice of scouts."

Giambo nodded to D'Shay and Jaym. Reya noticed Jaym's eyes widen. Surprised, she guessed, that he was chosen instead of one of the Nswibe warriors.

"Excuse me, Annja," said Reya. "Will there be any of us women going?"

"That's up to Giambo and Tarkin."

Giambo shook his head. "You and Nakhoza are still healing from wounds. Village people might be dangerous. You cannot help case there be a fight."

"But with a couple of women along, you might not seem as threatening."

"Maybe," said Giambo. "But not this mission."

"Finally something we agree on," said Tarkin. "No girls."

Reya wanted to reach over and slap the smirk off his face.

"No, I think Reya has a point," said Annja. "Tarkin, please add Reya's friend, Bettina to your group."

"But Annja—"

Annja held up a hand. "No, Tarkin. Bettina was a former SUN scout and has a great deal of experience in dealing with villagers. And she can fight if necessary."

"I mean no disrespect, Annja, but I think all of Giambo's crew and a girl are—"

"Bettina is a *woman,*" said Reya.

Tarkin ignored Reya. "They are all too inexperienced for a mission this sensitive. We still don't know if one of them may have—"

"No!" snapped Annja. "This is a chance for them to *gain* experience, Tarkin. And it is a chance to build a little trust between your groups."

Good for you, thought Reya. She grinned at Tarkin before he stomped from the room.

9

SHOW NO FEAR

Ezondwei (Ez-OND-way): Location: 13°43' South;
33°51' East. A village in the foothills of the Blue
Mountains of Chewena, S.E. Africa. Population approx
320 (in 2060). Wet season precip approx 200 mm/month
(Dec-March). Ezondwei was established in 2058 by
refugees from several Chewan villages who survived the
ravages of the Pan-Af Wars.

—GlobaPedia: fltt.GlobPed.gazetteer

──────────

'Shay didn't sleep much the night before the mission to
Ezondwei village. He kept thinking about his talk with
Nakhoza earlier in the evening. She said she had a bad feeling
about the mission; that the villagers might be hostile or that
'gades could be lurking and ready to ambush.

He had the same kind of worries, but this wasn't the time
to tell her. Instead he said, "It's gonna be okay. Besides, I need
to do this. If I do fight, it's for our survival—yours, mine … "
He almost added, *and for our kids,* but, God—where did that
come from? Hell, they weren't even matched yet. Not officially.

She nodded. "Yes, okay. But I want to be selfish. I want
you safe. So watch you buttocks."

He laughed. "Yeah, I'll be fine Babe. And I certainly will watch my rear."

When Nakhoza finally dropped off to sleep, he gathered his gear and threaded past tents in the near-darkness. Dawn was just beginning to glow through the cavern mouth. Giambo and Tarkin were already waiting. Soon the other members of the team straggled over. To the east, the blood-red sunrise threw fingers of orange light across the savannah far below. They waited for Annja in uncomfortable silence.

From the Nswibe group were himself, Giambo, and Jaym—Giambo's choices. He said each was fit and had proven themselves in the battle for Nswibe. D'Shay wasn't anxious to "prove" himself again, but here he was, an Af-Am mzungu with his future now rooted to Africa. Besides, he thought, he'd rather go after 'gades than sit around and wait for them to jump the outpost. He wouldn't let Nakhoza become a 'gade slave and go through the shit Reya had.

Never.

The other team was made up of Tarkin, Bettina—the girl who saved Reya—and Xian. D'Shay liked Xian. He was smart and funny. Xian once told of how Tarkin liked to call him "Shawn" to piss him off. Tarkin would pull that kind of shit, thought D'Shay. Well, he wasn't gonna take the Tarkin route. It might take some practice, but he'd get that Chinese inflection down perfect. "Zhee-*awn*." Not really that tough. Maybe he'd even learn a few Chinese words while he was at it. Yeah, thought D'Shay, Xian was alright.

Annja had instructed Giambo's team to choose weapons and pack rations for a two-to-three-day probing mission to the village. Xian and Bettina chose Zeno 9mm automatic rifles—

light, easy to handle, and deadly. But D'Shay decided on a vintage AK-47, simpler than some of the impossible newer models with their multiple switches, buttons, and LED indicators. Jaym carried the same. But Giambo only toted a machete and three throwing spears.

Tarkin broke the silence. He looked at Giambo and shook his head. "You going suicidal, mate?"

"You make joke?" asked Giambo. "I think you swallow you joke when you see how 'gades meet with these weapons of my grandfathers. Big noisy guns not be only answer, 'specially if we gotta fight 'gades in close."

Annja appeared from the back of the cavern. She looked at the teams with her fists on her hips. "Still bickering?" she asked. "You will *not* be two competing teams, but will work as one. And Tarkin, Giambo—remember your mission. Everyone keep your weapons on 'safety' and do not seek an engagement. We need intelligence, not needless killing. We have enough casualties to deal with as it is. Understood?"

Heads nodded.

"Good. Then this will be the team configuration. Tarkin will be overall leader, but his fighters and Giambo's will be intermixed to form the two teams." She looked at D'Shay. "D'Shay, you join Tarkin and Bettina's squad."

D'Shay, opened his mouth to object, but kept silent and walked toward Tarkin.

"Xian, join Giambo and Jaym." Annja looked at the morning sun and darkening clouds to the north. "It's about 0700 hours, time to depart. I expect this will be a two-day mission. If you are not back by nightfall on the third day ... well, just return. Be cautious, and again, do not engage unless attacked."

By noon D'Shay and the rest of the team were deeper into the foothills, pushing through brush as they struggled to follow the trail. So far it had been whacking through scrub, getting their hides seared in the blazing sun, and swatting at blood-sucking flies. But now they began to wind through small pockets of broad-leafed trees where the underbrush was thinning out. In one ravine, they stumbled across a shaded oasis near a rippling stream.

"We'll break here," said Tarkin. "Thirty minutes to eat, take a leak, and refill your canteens. No smoking. It can be smelled two klicks away."

D'Shay dropped his pack and propped his AK against a pine tree. *Huh*, he thought. Fewer bugs too. Had to be because a dozen orange-and-yellow birds were swooping through the grove and snapping up mosquitoes and flies. The place was a mini-paradise. It even smelled good—like one of those scented candles his aunt lit at Christmas. A fresh, alive smell. It was kind of like the lush smell of Nswibe valley before the 'gades came. Yeah, he thought. Nakhoza would like this sweet place.

Xian, Bettina, and Jaym dropped in the shade of D'Shay's pine tree.

Bettina cocked her head, casting Jaym a concerned look. "You are too red in the face, Jaym. Maybe you are going to get sunstroke."

Jaym smiled. "I'm okay, Bettina. I always look too hot. I blame it on my Swedish great-grandmother."

"Just don't get tanned as me," said D'Shay. "Hard to fight off the ladies with my glorious skin tone."

Bettina grinned as she opened her cloth of rations: a hard biscuit; dried berries; and some kind of jerky. D'Shay unwrapped the same and began gnawing on the oily jerky. "Anybody know what this meat is?" he asked. "Not bad."

Tarkin sauntered over, biting off a chunk of jerky. "It's an excellent source of protein," he said. "A succulent blend of creatures. Most live under rocks or slither through grass. Very nourishing, and all natural ingredients."

D'Shay stopped chewing.

Xian laughed. "Back in China during starvation years, people eat bugs, worms, even leaves." He grinned and raised his piece of jerky. "So, *Bon appetit,* yes?"

Jaym grinned at D'Shay. "Had to ask, didn't you. Might as well chow down. This is our only entrée until we get back to camp."

D'Shay sighed and began to chew again. "Got any soy sauce, Xian?"

"Sorry, no chopsticks either. Maybe ask for some in village."

"How much farther to Ezondwei," asked Giambo.

Tarkin shrugged. "Probably two or three more hours. It's just a dot on the map, and none of us have gone this far on the trail."

"You think they gonna be hostile?" asked Xian, now munching on a biscuit.

"We think they're friendlies," said Tarkin. "But to be on the safe side, we're not all going in at once. We'll send in one unarmed person to test the waters." He looked at Giambo. "Think you've got the *cojones* to go in alone, Giambo?"

Giambo's eyes narrowed. "Do you question my courage?"

"Hey, hey, guys!" said D'Shay. "Tarkin, why're you taking jabs at Giambo? Your idea of a New SUN hazing thing?"

Xian chuckled. "Tarkin often like this when Annja not around."

"Knock it off, *Shawn*," said Tarkin. "I'm just having a bit of sport with the new people. Pity they can't play along. I like to think of it as a team-building exercise, yeah Giambo?"

"I think you have more luck being civil," said Xian. "New people not used to your ways." He chuckled. "Fact, even we experience people not used to your ways."

"Okay, enough of this," said Tarkin. "Two minutes! Get ready to move your arses in two minutes."

As they continued, the trail became better, and shadier. The path grew wider and the thicker underbrush had been macheted for clearance. To everyone's relief, the tree canopy was dense enough to shade the trail.

Bettina walked just ahead of D'Shay. She was shorter than Reya, but carried herself like a soldier—rifle half-raised, and constantly glancing at brush and trees. "Hey, Bettina," said D'Shay.

"Yes?"

"That's a serious-looking weapon you're toting. You really know how to use all those buttons and switches?"

She turned and flashed a grin. "I can handle it pretty good. It is a 9mm Zeno-III model with I-R homing scope. It is, how you say, 'like my gun and I become one' if I need to use it."

"Hmm. That's very Zen, Bettina. I want to see you shoot that thing sometime."

She shrugged. "I hope you never do. It's a killing machine, and I have seen enough killing."

Tarkin, in the lead, suddenly raised his hand. The teams stopped, silent. Tarkin waved everyone to the side of the trail. "I heard a dog barking," he said. "We're probably less than a klick from Ezondwei village. From here on I want total silence. There's no breeze, so their animals shouldn't pick up our scent. When we reach the village clearing, stay hidden in the bush. Ready?"

Everyone nodded. He signaled to move forward.

Ten minutes later, D'Shay saw the forest's edge and a clearing beyond. Xian, Bettina, and Jaym crept into the scratchy underbrush and stopped just meters from the clearing's edge. D'Shay moved with Tarkin's squad to the other side of the trail.

Bugs crawled on D'Shay's neck while thorn-bushes jagged into his thighs. Through the trees and brush, he could see adobe homes and a few women working in the gardens. Chickens clucked and pecked at the plowed earth, while tethered goats ripped at patches of weedy grass. Kind of looked like Lingana's village—before the 'gades attacked.

D'Shay glanced at the team on the other side of the trail. Bettina clutched her robotic gun, but he was glad to see the safety light was on. So was Xian's. They'd be dead if someone got jumpy then trigger-happy.

Then, without a word, Giambo calmly laid his spears and machete in the underbrush, then stepped out onto the trail. He walked slowly into the clearing.

Damn, thought D'Shay. That took real balls.

A girl screamed and ran toward a cluster of huts. Giambo walked on, his palms forward in a gesture of peace. Men came running toward him, several armed with bows and spears, but a few carried high-tech automatics. They shouted at Giambo in Chewan.

Giambo raised his arms higher. *"Moni! Dzina lanu ndi, Giambo. Chone, thandizeni."*

Two men approached with rifles raised. After a couple minutes of posturing and shouting questions, the men lowered their guns. Giambo turned and waved his arm. "All New SUN peoples, come out! Put you weapons on ground and walk to me!"

Slowly, D'Shay and the others rose up and made their way toward the village clearing. They laid their weapons on the perimeter of the clearing in sight of the armed villagers, then walked slowly toward Giambo. Tarkin started forward toward the stack of weapons, but hesitated.

One of the Ezondwei men shouted and raised his rifle. Tarkin jerked up his automatic.

"No!" yelled Giambo, stepping in the line of fire. "Guns down!"

Neither Tarkin nor the village man made a move to lower their weapons.

"Put it down, man," D'Shay hissed at Tarkin. When Tarkin didn't move, D'Shay grabbed his gun barrel. "You looking to start a slaughter?"

Tarkin's eyes were wild. But slowly he lowered the muzzle and laid the gun with the others. "Never, *ever* give me a command!" he hissed. "You are under *my* command and don't forget it."

D'Shay didn't reply, but turned and walked toward Giambo. The one village man still had his rifle pointed at them. D'Shay walked erect, head high as he tried not to show the fear that lay like a hot stone in his gut.

Show no fear.

DIPLOMACY

The Black Mamba (*Dendroaspis polylepis*) is one of
Africa's most dangerous snakes and feared in East,
Central, and Southern Africa. It is aggressive when
cornered and will not hesitate to strike. It can reach
speeds of up to 20 kph. It is the largest venomous snake
in Africa with adults reaching an average of 2.5 meters
in length. Black Mambas live in savanna, scrub, tree
hollows, and sometimes people's homes. If a Black
Mamba encounters prey, it can strike up to 12 times,
each time delivering enough neuro- and cardio-toxic
venom to kill a dozen men.

—*W. R. Kubila. "Snakes of Southeast Africa."*
(Kenya Natural Hist. Soc., Nairobi, 2059)

After Jaym and the others were patted down, the Ezondwei villagers finally shouldered their weapons. The chief
and Giambo spoke in Chewan for a moment then turned to
the rest of the team. The chief pointed to D'Shay and said
something in Chewan.

Giambo motioned. "DuShay, please come here. I try to
explain, but chief has question of you."

D'Shay glanced at Jaym, as if for encouragement. Jaym
whispered, "Just be cool. Not the time for wise-assing."

"Moi?" said D'Shay as he stepped forward.

"You be mzungu, or you be African?" asked the chief in a rough baritone. "Or maybe you skin have disease? If you be diseased, must leave quick, quick."

"No disease ... Sir. In NorthAm there are a lot of folks like me—part mzungu, part African, you know, from the old days when whites took Africans to NorthAm as slaves."

The chief glared at D'Shay. "Yes, I hear such a thing happen, but not believe it." He reached out and grabbed D'Shay's wrist. He rubbed his thumb hard against the back of his hand. The chief released him and looked at his thumb.

"Yessir, it's my natural color."

Jaym breathed a sign of relief as D'Shay walked back to his side. "Nice job," said Jaym. "I worried you might've had the urge to mess with the chief—just a little."

D'Shay put a hand to his chest and feigned a shocked expression. "Jaymster, I'm stunned that you could think such a thing."

———————

That evening the villagers served Jaym and the New SUN people a light supper of soup made of hacked-up sheep bones with boiled stems that, to Jaym, might have been swamp reeds. It was so spicy he didn't have to worry about the taste. His tongue was numbed by the first spoonful. During the meal, he noticed that one of the serving girls kept giving D'Shay the eye. She'd brush her hip against him as she passed, and he'd grin.

"Hey," said Jaym. "Don't even think about it."

"Jaymo, I'm as monogamous as they come. It's just that,

the female figure is something God intended to be admired—as one would admire any of his gorgeous creations. It would be kind of a sin not to, right?"

"You so much as make a move toward that girl and I'm gonna tell Nakhoza. Besides, she might be one of the chief's daughters."

"Got it. I'll just concentrate on this throat-burning cuisine and think about Nakhoza's gorgeous bod. Happy?"

Jaym nodded. "Happy."

After the meal, they were taken to the men's lodge. Jaym and the others squatted on their heels, as did a half-dozen men from the village. The chief sat on a polished black chair—his throne—with legs carved into a quartet of spear-toting warriors. On either side stood two real warriors with AKs slung over their shoulders.

The chief wore traditional African sandals and a batik cloth around his waist, but also wore a flashy gold chain over his *TEAM CHEWENA* tee shirt. He gazed at his visitors through mirrored sunglasses. From one corner of his mouth jutted an unlit cigar. The chief snapped his fingers and one of the guards quickly struck a wooden match. The New SUN team sat in dead silence as his Highness puffed until he had a glowing ash. He coughed, blew a couple of smoke rings, then grinned. "Gold Brand specials," he said. "South African, and very expensive, but they be worth every kwatcha." He took another drag, then said, "Speak."

Tarkin cleared his throat. "As you know, Chief, the New SUN movement only wants to bring peace and stability to Africa."

The chief blew another smoke ring. "Yes, yes, I hear of you

peoples. But I also hear from other mzungu peoples that you New SUN peoples want Africa for selfs." He held out his arms. "So, who you expect this chief to believe?"

Jaym's mind flashed to an image of the firing squad wall again. *Come on Tarkin,* he thought. *Keep up the diplomatic tone. Don't lose your cool.*

"Yes, Chief. But *those* white men are 'gades. You must not believe them. Have they asked you or your people if your village has accepted any SUN blenders?"

The chief tapped ash from his cigar. "Yes, we have mzungu strangers—'gades, as you call them—come asking questions."

Jaym and D'Shay exchanged glances.

"'Bout month ago seven mzungu men with powerful guns come. First the leader, mzungu with beard red color of blood, be so, so polite and friendly, just like you being now. But not so friendly when they ask question about blender girl we have in Ezondwei. She been sent to marry my number-three son. She be a strong, strong mzungu girl and I think she gonna bear many children." He puffed more smoke. "First the strangers say, 'Well, chief, she be sent to wrong village. We gonna take her to her proper village.' I say that be kind offer, but they mistaken. This is right village and she gonna stay here. Then 'gade mzungu offer three gold pieces for our blender girl. They say the money is for 'trouble' of mix-up. I say, no mix-up. Girl not for sale. She gonna give me grandchildren."

He flicked ashes from his cigar. "I ask them so polite to go from village, but they point their big guns and grab my number-three son. Said they gonna machete him. Fingers and toes first, and so on."

Jaym saw Giambo's face tighten as the chief spoke. Had to

be thinking of the day his own blender bride had been dragged off by 'gade thugs; how they had bashed his legs with clubs as they torched the village.

"Their machete talk make me very angry." More smoke rings. He tapped off cigar ashes. "I act so frightened then and say, 'Oh, please, *Bwana,* I cannot give up blender girl, but do not hurt my son.' That's when they put his hand on chopping block. I be proud of son 'cause he not show fear. He just give blood-beard man a death look. That is when I hold up my arm. Red Beard smiles and think he win."

The chief chuckled. "'Gade men all look so, so surprised, like they get hornet sting in necks. Red-beard and others slap their necks, but that do no good. A couple 'gades try to shoot us before they fall, but my men ready and jump them to ground. Heh, heh. They be alive on ground but twitch like clubbed rabbits."

"Poison darts," said Tarkin.

The chief nodded. "Yes, poison from biggest black mamba snakes we find. God provide good when he create mamba snake. Poison for enemy, and fine, fine meat roasted by my cooks."

"The poison kill the 'gade men?" asked Giambo, his eyes afire.

"Was gonna do that in time. They be awake, but cannot move. I think they be in much pain, so we not let them suffer. Heh, heh. We used chopping block and their own machete. We cut off they heads like chickens. We sit up Mzungu Red-beard so he watch whole thing. We do him last. You can see heads behind village. They still be sticking on spears like gourds." He tapped his mirrored glasses. "Red-beard kind 'nough to give me these, heh, heh."

"Geez," D'Shay whispered to Jaym. "We need these guys on *our* side."

Jaym nodded, "Bet they've had blowguns trained on us this entire time."

Tarkin looked at the chief wide-eyed. "Um, we are impressed at your wisdom in dealing with such men. Our mission is to allow the blending process to continue and eliminate the 'gades—as you bravely did here in Ezondwei. We wish to assist you any way possible to prevent further attacks on this or any other—"

The chief waved him quiet and smiled. "I think you see this backward, young mzungu. I think we do not need assist. If there be more 'gade people come, maybe you the ones who need assist, yes?"

INTERVIEW

No hay mal que por bien no venga.
(There is no bad that comes without a good.)

—*MexiCal proverb*

———————

ack at the cavern outpost, Annja walked briskly toward Reya, who was watching the sunrise from the entrance. "Good morning, Reya. Assuming the drones are on holiday, perhaps we can complete your interview today."

Reya nodded and tried to smile, but she was a little shaky from the drone and rockets yesterday. Teams were still clearing debris. Only luck kept half the camp from being crushed by falling slabs of rock.

"Another glorious African sunrise," said Annja.

"Yes. Before I came here I didn't know there could be so many colors in the sky."

Annja smiled. "I think countries have their own tones and colors. My birth home of the Netherlands was a country of cool tones. Soft grays and blues, a little violet in a few sunsets. Maybe that's why the Dutch loved their wildly brilliant tulips so much. An antidote for too much coolness; too many drab skies. But here! The flaming sunrises and sunsets; the rich ocher and red hues of rock and earth … only in Africa."

While Reya made small talk about sunsets, her innards churned. Anytime now, Annja was going to grill Reya on her abilities. But what could Annja possibly think a blender with a lame arm might be able to contribute? She needed something beyond kitchen duty or other maintenance crap. Sure, maintenance was important, but she was a fighter. If she had to, she'd find another New SUN post that would let her fight. It'd be tough to leave her friends, but she needed a lot of payback. For herself, for Mai-Lin, and for all those raped, killed, or maimed by 'gades.

"What's the matter, Reya? You look troubled," said Annja. "If it's the drones, I don't think we will be bombarded again. We believe GlobeTran somehow intercepted one of our transmissions to another outpost. A confused intercept analyst probably assumed we were a 'gade command center. The drones shouldn't return."

"It's not the drones."

"Then what?"

Reya tried to smile. "It's nothing, ma'am... really."

"Okay, but I'm here if you need an ear."

Reya nodded. "Thanks."

She followed Annja to a savannah overlook. They sat in the shade of the towering cliffs on a piece of limestone, a perfect bench. It was going to be another clear morning.

Annja glanced at the distant clouds. "Reya, have you been in Africa long enough to experience our rains?"

More small talk, thought Reya. *Let's just get the real topic over with.* "Um... Yes, ma'am, when I was a captive at the 'gade camp. The rain and mud were almost as frightening as the 'gades. In MexiCal and NorthAm, we only had light drizzles a couple of times a year."

Annja smiled. "The monsoons used to be seasonal, but since the Meltings and the shifts in ocean currents, the rains are unpredictable. But we have no complaints. Vegetation and animals are beginning to thrive, and it is said even the great Sahara is actually shrinking." She looked at Reya. "By the way, feel free to call me Annja. No need for the 'ma'am.' We are equals here."

"Tarkin calls you ma'am."

She laughed. "He was in the Alliance military for a year. I think the poor boy would choke if he had to call me by my first name."

Reya smiled. "I understand, ma'am."

She gave Reya a look.

"Just kidding—Annja."

Annja smiled. "It's good to have a sense of humor after all you've been through. You are a survivor." She touched the red scars on Reya's upper arm. "How are you healing?"

"As good as could be expected. It's stiff but I can lift it. The nerves to my fingers don't work so well, but they're better. The first week my entire hand felt cold and dead. Now the tingling is getting stronger."

Annja turned to Reya. "Well, let us get to it. We're here to discuss what you can contribute to New SUN."

Finally! She cleared her throat. "I have training as a med-tech. Maybe I could join your medical team."

"We have enough med-techs, but we have many other needs that you can consider. We need assistance caring for the elderly that we're housing, and there's always a need in the kitchen for prep-work and—"

Reya shook her head. "No. Please, Annja. I want to fight 'gades."

Annja looked at her arm and pursed her lips.

Shit, thought Reya, *always the damn arm.*

"I know you have courage and battle skills, Reya, but to be blunt, you would be a possible liability in a battle. An automatic rifle is difficult enough to handle with two good arms."

Reya nodded. "Yes, but there are other weapons." She nodded toward the tall Chewan girl. "Like Maykego's weapon." Reya took a breath and just blurted it out. "I want to be an archer."

"But your—"

"I can do it. I've watched Maykego practice. My wounded arm only needs to lift and grip the bow. My good arm will handle the arrow and bowstring. I just want a chance. Please let me try."

Annja glanced at Maykego talking with another Chewan girl. "Maykego!" she called.

Maykego jogged over.

"Reya, this is Maykego, an expert soldier and trainer. Best archer in Chewena."

As they nodded greetings, Reya noticed Maykego sizing her up. She glanced at Reya's arm. "But Amai Annja…"

"Yes, I know. But let her try, then please report to me." Annja stood. "I'll leave you two now." She hesitated. "Maykego, give Reya a fair chance to show what she can do. But I want an honest assessment of her abilities."

"Yes, amai."

Reya read the doubt in Maykego's expression. "Yes," said

Reya, "my arm is a mess, but it's getting stronger. I'm sure I can hold a bow."

Maykego nodded. "Okay, first test. Show me you can raise your bad arm."

Reya took a breath and raised her left arm shoulder-high. It shook a little and ached, but no longer sent shock waves of pain. Although some of the muscle was destroyed, she'd been exercising the arm every day, lifting its dead weight and working to get back some rotation in the shoulder. This still hurt, but she wasn't gonna let Maykego know.

"Can you lock your elbow in place?"

Reya held her arm out stiff from her side—elbow locked.

"Yes, good. Now, can you move your thumb to grip bow?"

"Yeah, better than my fingers."

Maykego grasped her thumb. "Move it now."

Reya gave it all she could, straining to fight Maykego's grip. Sweat beaded on her forehead.

Maykego released Reya's thumb and smiled. "That is good. I think if you practice that often you can stop the shaking. You cannot shake when you be an archer in combat."

Reya nodded. "I will learn to control that. But one thing... if I do become an archer, will we really see combat?"

"Yes, but archers not gonna be with those fighting with guns. Sometimes a battle needs silent weapons. In heavy brush or a forest, a silent arrow does not give away the archer's position. A few unseen archers can loose arrows from different positions and create panic in an enemy." Maykego touched Reya's arm. "Rest your arm. I think you can handle the shooting, but there are other parts of archery you must be able to do. Are you ready for a test to prepare an unstrung bow for shooting."

Reya nodded. "I'm ready."

As they walked beneath the cavern overhang, Maykego asked, "Rey-yah? You ever shoot bow and arrow before your arm be wounded?"

Reya shook her head. "Never had a chance. Soon after getting shipped over here, I was captured by 'gades who made me a slave. I . . . can't talk about that shit."

Maykego nodded. "'Gades took me from my village and also kept me as a . . . prisoner." Her jaw tightened. "When they came to take me, there was a blender boy I was gonna marry. 'Cept 'gades killed him with machetes. They force me to watch. They took me and two other girls, then burned our homes before they left. I cannot speak of the things they did to me when I was their . . . slave. Every day I thank God for being rescued by New SUN peoples. That is how I come to be here."

Reya followed Maykego to one side of the cavern mouth where a lean-to of branches walled off a corner of the cave. The branch wall had been woven like a mat and camouflaged on the outside with brush and vines. Behind the woven wall was a room carved from the rock face. Three men sitting on stools glanced up. Each was working at sharpening blades and oiling wooden bows and spears.

Reya ran her hand across a smooth wall. On the back walls were traces of a mural depicting a herd of extinct animals—elephants and a mix of giraffes and zebras. Figures of hunters holding short bows had pin-cushioned a bleeding zebra with their arrows.

"Amai Annja says these rooms and wall pictures are very ancient," said Maykego. "She has a doctor degree for studying such things."

"Is this the only room they carved out?"

"Not at all. Amai Annja and Tarkin do exploring and say there be many more in hillside. They call all this a 'city dell'—a rock city for living in protection."

"A citadel," Reya whispered.

Maykego walked over to a dozen bows of different sizes and shapes. To Reya, they all looked the same—just straight sticks with strings dangling from one end. Maykego chose a bow about a meter long. "Let's try this one. Good for rabbits and other small game. But if you use it good, we gonna work you with bow like mine." She handed Reya the bow. "You gonna string it now."

Reya's face flushed. She sensed the others in the room watching. "How do I start?"

"First, put end already stringed against your foot. Yes. Now take loose end of string in your bad hand."

Reya tried to grasp the string with numb fingers, but it kept dropping to the floor. Maykego said nothing. Reya picked up the string with her good hand and draped the end across her other thumb. With great effort, her thumb finally behaved and she pressed the string tight to her palm.

"Now, bend the top of the bow down with strong hand. Push it 'gainst your foot and don't let it jump from you. The wood wants to stay straight, and fights when we force it to bend."

She pressed down. The damned stick seemed to have a life of its own. It took all her strength and balance to keep it bending without springing sideways from her grasp.

"It is only wood and string," said Maykego. "Show it who be boss."

Reya's shaking thumb and arm finally noosed the tip. When she eased up, the string snapped taut in the notch, and the wood was bowed. There was a patter of applause in the room. Reya grinned and made a little bow to the workmen.

Maykego beamed. "Now all we have to do is make you be expert shot."

PASSAGES

"A snake that you can see does not bite."

—*Mozambican proverb*

It was a quiet morning. Nakhoza stood outside her tent waiting for Annja. D'Shay and the rest of the team hadn't yet returned from Ezondwei, so Annja planned this morning for Nakhoza's orientation and assignment. A couple of children darted past, playing tag and squealing. Nearby, three women sat in a circle mending trail-torn clothes. They chattered and laughed as they worked. But Nakhoza was oblivious as she chewed a thumbnail, wondering what Annja had in mind for her future in this camp.

"Morning, Nakhoza," said Annja from behind.

Startled, Nakhoza whirled. "Oh, good morning Amai Annja." Although Nakhoza was tall for a Chewan girl, Annja stood half-a-head taller.

Annja looked at the women sewing and laughing, then dodged two kids tearing past. "Let's find a quieter place to talk."

They settled on two smooth boulders at one side of the cavern.

"I understand you were a SUN officer before GlobeTran took control of African SUN responsibilities."

"Yes, my father was an Alliance captain and got me an intern position with the SUN Intelligence Division."

"And from Giambo I hear you were largely responsible for defense logistics in the Nswibe incursion."

"Yes, I was able to use what I learned in Alliance counter-insurgence training. We did not have much to work with at Nswibe, but I had a motivated team and we created traps and diversions that held off many 'gades."

Annja nodded. "Nakhoza, I want you to be our defense specialist. We have some natural and man-made defenses, but we must do better. And we have little in the way of warning systems. Do you think you could assist us?"

Nakhoza sat straighter. "Oh, yes. I would be proud to assist your community as best I can, amai."

"Remember, Nakhoza, this is *your* community as well."

"Yes, yes of course, Amai Annja."

"Good, now let me give you a brief tour of the cavern's interior to see how you can best protect our outpost. I think you will be surprised at the unseen part of our compound."

Annja headed to the southwest corner of the cavern where there was a two-meter gap in the wall. A young African man sat on a wooden bench. "Nakhoza, this is Ndibeo. He's on guard duty at the moment."

They nodded to one another.

"Most of our people rotate the guarding of this entrance to the secure part of our fortress home. Only a few are allowed beyond this point for security and safety reasons. The main cavern with our living facilities is only the tip of the iceberg."

"Iceberg?"

"Sorry; extinct analogy. Like a crocodile nose barely visible above the river's surface. What you see is only the tip of what lies beneath."

"But, how could this great room be just a 'tip'? I have never seen any room so vast."

"Because there are so many passages and rooms dug deep into the hillside. There are so many, we have only explored some of the interior."

"Then, why do no Chewan people live here? It is cool, the water good, and if there are rooms and passages ... "

"The local people consider this place taboo. They think the spirits of the ancient people who lived here haunt the cavern and will devour their souls." She handed Nakhoza a wind-up lamp. They cranked up their lights and stepped through the gap in the wall. "This area is off-limits to most because it is easy to become lost in the passages and because we have sensitive equipment that cannot be tampered with. There are also deadly hazards that you should find useful as defense coordinator."

They followed the dank passageway for more than a hundred meters. Water dripped from above, and Nakhoza shivered from the chill of the cool rock. A sudden flutter overhead made her jerk her lamp's beam toward the ceiling. She could only make out the shapes of dark leaves moving high above them.

"Bats," said Annja. "They are harmless neighbors. We appreciate them since they love to devour our evening clouds of mosquitoes."

They continued.

"Okay," said Annja. "We're coming to the end of the natural passageway."

Up ahead, Nakhoza saw a glow of light. As they approached she could see that the ceiling was lower now, and the rock had been hewed into a hallway.

"We're now entering the underground city. *The Old Ones,* as the locals call them, probably cut this and the many other tunnels over hundreds of years."

They came upon the first section lit by tiny lights in the ceiling that cast the limestone walls in soft yellows.

"How can you have electric down here?" asked Nakhoza.

"We've scavenged solar panels from deserted villages and installed them on the hillside. There are natural cracks to the surface so it was relatively easy to drop wiring for lighting and communications."

Nakhoza followed Annja to a place where the tunnel forked. Annja shined her light at the ceiling. "Do you see that mark?"

"Yes, amai."

"We've made marks to keep from getting lost. A straight dash means you're on an escape route. An 'X' means don't go there. The builders of this complex worked to defend against invaders. Some of the X-ed passages turn into mazes from which it is difficult to escape."

They continued to a three-way fork in the passage.

"You choose the way, Nakhoza."

Nakhoza flashed her beam overhead and saw the mark. The passageway to the far right was chalked with a short black line. Not obvious, but there if you knew to look for it. The other two were marked with faint X's. "To the right," she said.

"Good. This leads to our communications center."

But a few meters further Annja stopped and held up her

hand. She flashed her beam across the passage floor. "Here is something important that you must know and remember. See that dark stone set in the floor?"

"This one?" Nakhoza stepped forward and toed the rock.

Annja lunged to grab her. *"Nakhoza!"*

Nakhoza heard herself scream as the floor fell away. She threw her arms out, grasping. Her forearm slammed to the stone floor, but slid as her body weight dragged her. The lower half of her body dangled in space. She clawed at the stone, eyes wide, panting. Her lamp tumbled and shattered in the darkness below.

An iron grip seized her wrist. Her heart pounded and her other hand floundered to grab Annja's arm. Fingers fumbled together until Annja had her tightly gripped. Annja leaned back, straining. "Nakhoza … can you … get your leg to the surface?"

Nakhoza was panting so hard she couldn't speak. *Please, dear God!* she pleaded silently. *Give me the strength.* With a last burst of energy she swung up a leg. Her knee caught on the edge of the floor.

Annja gave a final tug and grunt, and Nakhoza scrambled, gasping, to solid ground. She rolled away from the pit, her body shaking.

"Dear Lord, Nakhoza!" snapped Annja. "You should have recognized that as a trap. I even pointed out the trigger mechanism, yet you carelessly—"

"I'm sorry!" said Nakhoza. "Yes, I was careless, but I thought you would brief me on such dangers *before* we encounter them."

Annja made a dismissive wave. "Never mind," she sighed.

Annja retrieved her light from the floor and shone it toward the trap. The trapdoor was the width of the passage and about two meters long. It rotated on an axis so it could drop a person, then swing shut for the next victim. Annja triggered the stone again and pushed the trapdoor open enough to look down the shaft. When Annja shined her light, Nakhoza saw the remains of her own shattered lamp about ten meters below in a jumble of stalagmites and jagged rocks. Near the light was a scattering of chalk-white bones—ribs, skulls. Nakhoza stepped back and looked away.

"Yes," said Annja. "Others have fallen. There are traps like this throughout the passageways. Each has a brown stone trigger planted in the limestone. The traps are similar to the Punji pit-traps used by guerillas in past wars. Very simple. A false floor and a deadly drop to needle-sharp stakes." She pushed the door until it clicked back in place.

Nakhoza tried to read Annja's expression. At times she seemed calm, almost a mother figure to the New SUN people. But she had just shown a hardened side of herself. But then she had been through so much during her life—the drowning of her homeland; the neglect of SUN by GlobeTran; and here she was now trying to revive the hopes of SUN in the mountains with amateurs of every sort.

Without another word, Annja turned and continued along the passageway.

COMM ROOM

After the Great Solar Flare of 2058, gamma radiation destroyed the ability of satellites to relay communication and computer data. The Flare set communication technology back a century, forcing governments, businesses, and individuals to rely on antiquated point-to-point telegraphy and primitive cable and wire technology.

—*"Post-Flare Communication." GlobaPedia 1:338.sunprog.swz*

Here," said Annja. A light glowed from a doorway to the right. "This is our communications room." Although carved from solid stone, it almost looked the room of a village home. Walls were plastered smooth and painted white; only the floor and ceiling showed chisel marks.

A blender working at a vintage computer looked up and nodded. "Morning, Ms. Annja." The boy was dark-skinned and stocky. In a crowd, he might pass for an African, thought Nakhoza. Except for those sea-green eyes and his straight, dirty-blond hair that hung in dreadlocks. He appraised Nakhoza with his deep-set eyes.

"Good morning, Daku," said Annja. She smiled at Nakhoza. "Daku, this is Nakhoza, one of the new members of our team."

"Pleased to meet you," said Nakhoza, trying to read those eyes.

Daku nodded, no hint of a smile. He turned to Annja. "I've got a new intercept." He tilted his head toward Nakhoza. "It may be critical."

Nakhoza felt her face heat with a rush of anger. What kind of rude hyena does not return a simple greeting?

"Nakhoza has clearance to hear anything you have to say. She is now our defense coordinator."

Daku glanced at Nakhoza and shrugged.

"Daku and Tarkin arrived together, blenders from 'Down Below.'"

"Down *Under,* Annja. Queensland, Australia."

"Yes … 'Down Under.'"

Nakhoza looked at this boy, so different in appearance from Tarkin. How could they be from the same place?

Daku smirked. "I can read your thoughts. Tarkin and I became mates on the ship over. We had to sort a few things out—seeing how most whites don't think highly of Aboriginals, as they call us—when they're being nice. You'd think they'd give us a little credit for living in Australia for 50,000 years longer than themselves, but no. Anyhow, Tarkin and I had a bit of back-and-forth in the beginning, but we're good-enough mates now. But that's what mates do, yeah? Sort things out."

Nakhoza made a half smile and nodded.

"Daku is a weapons specialist," said Annja, "but he has comm training and assists Xian with the communications room. He monitors radio traffic and even Morris Code."

"*Morse* Code," said Daku. "A form of communication once dead and gone; now risen from the grave. A simple series of beeps—long and short tones that indicate letters and numbers. Not so different from sending drum messages from valley to valley, yeah?"

"Yes," said Nakhoza.

His glance went from her face slowly down her body. She crossed her arms and looked aside.

Daku leaned back and smiled. "You seem like a bright sheila. Maybe I could teach you a little code in your spare time, yeah?"

Nakhoza lifted her chin. "Thank you, but I have other duties. And, to let you know, I have a blender ... friend."

Annja cleared her throat. "Daku, please explain to Nakhoza what resources we have here and how this room works. Intelligence is a key to our defensive strategies, so she must become familiar with all our electronics and related capabilities."

Daku stood and made a sweeping motion across the long table at which he had sat. *"Voila!* This seeming jumble of electronics is the heart of our Comm Center."

Nakhoza stepped around to look at a flickering vid-screen attached to patched-together computer components that sprouted tangles of colored wires. On her right stood a black metal box with dials and switches that she recognized as a shortwave radio, an older version of what she had used in her former SUN office back in the capital.

"This," said Annja, "is our connection to the outside world."

"I am impressed," said Nakhoza. "Much is old, but it is

working, and all in the middle of a rock mountain. Is it all powered by solar?"

"All by solar," said Daku. "Xian and I have scavenged bits and pieces of electronics to patch together lighting and a variety of comm devices."

Nakhoza nodded toward the shortwave transmitter. "Could your signals be detected by 'gades? If so, they might be able to get a fix on your position."

"So far, so good. We compress our coded messages to our other outposts, then send them in a half-second burst. We also have spotty communication with Global Alliance in Geneva, but only when we can bounce our transmissions off the ionosphere—or what's left of it after the Flare. The 'gades may or may not intercept some of those, but we never send information that might compromise our location."

"Amai Annja," asked Nakhoza, "how do you suggest I use these resources? I am trained as a defense specialist. I do not have the communications knowledge of Xian or Daku."

Annja nodded toward wooden ammo boxes stacked in a corner that overflowed with wiring and electronic parts. "You are an expert in explosive deterrents. Dig through those and see what you might use to detect and stop approaching enemies."

"Yes, I will need switches and wires to activate a minefield."

Annja frowned and nodded. "Yes, minefields. The thought of using mines rubs against my Quaker upbringing, but I'm afraid one must weigh the distasteful against the disastrous. So, Nakhoza, come down here and work as often as you need. And if you are lacking some kind of electrical gadget, we have people who are quite ingenious at creating amazing things from very little."

"Yes, Annja," she said. "I am honored to be a trusted member of your group."

"We're lucky to have you. I'd like you to set up a safety perimeter as quickly as you can."

"Of course, amai."

Annja sighed, her face weary. She crossed her arms, seeming to hesitate. She glanced at Daku. "I'm going to tell Nakhoza about the recent communication."

Daku frowned. "But, Ms. Annja, she's a newcomer."

"She is a former SUN officer, and she has skills we need. She needs to know what is in the works." Annja turned to Nakhoza. "Please do not pass on the information I'm about to tell you."

Nakhoza stood straight and attentive. "No, amai, I will not."

"I believe we will be tested soon enough. We have intercepted 'gade communications that units are converging on the savannah. Normally these 'gade units would be natural enemies—warlords and their thugs, each fighting for territory. This must be a temporary alliance to plan a coordinated attack and finish New SUN." Her eyes narrowed. "I will *not* have New SUN wiped out by killers who wish to trample Africa and its people!"

Nakhoza sensed a mixed shiver of fear and elation. The time of trial was approaching, and she would play a major role. "I will not fail you, Amai Annja. This is my homeland. I will give my life before letting the 'gades defeat us."

MAID MARIAN

"One arrow can knock down an elephant."

—*Kenyan proverb*

———————————

The next day, just after dawn, Reya watched Tarkin, Jaym, and the others straggle in from their village probe. They looked tired, but most seemed upbeat and even grinned as they talked and shed their packs. Tarkin was the exception. He just looked pissed and wasn't talking to anyone. One of the New SUN boys tried to intercept him on the way to his tent.

"Hey, Tarkin. Annja wants you to report to her as soon—"

"Bugger off!" snapped Tarkin. "I'll report when I'm ready."

Reya waved to Bettina, the last to come inside. Bettina walked over and smiled. *"Hola, amiga.* What you been doing? They give you an assignment yet?"

Reya laughed. "You'll never guess."

"Umm, they gonna make you chef lady in *la cocina* so we don't have to eat nothing but African mush, yes?"

"Sorry, *chica,* but you're gonna have to deal with the same Chewan chef. Okay, now don't laugh, but you are looking at— ta-dah—a future archer."

"You don't mean, bow-and-arrow kind of archer?"

"Yeah, I *do.*"

Bettina looked confused. *"Pero, tu brazo."*

"Always the arm." Reya shrugged. "Look...Annja says I can deal with the arm. She has me training with a master archer. An African girl named Maykego. You'll like her." Reya looked at the rifle slung over Bettina's shoulder. "I can't use a rifle, but Annja says archers can be—"

"Morning, Rey-yah," said Maykego, approaching them. "Ready for lesson?"

"Maykego. Um, this is my friend Bettina." The girls smiled, nodded, and exchanged light handshakes.

"Please excuse me," said Bettina, but I must take a little sleep. I will talk to you later, Reya. Nice to meet you Maykego."

Maykego smiled and nodded. As Bettina headed for her tent, Reya beamed. "I am proud to announce, Maykego, that I'm the boss, not the bow. I can string its skinny little neck in about ten seconds flat. Like you said: trap with foot and thigh; then bend and drop the loop. It's easy now, but for most of yesterday I thought I'd never tame that damn wood."

Maykego grinned. "I am glad you master it. We will get breakfast meal then start shooting practice, yes?"

"I can't wait!"

An hour later, Maykego led Reya on a trail that took them down a grassy ravine. "Maykego?" asked Reya. "How did you become an archer? Female archers must be kind of...rare over here."

"I was oldest of five girls and my father sometimes take me hunting. I be maybe thirteen when he die in the cholera. From then on I hunted to feed our family."

They stopped walking. "Here," said Maykego. "This be the practice place for archers. String you bow, Reya."

Reya wished she hadn't bragged about her ten-second bow-stringing record. It took her a half minute, but she did it. "Ta-dah!"

"That be okay, but you must be faster. You practice each day and you be ten-second stringer. Now, I think you find the next part gonna be more difficult, but you can do it. Take hold of bow with you hurt arm and draw string to you cheek with good arm."

"Yes, good." Maykego whipped a shaft from the leather quiver on her hip. She pushed the arrow's notch onto the string and lay the shaft across Reya's left hand.

"Okay, shoot at small red bush on hillside. Aim just above bush. Keep bow straight up and down. Okay, now."

Reya let the arrow fly. The shaft wobbled in a low arch and struck several meters from the bush. "Crap," she muttered.

Maykego shook her head. "Big miss. But what be important is you *can* shoot. Just take much practice to hit target. Here. Watch how I stand. Toes and shoulders in line with target. Bow straight up and down." She drew the string back and let the arrow fly.

The arrow hissed and vanished into the little red bush. "Damn," said Reya.

"I think you pick up skill fast enough." Her face grew serious. "Besides, Reya, I think we do not have that much time."

"What do you mean? You know something I don't."

Maykego hesitated. Finally she nodded toward the hillside. "Just practice. That red bush is a 'gade. Now kill it."

ADVICE

And when a woman's will is as strong as the man's
who wants to govern her, half her strength must be
concealment.

—*Mary Anne Evans (aka, George Eliot)*

After a morning of practice, Reya broke for lunch.
Although her arms ached, she decided to go back to the
range for another hour.

"Reya?" called Lingana.

Reya turned and smiled, her bow in hand and quiver of
arrows on her hip. "*Moni,* Lingana!" She held up her bow.
"Getting ready to practice at the range." She noticed Lingana's averted eyes. They were red, like she'd been crying. "Hey,
what's going on. This isn't the Lingana I've gotten to know.
What's up, Girl?"

Lingana still looked to one side. "I … just need to talk to
another woman. It is about Jay-em, and I think you gonna be
best woman who knows him, yes?"

"Me? I thought you'd know him best." But she read the
unhappiness on Lingana's pretty face. "Well, yeah. Sure, let's
talk." She glanced at all the people nearby; some at work sewing torn clothing; a few cleaning their weapons; a bunch of kids

heading for their makeshift "school" in one of the cavern chambers. "Come on Lingana. Let's head down the trail and find some privacy."

"Yes, that would be good. Thank you."

Although Reya's arm was still weak, her step was nimble as a mountain goat's as she skipped down the trail. A hundred meters down she veered off to the little patch of trees in the shelter of a cliff face. "I think this is private enough."

Lingana nodded. They sat cross-legged in a patch of lush grass. Reya laid her bow and quiver aside and touched Lingana's quivering chin. "You look miserable. What's going on?"

Lingana wiped her nose and looked at Reya. "Jaym does not want to go home with me."

"Home? You mean, back to your old village?"

Lingana nodded. "When we came to this place, I was very excited that we survived the terrible walk across the savannah. I was happy that my mother and sisters made it here, and thrilled that Jaym and I would have a life together. He could have been killed so many times, but thanks to God we both made it. It seemed that everything was going to be as I always dreamed." Lingana shook her head. "But Jaym does not want to go back with me."

Why me? Thought Reya. She was no good at counseling about relationships. Her luck with guys had always been shitty. And it looked like it was going to continue to be shitty. No prospects here in camp, and she didn't even want to think about the future. If they couldn't stop the 'gades, it was all over anyhow.

But Lingana looked so miserable that she had to try. "Look, Lingana. I think you've got to give it some time. You've only been here a few days. It hasn't been that long since your village was destroyed and you had to bury your father and friends. That's enough to make anyone unhappy. I'll bet Jaym just wants to get you through the next few days alive. If you're really set on moving back to Nswibe, wait till this is over to talk about it. Don't push him right now."

"If he doesn't want to go back with me, then he must not love me."

"That's not true," said Reya. "I know he's crazy about you. He's always saying how he's so lucky to have you and he wants to be with you. I know he wants to marry you...when all this shit is over. And, no offense, but Nswibe is gone. It's just cinders and graves."

"My family has lived there since...forever. Giambo, my sisters, and I can begin a new Nswibe nearby. The valley there is rich with fine soil and clear water. It would be a wonderful place for our children. But Jaym says it is too full of death, and he did not like the old village nearby that is said to be full of ghosts. He thinks it is better to make a new start. Maybe near wherever D'Shay and Nakhoza decide to go."

Crap, thought Reya. Okay, *what would I say to soothe my own sister?* She leaned close and took Lingana's hand. "Look, sweetie, I know you've got to be confused and grieving; wondering what's gonna happen. Jaym's a great guy, and you are perfect for him. We still have a lot of things to get through before we can decide where to settle down." Reya patted the bow beside her. "We're still fighting for survival. 'Gades want us wiped out, and the GlobeTran assholes in Wananelu don't care what happens to us."

Lingana nodded. "Yes, maybe it is best if I don't talk about

Nswibe to Jaym. It seems to make him angry. Then I get upset and we don't talk sometimes. It is hurtful in my heart."

"Yeah, probably it hurts him too. Let's get through the next few weeks—maybe months, and when things settle out, then maybe we'll all talk it out together." Reya smiled. "When the time comes, I might be able to nudge Jaym a little."

They stood and brushed off their legs. Reya smiled and noticed Lingana's face wasn't as tight and miserable as when they started talking.

"Thank you, Reya. You are a true friend. I will concentrate on the coming days, and I will keep from talking about Nswibe to Jaym." She managed a crooked smile. "You are like a sister now." She hugged Reya, and then slowly walked back up the trail.

Reya picked up her bow and quiver and thought, *Hassling over where to live?* Hell, at least Lingana had a decent guy and a future. She wondered if D'Shay and Nakhoza were also quibbling over some stupid little thing. Would she do that when—if—she got her African guy. Probably. She knew she wasn't the easiest female to live with, but that was because she had to be tough. Tough to survive the Corridor 'gee camp and tough to protect her mom and sister from gang boys and camp guards. And tough to have survived being a 'gade "bitch" held prisoner in their mountain headquarters.

But enough of that. She had to take her own advice and get through the present. And the present for her was to become a useful soldier in this new community.

She turned and headed down the trail to the archery range.

WOMAN TO WOMAN

"A person who has children does not die."
—*African proverb*

Nakhoza gathered with a dozen other New SUN leaders. Annja had called them into this whitewashed room carved into one side of the cavern. Sitting and standing was a cross-section of the present camp: Lingana, Jaym, D'Shay, Xian, and Annja's New SUN lieutenants—Tarkin and Daku.

Annja leaned forward, hands splayed on the table and her face determined. "It seems most of you already know that Xian now has solid 'gade intel. As many as a dozen 'gade camps appear to be planning some sort of unified attack on our three main outposts. We at Post-1 expect to face a force of 150 to 200 men. For our mutual survival, we *must* convince the Ezondwei villagers that without joining forces with us, this outpost and their village could be plundered and destroyed in a single 'gade attack." She glanced at each face as she continued. "I will appoint several of you to approach the chief and the village men again."

Nakhoza heard Tarkin whisper something to Daku.

"Tarkin?" said Annja. "Perhaps you would like you share your opinion with the group."

"It's just that we've been to Ezondwei and did our bloody best to convince the chief to ally with us. He thinks they can handle any 'gade force. But I don't think it's a loss for us. Allying with villagers could cause more harm than help. Villager warriors like to show how macho each bloke can be in battle. They don't work as a fighting team, so how could they ever work with us in a coordinated offensive?"

Annja crossed her arms. "Do others of you agree with Tarkin's logic?"

Daku spoke up. "Those natives are superstitious. No offense to any present company, but they have been so isolated they might think voodoo and spells will turn back 'gade lorries and crawlers."

"That is offense to me and my people," rumbled Giambo. "And it is not so! 'Member the 'gade heads on stakes? Ezondwei people make fine, fine plan to do that—not voodoo or macho warrior fighting. I think you insult 'telligence of Chewan peoples."

Good for you, Giambo, thought Nakhoza. She glared at Daku and Tarkin.

Annja raised her hands for silence. "*No more!* I must agree with Giambo." She looked at each person as she spoke. "Giambo, you take the lead. I believe the people of Ezondwei respect you after facing their warriors during your previous attempt. And you, Xian, as intel officer you may be needed to convince them of the truth of the recent 'gade intercepts. Then the others who went last time—Jaym and D'Shay, will also go. Finally I want either Tarkin or Daku to join you."

"But Annja—" began Tarkin.

"You two are doubters, so I would like to see you convinced that those villagers can indeed work with us. Test them, if you must. Give them a tactical scenario and listen to their solution. I believe you will be surprised."

"Then send Daku," muttered Tarkin.

"Gee, thanks, Mate," said Daku.

"Very well, Daku it is. You have your orders, I wish you well tomorrow."

"Amai Annja," said Nakhoza. "Please! I think it would be good for some of us women to go as well. Bettina went on the first mission. We could be helpful."

Annja pinched her lips. "From what Giambo has told me, the Ezondwei chief was a bit miffed that women were included in the diplomacy."

Reya said, "But that's just…"

"Sexist?" said Annja. "It is. But once we become allies, the villagers will see the prowess of you women. But this is not the time."

Nakhoza stood. "Forgive me, Amai Annja, perhaps we women could speak to you alone for a moment, yes?"

Annja nodded. "Very well." She looked at the men hesitating. "Let us women talk alone. Prepare for your journey, gentlemen." The men ambled away.

"What is it, Nakhoza?"

"We can help," she said. "I think we have something to tell villagers that men cannot." She turned to Lingana. "Remember how I convinced your mother to let Jay-em to court you?"

Lingana grinned and nodded. "Yes." She turned to Annja. "Nakhoza is right. We can make a difference."

———

The next afternoon Lingana and Nakhoza hesitated when they arrived at the edge of Ezondwei. Nakhoza noticed a tangle of vines grown over a burnt-out crawler. It had to be the 'gades' crawler. She wondered where their heads were impaled. She shuddered and hoped she would never see such a sight as D'Shay had described.

Nakhoza turned to see Jaym, D'Shay, Giambo, and Xian, all unarmed except for Giambo with his machete. Their tee shirts were sweat-stained and dusty from the trek. She glanced down at her own sweat-damp shirt. If only she had a sheet of *chitenge* cloth to change into. With a traditional garment wrapped around her waist like a long skirt, these village women would see her more as a decent Chewan girl rather than an immodest tramp daring to wear shorts on a first visit. She brushed dust from her shirt and shorts, then took a deep breath. "I think we must go in now," she said.

"We'll be right behind you," said Jaym. His voice was calm, reassuring.

Nakhoza glanced back at D'Shay. He gave her a wink. "Go on, Babe. Impress those ladies with your diplomatic charm."

Nakhoza forced a shaky smile. "Do not worry. Lingana and I will fulfill the mission Annja has allowed us."

Giambo nodded. "And we will deal with the chief."

Lingana looked at Giambo's machete swinging at his side. "Brother, do you think it wise to bring big knife to village? They maybe see you as big danger."

"I need to protect you if I have to."

"I think it can only bring distrust. Please leave it here."

Nakhoza nodded. "Lingana is right. We will both be fine.

'Sides, one knife gonna be nothing against many village men. Show them we come in peace."

Giambo hesitated, but finally leaned the machete against the village's thorny fence.

Lingana and Nakhoza walked into the village square, their chins high.

Nakhoza looked back to see D'Shay and the others heading toward a large thatched building. Probably the Chief's home.

Children running around the square stopped to watch the two women strangers. The village was silent except for the cackle of chickens pecking at the dirt.

"Oh!" said Lingana. "That blue house looks so much like my old home in Nswibe—how it used to look."

"Yes," said Nakhoza. "This somewhat like my village. The smells are the same—*chamba* stew cooking somewhere. And I smell peppers hanging out to dry." The scents and sights of adobe homes were so much like her old village that they made her heart swell with longing. *No,* she thought. She must not think of home now. It would make her weak. It was so important to be strong right now.

They approached a young woman fetching water from the well. She stopped in her tracks, her eyes wide.

Nakhoza and Lingana touched their fingers to their lips to show respect. *"Moni,"* they said in greeting. The woman, wearing a black and green *chitenge*, eyed Nakhoza's tee shirt and shorts. She did not return the lip greeting, but finally murmured a soft, *"Moni."*

Lingana spoke to the woman in Chewan. "I am sorry that we are not dressed appropriately for a visit. But we are refugees and have traveled many days across the Great Savannah. We came to the Blue Mountains to escape the 'gade killers."

The woman nodded, but did not change expression.

"I am Lingana Zingali from Nswibe, a Chewan woman like you. And this is my friend, Nakhoza, also Chewan."

The woman's face was still unreadable. Her fists were clutched at her side, knuckles white. "What do you want from me?"

"We come as friends," said Lingana. "We are with the New SUN people, working to rid our country of 'gades who plague all our villages, and our country."

Nakhoza spoke up. "We would please like to speak with the women of Ezondwei. We have something important to tell you all."

———

Within half-an-hour, the village women were gathered in the meetinghouse. The head woman told Lingana and Nakhoza that she was the chief's number-one wife. To Lingana she looked about her mother's age—the same weatherworn face and swirls of gray sprinkled across her head.

"What can you tell us women that we do not already know? After all, you are only girls," said the woman with a scowl. "I know your men are talking to our men. My husband, the chief, does not want to do your bidding. So what do you think you can say to make a difference, eh?"

"Yes, amai," said Nakhoza. "Although we are girls, we have seen much killing by the 'gades. We only ask that you hear our words, then decide if they have worth."

The older woman shrugged, then squatted with the others to listen.

Nakhoza swallowed and hoped her voice would hold steady. She tried to avoid the judgmental eyes of the head-woman. "Like you, we are Chewan. We have escaped death at the hands of the 'gades who intend to rule our land. We know many of you do not think you need the help of New SUN—"

The headwoman chopped the air with the edge of her hand. "We do not need help of runaway girls and your mzungu friends. Our warriors can defend our village. Did you see the 'gade heads on spikes?"

"We know your men are brave," said Lingana. "You might be able to fight off more 'gades by yourselves. But there is an important reason to embrace New SUN as your ally, yes?"

The women whispered to one another. Some nodding.

"Yes," said Lingana. "You all know of the curse sent by the Great Flare. What will happen if you do not allow New SUN into Chewena's future?"

A young village woman began to sob. "My babies," she wailed. "All born dead. God has cursed us."

"No, no!" said Lingana. "It was a terrible thing sent from the sun, but was natural as a typhoon or an earthquake. God protects, does not destroy. And through God's grace, Chewan women can have children. Blenders from many countries have *not* been affected by the Flare. With them you can make many babies. And your Chewan blood will carry on to beat in the hearts of your children."

"But they will be mzungu children!" shouted a woman. Heads nodded, others called out.

"They will also be Chewan," said Lingana.

Nakhoza stepped forward. "Hear me, women of Ezondwei! Do you want children? Or do you want your people to fade to nothing. New SUN may be not be your choice, but it is the only hope for our people."

Silence. The women looked at one another.

"Think on this, then talk to your men. *They* may not think they need to accept us, but I think you women will see what is necessary."

17

DEBRIEFING

In times of danger people will act together.

—*Kenyan proverb*

Outside the cavern, the woman on guard duty scanned the ravines and pathways below. *There.* On one of the trails straggled a column of people. She focused her binoculars and waited. *Yes!* She turned and shouted. "They have returned."

Annja, Reya, and a dozen others came running to the cavern's edge to meet them.

Jaym and Lingana were in the lead, followed by Nakhoza, D'Shay, and the others. Lingana smiled and waved.

As they stepped into the cool shade of the cavern, Annja said, "We were so worried about all of you. When you didn't return yesterday, we feared 'gades found you, or that the village chief might have..."

"No," said Jaym. "All heads are present and accounted for."

"But, three days! What happened?" asked Annja.

Giambo stepped forward. "We men talk to the chief and warriors, but they mock us. Kept saying they so strong and brave—don't need us. We talk for three hours, then they shoo us 'way like flies." He turned to Jaym and D'Shay. "Come.

107

We get some food. Let Lingana and Nakhoza tell what happen after that."

D'Shay winked at Nakhoza as he and Jaym headed to the kitchen with Giambo.

"So, what happened?" asked Annja.

Nakhoza smiled. "Over cups of bush tea, we explained to the women importance of the Blending Program. We tell them how 'gades wanna crush it so they have Africa to their self. When we finished, the chief's number-one wife kept asking questions: 'Will blending babies have more mzungu in their blood than Chewan? Will blenders make us worship a Holy Ghost? Are blenders brave as their Ezondwei men? Will their babies speak mzungu talk or Chewan?' Then other women asked questions. I think we talked 'bout two hours."

"At *least* two," laughed Lingana.

Nakhoza nodded. "We did not give up, and it was worth it. The women invited us for evening meal and to stay the night. They say they want to talk to their men and hear more from us."

"The next day," said Lingana, "Chief's number-one wife has loud talk with her husband. We be polite and walk 'round village so not to listen to private words. But as we walk we can still hear loud words."

"Chewan men think they run village life," said Nakhoza, "but we know who are really village bosses. So the number-one wife finally brought us to common house to speak to men and women together. We make the same arguments like we did for women. When men yell that we lie, their women shout them down."

"We decided to let Lingana do most of talking 'cause she

is small, looks so innocent. They sensed she would not lie to other Chewan women, and I think she convince many men."

"Some men puffed and blustered," said Lingana, "but the chief finally gave in. Says the matter is not that important, not worth so much talk, 'Let the women have this small victory,' he says. 'My men too busy to waste time talking more.'"

"So they're joining forces with us!" said Annja. "That's wonderful." She looked around and motioned to Daku.

Daku trotted over.

"Where's Tarkin?" she asked.

"Um, I think he took a walk...maybe went to relieve himself."

"He should be here. This is important news. Now that we have native allies, we can plan some serious strategy."

Daku nodded, but avoided her eyes.

Nakhoza said, "I think Tarkin is not too pleased with this new alliance. He is concerned that villagers will not follow strategy when we finally face the 'gades."

"Yes," said Annja. "I know he has reservations, but I expect he will come to accept the alliance as he gets to know the villagers."

"Absolutely," said Daku.

The next morning, Annja gathered the group leaders in a chamber off the main tunnel. In the center of the room stood a rough wood table, one end blackened as if by fire. Jaym wondered if it had been salvaged from a common-house in some torched village. He and the others were seated on rough-carved three-legged stools. Annja and Tarkin sat across from Jaym. He tried to read Tarkin's expression, but he didn't show a trace of emotion.

When everyone was seated, Annja spoke. "We knew we had to face 'gades sooner or later. According to what we gather from their chatter, they are aware of the basic locations of each of our three New SUN outposts in these mountains. Some of you may not know that we are the largest of the outposts. Each is about thirty kilometers apart. When the 'gades come—and be assured, they will come—we will need a joint battle plan coordinated with the other two posts. All three New SUN groups *must* work in concert. Xian? Please give us a briefing on the readiness of the other outposts."

Xian nodded. "Posts 2 and 3 also trying to ally with local villages. Chatter we pick up from 'gade militias say their warlords joining together to attack us. Communications don't tell if they're gonna hit our posts one at time or divide to attack all three at same time. Also don't know date 'gades plan to move. But we think it will be soon."

"Any idea of how soon?" asked Jaym.

"Soon," said Annja. "Perhaps a week or ten days, if the increase of radio traffic is any indication. And since we know the 'gades are coming in force, it is important for us to take the initiative. If they are truly massing all their forces, they could easily overwhelm our three posts at once. My instinct is that they will indeed make simultaneous attacks."

Bettina raised her hand. Jaym was surprised by her expression; tense, yet determined. Bettina had been so quiet most of the time that Jaym rarely noticed her. Her only real friend seemed to be Reya, and when they spoke it was often in Spanish.

"*Señora* Annja," said Bettina, "my home base was Number-2. It is small, only two-dozen scouts and a handful of trained fighters—all good people and my friends. I do not wish to desert you and the others, but I must be with them when they are attacked. If I leave now I should make it before the 'gades arrive."

Reya looked stricken. "But...we need you, and it could be suicide if—"

Annja waved Reya quiet. She pinched her lips and stared at the tabletop. "Bettina, perhaps we could order the Post-2 people to come here. We could certainly use all the reinforcements we can get."

Bettina shook her head. "I think there is not time. The post has several elders. It would take them days, and I fear the 'gades could find them in the open before they arrived. I can make it there in thirty-six hours if I do not stop."

"Travel at night?" asked Annja.

"I am a former SUN scout. Most of my journeys were made at night."

Annja nodded. "Then you should be with your people. We will miss you, but Godspeed, and we wish you well, Bettina."

Jaym glanced at Reya as Bettina stood to leave. Reya looked stunned, her mouth open. Jaym figured he and Reya were thinking the same thing: If a force of 'gades hit the two smaller posts first, Bettina and the others wouldn't have a chance.

"*Hasta luego,* my friends," said Bettina on her way out. She paused and made a forced smile toward Reya, then was gone.

After Bettina left the room, Annja cleared her throat and

continued. "I'd like you all to know that although my second-in-command, Tarkin, at first did not agree with joining forces with the Ezondwei villagers, he now accepts the fact that we need everyone's fighting power and skills." She looked toward him. "Yes, Tarkin?"

Tarkin showed no expression as he said, "Of course, Annja. I now agree in the tactical need for New SUN and local villagers to join forces. I'll do my part to make that alliance work."

Jaym knew this was pure Tarkin bullshit. Annja hadn't heard the nonstop crap Tarkin had spewed on their trek to the village—about the worthless natives and how they would mess up any kind of battle plan. So, why all the kiss-ass talk to Annja? Had she threatened to take away his command?

"Thank you," said Annja. "Tarkin and I have worked out offensive and defensive team assignments. I will meet with individual teams later, but for now I want everyone to hear who is being assigned to which team."

Jaym tried to read Tarkin's expressionless face. Tarkin had helped choose the assignments, and since Tarkin hated Jaym's guts, it would be just like the bastard to put Lingana in a lethal front-line position. No matter what, he wasn't going to let that happen.

"Nakhoza and I will be co-commanders of base defense," said Annja. "She successfully helped defend the village of Nswibe against a powerful force of 'gades. She has SUN training in counterinsurgency. I feel most confident in her abilities."

Nakhoza lifted her chin. "Thank you, Amai Annja."

"Lingana will be co-leader with Nakhoza. They have proven to work together well." Lingana tried to suppress a smile as she glanced at Jaym.

Thank God, thought Jaym.

"We leave the selection of the rest of the defense team up to Nakhoza," said Annja.

"Next, the offensive teams. Tarkin will be in overall command of both teams; his own, and Giambo's. If—God forbid—something happens to Tarkin, Giambo will take over general command. Xian will go with these teams to keep us in touch. Tarkin will take his experienced fighters, and Giambo will choose his team from the Nswibe refugees."

Jaym raised his hand. "Annja, what about the Ezondwei warriors? There are about a dozen village men with 'gade weapons."

"Yes, thank you. They will join you as you move to intercept the 'gade force. Giambo and Tarkin will each add Ezondwei fighters to their teams."

"Annja?" said Tarkin. "Why not have them all on Giambo's team? Chewans with Chewans."

"Tarkin, we've been over this before. I know you doubt the villagers' abilities to work as part of a team, but we need them, and I want them to feel included in New SUN—not separated because they are villagers."

Jaym noticed Tarkin's face redden, trying hard to contain himself. But Tarkin remained silent.

"Next," said Annja, "we need a team to lead the Ezondwei archers. Maykego will head this team. She is a superb archer, and a Chewan." She smiled at Maykego. "Do you think you can handle those Chewan men?"

Maykego smiled. "Oh, yes, Amai Annja. I am taller and maybe better archer than any of them. If they give me trial, I will show them who is in charge."

Jaym and the others laughed. Only Tarkin did not smile.

"And Reya will be with Maykego."

Reya bit her lip. "Annja, I've only had—"

Annja held up her hand. "No, Reya. Maykego says you are a natural archer and have the gift of handling a bow."

Reya cleared her throat. "Thank you, Annja."

Annja was silent for a minute as she looked at each face. Finally she said, "We are going to win this battle. Then we are going to move on to build a greater New SUN. We will not fail."

FIELD OF THE DEAD

"Osaman tee ne nsa kyia wo a, wopono de mu."
(When a ghost stretches its hand to greet you,
pull yours back.)

—*Akan saying, West Africa*

It was early morning on a blessedly cooler day when Nakhoza and Lingana arrived at the village of Ezondwei. Six women waited for them in the village square.

Nakhoza nodded a greeting and asked in Chewan, "Are none of your men going to help us?"

One of the women, stocky—maybe in her forties—chuckled. "You know Chewan men. 'We are not beasts of burden,' they say. 'That is women's work.' So you have us. But we are strong and used to carrying heavy loads."

Lingana smiled. "Yes, it was the same in Nswibe."

"We are glad for your help," said Nakhoza. She pointed to the southeast. "The old battlefield is four or five hours from here. Do you have food and water in case we have to spend a night on the savannah?"

"Yes. We are prepared fine. We often have to make long treks for firewood; and for water in the dry season."

"Good." said Nakhoza. "Then let us begin, and pray that we can find what we need to stop the 'gade devils."

The trail from the village wound down the canyon bottom toward the savannah. In most places it was little wider than a goat path. As they walked single file, one of the women began to sing. Within seconds everyone joined in.

O leopards, dearest leopards,
I've traveled far along this trail,
Please don't harm me now.
O baboons let kindness prevail,
Like others, please spare my life.
O hyenas please go back to your vale.

Lingana laughed as she sang the familiar traveling song she had sung with other Nswibe girls during their treks to the city. Now the Ezondwei women sang it over and over, changing the names of the animals, sometimes joking that the beasts were welcome to take any unfaithful husbands they found on the trail.

When they finally reached the edge of the savannah they stopped their singing and joking. The coolness of the mountain trail vanished as they walked into a wall of searing savannah heat. Now it was time to watch in the distance for telltale dust plumes of lorries and crawlers. Time to be prepared to find cover if a drone appeared. Lingana figured any passing drones would likely not target a group of unarmed women. But who now controlled those remote-controlled killing machines? Rumors flew that 'gades might have already taken the drone command post. If so, they could target villages suspected of harboring blenders, as well as bombard New SUN outposts.

Soon after entering the tinder-dry grassland, Lingana's tee shirt became damp with sweat. Out here on the savannah, the heat danced above the grasslands and created ghost lakes and phantom forests that wavered above the distant horizon.

Around 1500 hours they arrived at the site of the battlefield. Blackened rovers, supply lorries, and robotic tanks lay shattered and askew across a kilometer-wide area. The savannah grasses were shin-high, so the women had to tread carefully to avoid shards of metal and unexploded ordinance.

One of the Ezondwei women hugged herself as she looked wide-eyed at the carnage. "I heard the sounds of this battle when I was a girl," she said. "It was a Sunday afternoon when drones hummed toward our village. Mother screamed and ran us into the forest. But the drones passed over and headed for the savannah. They sounded like angry hornets. Minutes later we heard explosions like mountain thunder. It was over so quickly." She gazed at a crawler lying on its side like a bloated rhino. "Mother never let me come down and see. Said it was dangerous because of hyenas coming for the dead. She said vulture birds would come next to pick at the bones. None of our people have come here since our village shaman had a vision. He saw in his dream that spirits of the dead trapped in these death cages haunted the battlefield. He said he heard their death cries and saw their angry faces swirling around him."

Nakhoza fingered her elephant necklace. "See this amulet? Lingana and I each wear one. I believe your shaman was truthful, but the wooden elephants will protect you from any lingering spirits. They have the power of New SUN. They will put any spirit to flight."

"If I touch it," asked a woman, "will it protect me?"

"It has protected me."

One by one the women approached Nakhoza and Lingana to rub the wooden elephants between their fingers. Some made the sign of the cross as they touched it.

"I did feel the power!" shouted a woman.

"Yes," said Lingana. She walked to the nearest crawler and placed her palm against the bomb-twisted armor. "See? Nothing to fear."

"Good," said Nakhoza. "Now let's begin our work." She pointed at two women. "You two, please check out that supply lorry. The cab is shattered, but there may be unexploded munitions in the back. Be careful of jagged metal. Lingana, please check out that rover for anything useful. The rest of you, separate and search other wreckage. Watch out for unexploded bombs in the grass. If you find shoulder rockets or large shells, tell me, but *don't* touch them until I can check them out. And remember, Chewan women, if you see bones or burnt bodies in the cabs, be brave. You are doing this to help save your village."

Lingana cautiously pushed through the dry grass toward the carcass of the rover. As she approached, she stepped around white shards of bones and tattered pieces of clothing bleached by the sun. The bones were so scattered and gnawed they didn't look human. *Were those ribs? Finger or toe bones? Thank God no skulls.* Or if there were, she figured, they had been crushed to fragments. She remembered how a hyena had once snapped off an Nswibe hunter's forearm with a single bite.

She shivered as she looked into the rover's open door. At least no skeletons. A gun lay across the floorboards. Some sort of automatic rifle. When she stepped back to inspect it, her heel crunched into something. She looked down to see a jawbone she had crushed. Lingana quickly moved back toward Nakhoza.

"Are you okay?" asked Nakhoza.

Lingana swallowed and nodded. "I think this gun is good. It was in the cab so maybe hasn't been ruined by the weather."

Nakhoza took the rifle and removed the ammo clip. She flipped some levers, then slid the clip back into place. "It's like new. It's a Vektor C-27, a South Africa assault rifle. A little dated, but reliable and deadly." She smiled. "Excellent find. Did you see additional ammo clips?"

Lingana forced an apologetic smile. "I'll go back again. I was little nervous. With all the bones, I begin to think like the village women—spirits in the air." She tried to laugh.

"No, you have a right to feel the sense of death. This place is like a violated cemetery."

Lingana went back and found a dozen clips under one of the rover's seats. She laid them in the pile of weapons and ammo the women were gathering.

A woman leaned out of the back of an overturned lorry. The cab had been blown apart, but the back end was intact. "Lingana, what you think this thing is?" She held out a metal tube. It looked about a meter and a half long with a grip and trigger.

"I think it's a rocket launcher. Did you see any rockets with it? Like a small missile with fins?"

"Yes, two. I'm afraid to touch them."

"Nakhoza," shouted Lingana. "I think Njemile has something important."

Nakhoza jogged over. "Oh my lord. That launcher can knock out a tank or crawler. Njemile, you have struck gold!"

An explosion tore through the silence of the savannah. A scream, then cries of women.

Lingana ran over to the blackened crater where a village woman lay, her legs blasted to stumps, her bleeding torso ripped by shrapnel.

A woman shrieked. "Biskisa! No, not my sister!" She clutched the girl's legless body and wailed. She screamed at Nakhoza. "You promised the elephant necklaces would keep us safe. But look, my sister is dead!"

"Dear God, I am so sorry for your sister. But it was not ghosts," said Nakhoza. "It was the filthy weapons of the 'gades."

The woman wailed, rocking the limp body of her sister like a child.

Nakhoza glanced at Lingana. "I think we must leave before we have another tragedy."

––––––––––––

Nakhoza, Lingana, and the women of Ezondwei village struggled back toward the trail, each carrying half their weight in munitions packed into makeshift slings fashioned from their chitenge sheets. Lingana toted three 250mm mortar shells, as thick as her thigh, carefully separated by fistfuls of savannah grass.

"Nakhoza?" said Lingana. "Are you certain these will not blow up if I fall?"

"Yes, the detonators are not locked into firing position." In truth, Nakhoza wasn't sure that the safety locks were completely secure. Some had rusted over the years and couldn't be twisted all the way to the "safe" position. But they had no choice.

Without these explosives they'd have no defensive perimeter for the outpost.

The rumble of distant thunder rolled across the savannah. Nakhoza and the others stopped.

"It is only a mountain storm, yes?" asked a woman.

Another rumble. "Perhaps," said Nakhoza.

"Is it coming from our outpost?" asked Lingana, her voice high, strained.

"We must not think…" She cleared her throat. " Come. Let us hurry."

19

UNREST

Although each person chosen for his/her Blending assignment has passed thorough background checks, there may be cases when assignees are insubordinate. Infractions may range from minor incidents to treason. Global Alliance law deals with each level of insubordination as detailed in Global Alliance Statutes B117–119.

—*Blender Handbook, chapter 21. "On Discipline."*

Jaym, D'Shay, Giambo, and others ran down the trail to meet the returning women.

D'Shay hoisted the heavy pack from Nakhoza's back. "Damn, Girl!" he said. "You scared the crap out of us. Gone three days? We were about to send a search party in case 'gades had you pinned down."

Nakhoza grinned. "You just gonna talk, NorthAm boy? You not gonna give me a welcome hug?"

"Oh hell yeah." His hug lifted her in the air. She giggled and rubbed her cheek against his. After a few seconds he looked her in the eyes. "Whoo! You've got enough voltage to power a village."

"Jay-em!" shouted Lingana. "We thought we heard explosions. I was so worried."

"Nothing to worry about." He pulled off Lingana's pack and swept her up.

She laughed. "You gonna carry me 'round like—"

Jaym kissed her. *Her lips were so soft—and hungry.* He pressed her closer as their mouths moved against each other's. Lingana's hand pulled his head toward her, making him dizzy—and, he realized, aroused.

"Hey, lovebirds," said D'Shay. "I think that's against New SUN rules. Geez, making out like that could set off some of those explosives."

Both Jaym and Lingana blushed as Jaym eased her down. Lingana touched her lips.

"C'mon, bro," said D'Shay. "Let's get these shells up the hill." D'Shay hoisted Nakhoza's pack. "My God, Nakhoza. How'd you lug this so damn far? Not sure I can make it a couple hundred meters."

Jaym shouldered Lingana's pack. They held hands in silence as they made their way back to the sanctuary of the cavern.

————

Nakhoza had her munitions team carefully unpack and store the explosives in a cave a hundred meters from the cavern entrance. Then she introduced the women of Ezondwei to Annja.

"Welcome," smiled Annja. The women looked puzzled. "No English?" asked Annja. "Well, my fractured Chewan will have to do." *Moni,* she said as she led them toward the dining area. On the way she pointed out the tents and work areas. The women gawked at the immense size of the cavern-fortress.

Jaym turned to Lingana and couldn't help but look at her lips and remember their lush warmth. He wanted to lift her again and feel her arms wrap tight around his neck. To feel the heat and curves of her body press against him.

She gave him a coy smile. "You think I have voltage too, Jay-em?"

He feigned a puzzled expression. "Hmm. I'm not positive. Maybe we should try again just to be certain."

She laughed. "I think maybe so, but not here. I think we should make a private test."

Jaym grinned. "Let's get you something to eat. You gotta be worn out."

"Yes, worn out...and sad. We lost a good village girl. She stepped on a mine. Her sister and a friend take the body to Ezondwei for burial."

"God," said Jaym. "It could have been you. I always worry about you when—"

She held up her hand. "Yes, we worry about each other. I was afraid for you when we heard thunder or explosions come from here. What was that?"

"Another drone," said Jaym. "No one was hurt, but two rockets took out our comm dishes and antennas. Xian's up there now trying to patch up what he can. The last communications he intercepted said 'gade forces were converging on the savannah about fifty klicks from here."

"Then they could be here in a day!"

Jaym nodded. "But Xian thinks they are still gathering. We probably have two days."

"Two days," whispered Lingana.

———

After the Ezondwei women left for their village, Annja and Tarkin gathered everyone together. For the first time, Annja was able to address all the Nswibe newcomers and the seasoned New SUN people at the same time. Jaym guessed there were about seventy-five gathered near the cavern's entrance. Some sat on boulders, others squatted or sat cross-legged. About half were Chewans of all ages, from pre-Flare kids to elders. He spotted Lingana's mother and two sisters across the way.

Jaym hardly knew Lingana's sisters. They mostly stayed with the mom and helped around the camp. They were pretty girls, he thought. They looked a lot like Lingana, just a couple of years younger. The others gathered with the Chewans were blenders—from pale blondes to D'Shay's "chocolate light," as he liked to refer to his skin tone.

"Please, sit," said Annja. She and Tarkin stood together to address everyone. "As you all know by now," said Annja, "'Gade warlords and their forces are gathering on the savannah." She paced for a moment, fingering her chin. "We have to prepare for the worst-case scenario—a combined attack on this post."

Lingana took Jaym's hand. He looked at her anxious expression and gave her a reassuring squeeze.

"Our council has agreed that if they come our direction, we will attack before they reach the cavern. If we cannot defeat them outright, we and the Ezondwei warriors will inflict as much damage as possible before retreating to the Post-2. Now, each of you here, and the Ezondwei fighters, will be assigned to one of our offensive or defensive teams. Tarkin and—"

"No, Annja!" snapped Tarkin. "That is *your* plan and many of us agree it is foolish."

Annja looked at him wide-eyed.

What the hell ... thought Jaym.

"Tarkin!" said Annja. "This is not what you and I—"

"*No!* You never seriously considered the plan Daku and I urged, did you?" He looked at the crowd of stunned people and shouted. "Annja wants to integrate a horde of untrained villagers into our fighting teams. That would be a disaster, and we cannot allow that disaster to happen. Therefore, it is time for new leadership if we hope to succeed."

Annja stood stunned, her mouth half open.

"Now, Daku," shouted Tarkin.

Oh shit, thought Jaym.

Daku and half-a-dozen of Tarkin's followers stepped inside the cavern with their assault rifles and pistols raised.

SURPRISE

I have learned to hate all traitors, and there is no
disease that I spit on more than treachery.

—*Aeschylus (500 BC)*

———————

"Just a few more shots?" asked Reya.

Maykego shook her head. "Rey-yah, you strain youself
too hard."

Reya grinned. "I'm fine." She held up her healing arm.
"This brace of yours did the trick."

Maykego shrugged. "That is good, but you still practice
enough today."

"But if we're going into battle I need—"

"Come, now, stubborn girl. Must go back."

As they approached the level of the cavern, Maykego
stopped. "Where is the guard? There is always a guard. And I
don't see any of our people."

Reya crept behind Maykego, scanning the giant rocks
ahead. "Maybe the guard is just taking a pee break."

Maykego shook her head. "Keep low," she whispered. "Stay
behind and do not show youself when we get to the entrance.
And get ready with the bow. I hope nothing gonna be wrong,
but must be ready."

Reya felt her heart beating faster. Yeah, something definitely was not right.

Together they edged along the rock face toward the cavern entrance. Maykego held up a hand and whispered. "Listen."

Voices. Reya couldn't make out the words. But there—she heard Annja's voice. "It's okay, Maykego, they're just having a meeting."

A shout from Tarkin: *"No!"*

Others began yelling.

"Oh my God," said Reya, "What the hell's—"

Maykego clapped her hand over Reya's mouth. From the shadow of a rocky crag stepped Daku and five other armed men. They walked into the cavern.

Maykego whispered, "Do as I do. Step softly." She moved along the wall to the edge of the cavern. The voices were clear now.

Tarkin was bellowing. Then came angry shouts and cries of *traitor*.

"Notch an arrow," said Maykego. "Ready?"

Shit, shit, shit, thought Reya. She drew an arrow from her quiver.

———

Daku raised the muzzle of his rifle. "Do as I say, Annja," he said. "Nobody's gonna get hurt. Now, just sit over here on the floor."

Tarkin moved toward Annja. "Everyone settle down!" he shouted.

Jaym noticed Tarkin's hand slip to his holster.

Someone hollered, "He's a bloody 'gade! Come on, we can rush him and—"

Tarkin pulled his pistol and fired over their heads. A girl screamed.

"Listen to me!" said Tarkin. "I'm no bloody 'gade. I am loyal to the New SUN cause, but Annja's plan is going to get us all killed. We *can* defeat the 'gades without allying with those village natives. *We* will take on the 'gades and destroy them. We will show the 'gades and anyone else that we of New SUN are able to defeat our enemies."

D'Shay shouted, "Get real, man. Without other fighters we'll get slaughtered. You looking to be our General Custer?"

"Shut up! My plan *will* work. Daku and I tried to make Annja see reason, but her ideals are unrealistic. If she chooses, Annja can still work with us, but will no longer lead us. Her strategy of fighting with untrained villagers will not defeat a force of 'gades."

Giambo stood. "What be you plan, small man hiding behind gun?"

"Sit down with the others!"

Giambo crossed his arms. "I think I gonna stand while you tell of big, big plan."

Jaym noticed Tarkin's jaw twitch.

"We'll use the villagers, but only as a diversion. They'll hit the 'gades from several fronts."

"Then they all gonna be butchered," said Giambo.

"Sacrifices may be necessary for a greater cause."

"So, after you send the warriors of Ezondwei to they death, then what you gonna do?"

Tarkin's face reddened and he fired a shot over Giambo's head. *"Sit down!"*

Giambo shrugged. "Floor not be so comfortable. You go 'head and tell us how you gonna save New SUN, Tarkin boy."

Lingana squeezed Jaym's fingers tighter.

"It'll be okay," whispered Jaym. *God,* he thought, *how could this ever turn out okay?* He'd never felt so helpless. He had to do something. Say something. He stood and hoped his voice didn't quaver. "Tarkin! If we don't fight alongside the villagers, then give them their own team. They can attack from one flank as we come in from another."

Tarkin acted as if he didn't hear Jaym—didn't even look his direction. He paced from Annja back to Daku as he spoke. "Although the natives will do little damage to the 'gade forces, they will divert them for a time. Meanwhile we sweep in from the 'gade's west flank. We'll have the high ground. We have armor-piercing bullets and shoulder-launched missiles. We can take out their forward armor and the rest won't be able to get by on that narrow road. There's a cliff on one side—where we will be positioned—and a ten-meter drop-off on the other. They will be sheep going to slaughter."

Giambo chopped the air with his fist. "No! You just gonna let 'gades butcher village people. Amai Annja's plan does not do that. Her plan—"

"Enough talk!" shouted Tarkin. Those who want to join me and defeat the 'gades, step over here."

People muttered, some shouted. Finally fewer than a dozen stood and made their way through the crowd to Tarkin's side.

Giambo laughed. "That gonna be your army? I think you be done now, Tarkin boy. Time to put big gun down.

Here, you give it to me. I keep it safe for you." He began to move forward.

"Stop!" screamed Tarkin. "I'm warning you. We want this to be bloodless, but we will do whatever is necessary for this change."

D'Shay stood, then Nakhoza. Jaym squeezed Lingana's hand as they, too, stood. Others began to rise. Meanwhile Giambo kept moving toward Tarkin.

"Daku. Shoot Giambo if he comes any closer."

Daku shook his head. "Look mate, we didn't—"

Tarkin stepped behind Annja and put his pistol to her skull. "Okay, Giambo, and any other heroes. Get any closer and I will be forced to shoot Annja. Her blood will be on your hands."

Daku looked confused. "Jesus, Tarkin, you said—"

Tarkin's eyes flashed. *"Shut up!"*

————————

"Count of three," whispered Maykego.

Reya bit her lip and nodded.

Maykego counted. "… two, three!"

Together they stepped in view. Giambo was still moving forward showing no sign of fear. Daku and the other men near Tarkin seemed to be arguing with each other.

Lingana, Jaym, and others were moving forward with Giambo.

"Drop your guns!" shouted Maykego. She and Reya stood with bowstrings drawn to their cheeks.

Daku and others threw down their weapons. But one of Tarkin's men swung his automatic toward Maykego.

Maykego and Reya loosed their arrows at the same instant. Maykego's arrow sank deep into the man's right eye. Reya's shaft punched deep into his shoulder. As he fell, his automatic traced a shower of sparks across the rock ceiling.

There was a moment of stunned silence as Giambo stepped forward and took Tarkin's pistol from his hand. Tarkin shook his head slowly. "I don't understand," he muttered.

Daku moved back, hands still in the air. "Tarkin said everyone would hear reason and come over to our side! He said nobody would get hurt."

People stood, dazed. Jaym hugged Lingana.

"Why is the shooting?" came a voice from the tunnel shadow. It was Xian. "What happening?"

Giambo helped Annja stand. "Maykego just kill a rat."

Annja seemed dazed. She looked toward Maykego and Reya. Reya couldn't read the expression on Annja's face as she approached them. Tears streamed down Annja's cheeks, but her eyes had narrowed and her mouth was drawn tight.

Her voice shook. "I've always said archers have their place in this world of laser-guided weapons." She glanced at the body of Tarkin's man. His left leg twitched in a final death shudder. She turned back to Maykego and slapped her hard across the face. "Why, Maykego! Why did you shoot to kill one of our own! You are a crack shot. You could have disabled him. Instead you *killed one of our own!*"

Maykego stepped back, her eyes wide with hurt. She put her hand to her stung cheek and wiped blood from her lip. "But Amai Annja," she said, "I *had* to. I could not take a chance that he still might—"

"Nonsense!" Annja turned away and placed her hand on Reya's shoulder. Reya flinched, waiting for the slap. "Reya did the right thing by trying to disable him."

Reya slowly shook her head. "Annja... I should have killed him, but I... couldn't. Maykego did what was necessary. He was going to kill—"

Without a word Annja whirled and strode to Tarkin and Daku, her fists balled. "Why, Tarkin! Why, Daku! I never thought you would go this far."

Giambo came over and nodded to Maykego and Reya. "You did nothing wrong. I be glad for you both to come to stop them. Annja should not slap you, Maykego. She is not thinking right at this moment. I think she be too upset about Tarkin. It is not right that she be takin' it out on you."

Tarkin's eyes darted. "I... thought everyone would see that it was necessary. They were supposed to join us."

"Annja," said Daku. "We believed Tarkin's plan was better. And we were mates. I didn't think any of this..."

Giambo walked over and picked up an auto-pistol. "Amai Annja, you want me take a walk with these two traitor rats?"

Tarkin's face paled.

Annja shook her head. "No more killing of our own. We need all our soldiers." She crossed her arms and stared at the two. "I don't know what to do with you now."

Tarkin looked too stunned to speak.

"We're not traitors, Annja," said Daku. "Tarkin really thought everyone would see his point and join us. We know we've lost. Give us another chance."

Tarkin hung his head. "Daku's right, Annja. I can still follow and be useful. I apologize. I swear I will follow your command."

She nodded. "I want to believe you, but you have trust to earn. You will not get your weapons back until we face combat."

Giambo shook his head. "If you change mind, Amai Annja, my machete be grateful for little bit of use."

"No more, Giambo, please. I think Tarkin and Daku have learned a lesson. Yes, gentlemen?"

Daku nodded. "Yes'm."

"Tarkin and Daku, for now you will now be under Giambo's supervision. Giambo, you will replace Tarkin as my second-in-command."

"That be honor, Amai Annja."

Annja raised her voice so all could hear. "I regret taking my anger out on Maykego." She seemed to weigh her next words. "I did not want to lose a single New SUN soldier, but Maykego—and Reya—did what was necessary to save lives. This is a dark day for New SUN, but it will pass." To Giambo she said. "I'll be outside. I need some time alone."

BATTLE PREP

Every morning in Africa, a gazelle wakes up.
It knows it must run faster than the fastest lion
or it will be killed.

—*African proverb*

Annja was already at the planning table as the team leaders came in to take their seats. She did not greet the others as she usually did, but stared at her folded hands as if lost in thought.

It was past 0300. D'Shay fought to stay awake.

"D'Shay?" said Annja, "Are you with us?"

He blinked his eyes open. "Oh, yeah. Sorry. Um, no disrespect, Miss Annja, but I think we've all got the plan memorized."

Annja leaned back and crossed her arms. "Then you do the final run-through, D'Shay."

"Sure." He rubbed his face and leaned forward. "'Gade chatter says their main column is going to attack us from two fronts—those arrowed lines you have on the battle map. One will consist of ATV attack vehicles. They're gonna send a smaller group toward—"

"Miss Annja," came Xian's voice from the doorway. His face was anxious.

Annja stepped out to talk with him. When she returned her eyes were wide, her face pale.

"I have … terrible news," she said. She glanced at Reya. "I am sorry to report that Xian just received a distress transmission from Post-2."

Reya put her hands to her face and whispered, "Bettina."

"I'm afraid the post has been lost," Annja said. "The last message was cut short, but said they intended to fight to the end. They expected no mercy from the 'gades." She looked at Reya. "Bettina was a selfless warrior. We will remember her as we prepare to engage these killers."

Reya swiped away tears and nodded.

Damn, thought D'Shay. It just wasn't right. Reya had been through more than any of them, and now she loses her best friend.

Annja cleared her throat. "We must go forward and be sure that does not happen here." She looked around the table. "Are teams fully prepared? Giambo, you first, please."

Giambo nodded. "Each of us know what to do. Jay-em gonna be number two in command. DuShay, number three. If I be killed or wounded, they command."

D'Shay sensed a prickle of fear. If 'gades could take out Giambo and Jaym, they'd probably take out the entire team. Including himself.

"Good," Annja said, "but I want Xian to join you to send us communications. I have to know if our plan needs revising—if something goes amiss." She looked to Maykego. "And the archers?"

"My archers be forty in all. Reya and five others from our people, plus all the Ezondwei archers. My team gonna meet villagers tomorrow. We will explain battle plan to them. We gonna be outnumbered by 'gades, but I think we make a strong stand."

"Reya?" asked Annja. "Are you positive you are able to be second-in-command?"

"I'm up to this, Annja. The arm brace makes all the difference." She lifted her chin. "And I will fight to the end, like Bettina."

Annja nodded. "God willing, that will not be necessary. And let us hope no second-in-command will need to take over in any team." She looked at Nakhoza. "You and I will be in charge of defense here. For those 'gades who might make it this far, we will be prepared. Nakhoza is my second-in-command. She and Lingana, with the rest of the team, are finalizing our work." She looked at the weary faces before her. "Any last questions?"

"Just one," said D'Shay. "What about Tarkin and Daku? They still gonna be part of this?"

"Yes," said Annja. "But I think it is best to separate them—at least for this operation."

Thank God for that, thought D'Shay.

"I'd like Daku to join Giambo. Is that acceptable, Giambo?"

Giambo nodded. "Yes, amai."

"Tarkin and I will remain here with the defensive team, and if necessary, make a last stand. Tarkin is trained in guerilla warfare. This stronghold will be difficult to breach. Sometimes a strong defensive position can wreak more havoc on an enemy than an offensive force." She scanned the faces in the room. "But I expect both offense and defense to succeed. We will take the 'gades down." Annja suddenly looked so tired. "If there are no more questions, we are adjourned. "Get some rest, then prepare to fight for the survival of New SUN."

As people filed out, D'Shay sat a moment, staring at the battle map. *Damn.* In a couple of days he'd either live or die on one of those arrows.

INSOMNIA

Dios te salve, María, llena eres de gracia,
el Señor es contigo.
Bendita tú eres entre todas las mujeres,
y bendito es el fruto de tu vientre...

———————————

Jaym lay wide-awake on his sleeping mat next to Lingana, snoring softly. The light of the full moon threw sharp shadows at the cavern's entrance. He gently rolled off his mat and threaded his way through the sleepers toward the moonlight.

"Hey, Jaym," whispered a voice. "Over here."

"Reya? D'Shay? Figured you'd be sound asleep. What're you guys doing outside?"

"Probably same as you," said D'Shay. "Pre-battle jitters."

"I keep thinking about Bettina," said Reya.

Jaym settled cross-legged on a block of limestone, still warm from the day's heat. Back in the Corridor, there were no slabs of natural rock, only slabs of concrete in vacant lots. And you couldn't sit on those. First, because an Alliance cop would wonder what the hell you were doing, and second, because the lot and concrete would be covered with broken glass and dog shit. But here in Africa—at least out in the boonies—it was like the planet was meant to be. No plastic bags whirling in dusty streets; no vid-cams watching from every corner; no surveillance balloons looming overhead.

The moonlight flooded the valley below. D'Shay and Reya sat with their legs dangled over the cliff face as cooler air wafted up from the ravine.

Jaym sat quiet, watching D'Shay toss small rocks out over the canyon edge to the creek a half-klick below their feet.

"Think we'll ever stop fighting with 'gades and get on with our lives?" asked Reya. "I'm so sick of running from 'gades. Sick of people getting killed by those bastards."

"Amen, sister," said D'Shay. "I just want a nice little village condo where Nakhoza can pamper me day and night."

"Good luck with that," said Reya.

"What're you making, Reya?" asked Jaym. "That a necklace?"

She lifted what looked like a dried berry from her lap and skewered it with a sewing needle. "Guess again," she said. "I'll give you a hint. In two weeks it's gonna be ... what?"

"Christmas," said Jaym. "At least Annja says it is. I can't even believe it's December. Hotter than ever in the day with such short nights."

"And the toilets flush backward south of the equator too, right?" said D'Shay.

Reya chuckled. "Urban myth. Anyhow, I'd love to have you find me a flush toilet. Even a roll of TP would be a nice Christmas gift from you guys."

Jaym watched Reya thread the berry onto a string with others. "So, a Christmas present."

"Yeah, for myself," she said. "Assuming I survive the battle."

"Hey!" said D'Shay. "Don't even mess around with that kind of talk. You're a survivor. We all are." He tossed another pebble. "We're gonna be okay."

"Sorry. I just get … never mind. Okay, back to my creation here. Jaymo, you still have to figure out what it is. Hint number two: In case you didn't know it, we MexiCal girls are mostly good churchgoing Catholics."

Jaym shrugged. "Still looks like a berry necklace."

D'Shay chuckled. "Jaymster, you are such a heathen. It's a rosary. Am I right, Reya?"

"Bingo," she said. "It's gonna replace the one I made in 'gee camp out of knotted string." She held it up, quiet for a moment. "You know, I used to have my grandmother's rosary made of jade and silver. It was the most precious thing I ever owned." She skewered another berry. "But Mom had to sell it in 'gee camp for ration coupons. We had to sell everything just to stay alive in that goddamn place."

"So," said Jaym, "with your rosary you're gonna do Hail Marys and stuff?"

"Yep. Hail Marys and stuff." She pulled another berry in place.

"Think those Hail Marys help when you're praying for things?"

"I don't pray for 'things.' My rosary helps me get through shit. Like tomorrow." She wiped her nose. "Sometimes … I think I'm gonna crack. My head starts flashing images, sounds, and even smells—if something triggers it. I'll see one of our New SUN people packing a big gun and, zap. Suddenly he's one of the 'gade guards where I was a captive. Once my brain gets freaked like that, I freeze up. Post-traumatic stuff, I guess."

She held up her half-completed rosary. "When that crap starts to bubble up, I take my rosary and start my Hail Marys."

"Sorta like meditation?" asked Jaym.

"I guess. I just know that if I can finger my rosary and concentrate on the words—really concentrate—the crap in my head can get pushed aside till I can handle myself. It's not as bad as it was at first, but it still happens." She made a crooked smile. "Thank you, Father Jaymo; Father D'Shay. I trust you will keep my confession to yourselves."

D'Shay nodded, his expression serious for a change. "I get those flashbacks too. I haven't been through half the crap as you, but I've got my triggers. Like there's this one older Chewan lady here in camp. She looks so much like my aunt that when I first saw her I had to keep from rushing over and hugging her. And like you said, zap, my brain yanked me right back to my Corridor hood and my aunt crying and hug-crushing me when I got on the Alliance bus. Hell, I could even smell that lavender goop she used to straighten her hair.

"How 'bout you, Jaym," asked Reya.

Jaym smiled. "You're gonna laugh, but the other day I saw this bird about the size of a robin, only it was bright yellow. The same canary yellow Mom had to wear at her job on the assembly line. I can still see Mom in the kitchen in her yellow outfit scrambling to get us both out of the flat before our daysleepers arrived." He was quiet for a minute, watching Reya stringing her berry-beads.

"Well," said D'Shay. "I'm gonna try to get some shut-eye before dawn." He stood and tossed a final rock far into the valley. Reya held up her completed rosary. "Ta-dah! Better than the Pope's." She glanced at Jaym. "Is Lingana sleeping okay?"

"Yeah, in there purring like a kitten." He stretched. "Come on. We should both try to get a little sleep."

"Easy for you guys. At least you've both got somebody to snuggle up to."

Jaym nodded. "You will too, Reya. We just gotta get through this crap and start to make a real life. You'll have your day."

She nodded. "Good to spill my guts a little. Thanks for listening."

"Hey, 'One for all…'"

"'And all for one.'"

AMBUSH

Caution is not cowardice; even the ants march armed.

—*Ugandan proverb*

One of the Chewan members of Giambo's team knew this little-used trail snaking toward the valley. Jaym, D'Shay, and the other team members watched their footing as they trod the narrow ledge across the face of a sheer cliff face. Jaym could hear the whisper of a stream within a ribbon of willows a hundred meters below. *Don't look down,* he thought. It wasn't the time to pass out or stagger. This terrain was terrifying. He'd spent his entire life on the streets of the Corridor—everything flat as a tabletop.

Up front was Daku, followed by Giambo, who watched him closely. Annja had insisted he'd be a good fighter; he just needed to be watched.

Right, he thought. If it had been up to him, Daku and Tarkin would be locked in some inner cavern room with an armed guard—at least till this was over. Annja had too much faith in the human race. Had to be that Quaker upbringing of hers. Daku might be salvageable, but Annja just couldn't see that Tarkin was about as trustworthy as a black mamba in your sleeping bag.

Behind Giambo were Jaym, D'Shay, and the rest of the team. Jaym stepped carefully, one hand against the rock face, the other balled into a fist. Was D'Shay as freaked as he was? Had to be. D'Shay was a Corridor Rat like himself, and the highest terrain in the Corridor was the Heights where the Council leaders and corporation heads had their gated mansions with double electric fences and security thugs with orders to shoot to kill.

Ten minutes later they'd made it across the cliff face. The trail now wound down through rocky scrabble and brush. "Hey, D'Shay," asked Jaym. "How many klicks you think we've come?"

D'Shay shrugged. "Maybe ten. It took forever to get across that mountainside. We're flatlanders, not mountain goats. About messed my shorts in a couple of places."

They were now pushing through dense underbrush and briars. The gnats came in clouds so thick it was hard not to inhale the damned things. Jaym waved them from his face and swat at green flies trying to bite off chunks of his flesh.

"Goddamn!" said D'Shay. "These flies are gonna eat us alive."

"Quiet back there," growled Giambo up front. "We getting near where 'gades gonna be. So get serious now and check you weapons 'stead of acting like children."

Jaym glanced at his automatic rifle. It was a standard Czech workhorse, maybe forty or fifty years old. But the thing never seemed to break down or jam like the whiz-bang 14-X Alliance models. If one thing went wrong with the Alliance rifle in combat, it was only useful as a high-tech club.

The underbrush was giving way to more open forest. Only

a few flies followed them now. The village guide with Giambo waved ahead and held up two fingers.

"What's that mean?" whispered D'Shay.

"Not sure," said Jaym. "Two minutes? Two klicks?"

When they reached a clearing, Giambo held up an arm and signaled for a huddle. "Guide say only two klicks now." He looked at Daku. "You gonna be one of us when we fight 'gades?"

Daku glanced at the faces around him. "Look, mates. I hate the bloody bastards as much as you do. Besides, we all got to fight for our lives, yeah?"

"Good," said Giambo. "We all gotta be New SUN brothers now." He turned to the Chewan guide. "Take us where we make best ambush place."

The guide was a wiry Ezondwei man in his forties. He was barefoot and only wore a pair of tattered shorts. "We be 'bout twenty minutes from where 'gades gonna be." He grinned. "There be a fine ambush place."

———————

After twenty minutes of hacking through brush, they arrived at the ambush location. The area overlooking the road was a tumble of weathered granite boulders. Giambo, Jaym, and others scrambled over smaller rockfalls. "Here Jay-em," said Giambo pointing with his machete. "Your position. D'Shay, you be here. Daku gonna be by me." He went along the ledge overlooking the mountain road, positioning each person near a boulder or rock slab.

Giambo gathered everybody in close. "Xian, you hear anything yet on radio thing?"

Xian had rigged up a small solar receiver-transmitter. "Only little bit of 'gade static. They not close 'nough to hear words. But I get some pop music from Cape Town. Maybe I turn it up for entertainment?"

"Quit joking 'round," said Giambo.

Xian giggled. "Music more fun. But yes, boss. I listen for 'gades. Always do."

"Xian," said Jaym. "Can you guess how close they are from that static?"

"Ten kilometer if we lucky. But if they go to radio silence, then we must listen with own ears to hear them come."

Giambo frowned at the guns the men carried. "Okay, everybody's barrel still shine too much. 'Gades gonna spot us easy."

Jaym glanced at his. Yeah, most of the charcoal he'd rubbed on the barrel this morning had been swept off by brush.

"Do what I do," said Giambo. He walked to a patch of windblown dust at the base of a large rock. He unzipped and pissed a long stream in the dust. He zipped back up and nodded to the men. "Now I have mud. Hold out you gun, Jay-em." He scooped up a little piss-mud and rubbed it on his barrel. "No more shine. Just look like stick. Rest of you make own mud then take positions." He looked at Jaym. "Jay-em, you and other white boys, put mud on you faces. You shine like moons."

Jaym wrinkled his nose.

"Don't make such a look," said Giambo. "Only be you own water and good African dirt."

Jaym hesitated, then took a leak. He took a breath, then smeared mud on his face and arms. Then he and the others took their positions and waited.

———

After half an hour of shooing flies and roasting in the sun, Xian shouted, "Radio contact! They coming in range. Maybe have fifteen or twenty minutes."

"Radio a warning to Annja and others," said Giambo.

"I try, but my signal pretty weak down here," said Xian.

"We could always send a runner to warn them," said D'Shay.

Giambo shook his head. "We need all men here. Outpost will hear our guns and 'gade cannon. That be their warning. Annja's team gonna be ready."

Giambo's men were spaced over a seventy-meter firing line. Jaym lay in a prone position, D'Shay a couple meters to his left.

"Like old times, eh Jaymo?" said D'Shay, his voice tense.

"Yeah ... right." But this was different. When they fought back in Nswibe, those 'gades had been on foot. But these had armored APC crawlers and rovers with heavy firepower. He lay in the beating sun. So thirsty, but not the time to fumble for his canteen. Any minute the—

He felt a low rumble.

"They be coming," shouted Giambo. "Maybe one klick now."

Daku said something to Giambo. Giambo nodded.

Daku called out, "Double-check your safeties!"

Jaym saw that his safety lever was still on. *Idiot!* He snapped it to *fire*.

"And be sure your weapons are not on full-automatic," said Daku. "Can't waste your ammo. Take single shots or short bursts—unless they try to rush us."

Jaym threw the mode switch to semiautomatic. Now he had to calm himself. He looked down the line. Besides his machete, Giambo cradled an old carbine tipped with a vintage bayonet—his choice. Said he preferred to take on 'gades close in with the bayonet and machete.

Jaym could hear the 'gade column clearly now. Sounded like huge convoy rumbling toward them. But maybe some were harmless supply trucks. Yeah, there'd have to be supply and troop trucks.

He saw the glint of a windshield as a rover rolled into view. His guts suddenly cramped. It was an eight-wheeler, fully armored with steel plates covering the tracks nearly to the ground. Its turret had a swivel-mounted cannon that looked like it could fire 80-millimeter shells.

On a hand signal from Giambo, Daku scrambled to the rear to take up the team's only rocket launcher. Xian helped Daku lock and load a hornet missile into the shoulder launcher. Daku knelt beside a boulder overlooking the road. Xian cradled another hornet—the only other rocket the women had managed to salvage from the savannah carnage.

Jaym watched Daku's eyes. He didn't completely trust Daku, but he was the only one trained to use the launcher. But Daku kneeled steady, eyes looking down the sights of the launcher, waiting for the right moment.

Jaym looked back the half-track, now fully in view. Like a

great armored beetle, it lumbered at a steady pace over fallen rock and deep ruts.

Damn! thought Jaym. Why the hell didn't he fire the rocket? Another few seconds and—

"Fire, Daku!" shouted Giambo. "Now!"

Daku took a quick breath, and then jerked the trigger.

24

CANNON FIRE

Until lions have their own historians, tales of bravery
and courage will be told about the hunter.

—*African proverb*

Lingana paused at the cavern entrance, shading her eyes
and squinting down the trail that Jaym, Giambo, and
the others had taken at dawn. The late morning was warm, but
she hugged herself against a shiver of fear. She listened. The
only sounds were the wind rustling brush and the chirrs of a
flock of firefinches swooping down the canyon.

No gunfire … yet. Only a couple of months ago the
thought of Jaym being in danger would not have bothered her.
But now …

"Lingana?" called Nakhoza. "Help with this mine."

Lingana hurried over to the path twisting up from the
savannah—the very path she and Jaym had staggered up when
the Nswibe survivors arrived. She knelt beside Nakhoza, who
had scraped a shallow hole in the trail. Lingana looked at the
mine—a dirty metal thing the size of Giambo's fist.

Nakhoza made a sympathetic smile. "Don't worry, it's not
armed, yet."

"What kind is it?"

"A nasty kind. It blows fragments of iron ten or fifteen meters. Can take out several 'gades."

Lingana nodded. "Nakhoza, do you … worry about D'Shay?"

Nakhoza made that smile again. "Like you been worrying about Jaym? Of course I do. I know they are worrying about us just as much."

"But how do you keep so calm?"

"I work. I think only about mines and defense now. I could not focus if I constantly worried about D'Shay. You must do the same. Here, hand me the mine."

Lingana picked up the small, heavy mine. A handful of death.

"Put it in the hole. Yes, just deep enough. The trigger will be only a couple centimeters below the dirt."

The two pushed dirt and bits of rock into the hole, packing the mine firmly in place. "Now to arm it," said Nakhoza. She unscrewed a metal cap and gently slid a pin from the trigger mechanism. "Okay, I'll finish while you watch and learn." Nakhoza sprinkled fine dirt over the armed mine until it was just covered.

"But the fresh dirt shows," said Lingana.

"Get a handful of grit and leaves from the trailside. Yes, good. Now sprinkle it over the mine."

Lingana held her breath as she gently spread the debris.

Nakhoza laughed. "Don't need to be that dainty. It takes at least a couple of kilos of pressure to set off this kind of mine."

Lingana let out her breath. "Why did you not tell me? I thought I might blow us both up!"

Nakhoza spread the grit over the area and used a leafed

twig to blend the edges. "Now the final touch." She took a light gray pebble from her pocket and laid it at the trail's edge. "Just like in the tunnels. Look for the brick or stone that does not belong." She stood and brushed the dirt from her hands. "Now, did you worry about Jaym so much the last few minutes?"

Lingana forced a smile and looked aside.

Nakhoza handed her the small shovel. "You do the next one, five meters up the trail. I've got to supervise inside. We're placing more mines, trip wires, checking the tunnel traps."

"Nakhoza? Will we hear the guns from here?"

Nakhoza pinched her lips. "Hard to say. Probably not small-arms fire, but we will hear any big guns—cannons, missiles." She squeezed Lingana's shoulder. "You must not think the worst. Just keep working and know that we have clever men and women out there. Besides, we have no choice, yes?"

Lingana forced a smile. "Yes … of course."

An hour later, Lingana was digging the last mine hole. She had almost made it up to the cavern mouth where Annja and Nakhoza had a squad of workers now rolling boulders and stacking slabs of rock across the entrance, building a rock wall from which the defenders could fire on surging 'gades.

The noise of workers almost drowned out distant rumbles. Cannon fire?

Everyone stopped to listen. Lingana glanced back at Nakhoza staring across the valley. Her eyes wide, fists to her chin.

WARRIOR WOMEN

A battle can be lost by a weak bowstring, inferior fletching, or a single arrow whose shaft is not true.

—*Jacob Ndiche, "Postmodern Warfare."*
(Cape Town Press, 2058).

———————

Maykego went over last-minute details with Annja, then finally managed a few hours of fitful sleep. The next morning she went to awaken her team, but found Reya already up and strapping on her elbow brace. "You feelin' okay, Reya?"

She smiled and nodded. "I may not be your finest archer, but I'll do okay. I want some payback for what those bastards did to me. And for what they did to my friends Mai-Lin and Bettina." Tears started again. "Damn. I feel like such a baby."

"No. You mourn for your good friends. Babies cry for nothing. You cry for something most important in life."

"Thanks." She tried a shaky smile. "You know, I'll bet Bettina fought like a wildcat. Probably took a dozen 'gades with her."

Maykego nodded.

"Well, let's do this," said Reya.

Maykego and Reya gathered their small team at the cavern mouth. Maykego whispered to Reya. "You do the check-off. I want them to have confidence in you since you be second-in-command."

God, don't get killed Maykego, thought Reya. She cleared her throat and stepped forward. "Has everybody checked your weapons? Strings, fletching, blades sharp as razors?"

They all nodded.

"Good job," said Reya. She paused, thinking about what Maykego would say before going to battle. She looked from face to face as she spoke. "You may have been hunters or competed in village contests, but today we are all warriors—hunters of men. Those are ugly words, but it is what we must do, and we will do it well to preserve New SUN."

Maykego, Reya, and five other archers from the outpost entered Ezondwei village square. Because they had jogged the entire way, Reya's hair was matted to her forehead and her cheeks coated with sweat and trail dust. She hadn't run like this since she and Mai-Lin made their escape attempt from the 'gades in the Mizambu highlands.

The Ezondwei warriors were waiting in the square. Reya counted about twenty men, all armed with heavy hunting bows. The warriors with guns must have left earlier to join Giambo's team on the trail.

A broad-shouldered archer came forward, but walked past Maykego and Reya without a glance. He scanned the faces of the handful of men from New SUN. "Who be you head-warrior man?"

Most of the New SUN men looked at their feet or off to one side. One finally motioned to Maykego with his chin.

The Ezondwei archer frowned. He turned to look at Maykego standing tall and strong. "Tell me this gotta be a big joke, yes?"

She returned his stony gaze. "It is no joke. I am to lead all archers to battle."

The man shook his head. "Girls do not lead. Girls do not go to battle. And what you doing with man's bow?" His warriors laughed with him.

Maykego narrowed her eyes. "This *woman* does lead. This woman *does* go to battle. And I intend to send many 'gades to hell today. *With this bow.*" She held her longbow over her head as she made eye contact with each Ezondwei warrior. "I am not a joke. I am going to take us to battle and together we *will* defeat the 'gades."

"This is foolish," said the man. He waved to his warriors. "We will wait for the 'gades to come to Ezondwei and we will slaughter them. I hope we have 'nough stakes to put heads on." The men laughed and began to drift from the square.

"Now what?" whispered Reya. "We need these assholes."

Maykego nodded. She whipped an arrow from her quiver. "You!" she shouted to the leader.

The leader turned, still grinning. But his face went hard when he saw Maykego's bowstring pulled to her cheek, the arrow aimed at his chest. He cocked his head. "What you think you doing, warrior girl?"

"We must stand 'gainst 'gades together. If not together, 'gades gonna win. You cannot wait here and hope you can defeat them. They will slaughter you. They will rape your women. Our only hope is to stop them in the forest—together."

The leader signaled to his men. They all drew arrows aimed at Maykego.

Maykego nodded to Reya and her New SUN archers. She and the others notched arrows and drew bowstrings.

Shit, thought Reya. *Outnumbered three to one. We'll look like pincushions.*

The man slowly shook his head. "Wait. Look, girl. You know we gonna kill you all for sure. But you might kill some of us. That not be good for us to defend Ezondwei. I think you just leave now and no one get hurt, yes?"

"No," said Maykego evenly. "We go together and I lead, because I know where 'gades gonna be and how we can stop them. But we must work as team."

"Let us not play games. I think it be best if arrows be back in quivers, then we talk. Yes?"

Maykego glared at the village warriors. There was nearly a minute of silence as everyone stood ready to shoot.

Geez, Maykego, thought Reya. Ease up and talk with the guy—even if he is a prick.

Maykego finally nodded. "We lower bows together. You give signal."

The leader raised his arm. They all lowered their bows and slacked their bowstrings as his arm came down. He walked toward Maykego, stopping a meter away. His face muscles twitched.

"I am a New SUN warrior," said Maykego, "so please do not treat me like a little girl."

The man shook his head. "You show me nothing yet, 'cept

foolish courage." He looked at her bow. "Maybe you show my men how good you are, yes? Big bow means nothing. You need a warrior's skill to face the enemy. Maybe you can hit sitting rabbit, but—"

Maykego stepped back and looked overhead. A flock of scarlet-winged pigeons were circling for a roost. "Pick one," she said.

He turned to his men and shrugged. "Okay, warrior girl. See bird with one white wing? It's in the—"

Her arrow sang toward the flock. The bird tumbled toward the square. In a blur of motion Maykego drew and fired a second arrow. The bird was still ten meters above ground when it was pierced again.

Silence. The leader and the village warriors stared at the mess of feathers impaled by crisscrossed arrows. The leader turned to Maykego. "What is your name, warrior girl?"

"Maykego, and do not call me 'girl.'"

"Yes." He paused. "You be a very different woman than I meet. I am Azibo, second son of Ezondwei chief. I think maybe it better if we talk alone, yes?"

Maykego nodded.

Azibo said loud enough for his warriors to hear, "Very good shooting for woman. Course, I could show off same way if I wanted, yes?"

The men dutifully nodded, but stared wide-eyed at Maykego.

———

The village warriors and Reya and the other archers of New SUN found shade while Maykego and the Azibo met inside one of the buildings. Reya looked at the sun. Had to be a little past noon. From Xian's 'gade intercepts, Maykego's squad would need to catch the flanking force in the forest no later than 1500 hours. Any later and the 'gades would make it to open ground and on their way to the New SUN outpost. The archers could not withstand heavily armed 'gades in the open, but in the dense forest they would have a chance.

One of the village archers sauntered over and squatted in the shade a couple of meters from Reya. *Oh great,* she thought. *Is he gonna go off on how mzungu girls can't shoot?* She gave him the evil eye, but he was intent on peeling an orange. He split the fruit in two and offered half to Reya.

"Um, *Zikomo,*" she said, accepting the orange. Reya bit into the ripe fruit and savored the wonderful scent and juice as she chewed. She closed her eyes as she savored this mouthful of heaven. She hadn't had an orange since she was a little girl in MexiCal.

"You like this fruit?"

"Oh God, yes! There're no oranges left in NorthAm."

He nodded. "Can you shoot good as the tall Chewan girl?"

Reya shrugged. "Nobody shoots like Maykego. But I'm not bad. I could take down a 'gade at a pretty good distance."

He stared at the angry scars on her arm.

She flushed. "Not very pretty, huh?"

"Bullet?"

"Yeah. Lucky to have my arm."

"Not pretty, not ugly. Just part of yourself." He sat quiet as he finished his orange. Unlike most of the Chewan men, he was at least as tall as her. She stole a glance at his face. Not bad looking. High cheekbones, strong jaw, honest eyes.

"I am Kwada," he said softly.

She smiled. "Nice to meet you, Kwada. I'm Reya."

"Reya. It is has a good sound. What meaning has the name, 'Reya'?"

She shrugged. "It really doesn't mean anything. My mother wanted to call me *Reina*—'queen' in Spanish—but I had two cousins with that name. So she just made up Reya, which sounds close." Reya glanced at his eyes. "No offense, but you don't seem like the other archers. Not sure what it is. And your English is really good. So, tell me about yourself, Kwada."

He smiled. "I enjoy archery, but only as a pastime. I am a potter much of the time, and teach English two days a week at our little school."

Damn, she thought. He's teaching English in this outback village? He's being wasted. "Where did you learn your English?"

"My family sent me to the English school in Wananelu, then I worked at the Alliance office as a translator. But I need to be here because of the 'gades. They been raiding villages on edge of the savannah." He smiled. "But I think it is time for you to tell me about you, Rey-yah."

She smiled. "We'll talk about me after the mission, okay? 'Cause we are going to kick butt and come back, yeah?"

"Okay," he said. "After the mission."

She looked to the meetinghouse. "I wonder what's taking Maykego and your man Azibo so long?"

He smiled. "I think maybe Azibo does not want to lose face. Maybe he's working out a bargain with Maykego."

"Are you bothered if she leads us?"

He shrugged. "I think it does not matter much who leads." He stared at the orange peels cradled in his palm. "At end of day, we kill some 'gades, but I think we not make it back. So man leader or woman leader, it makes no difference." He looked her in the eye. "Arrows not gonna win 'gainst 'gade bullets."

Reya shook her head. "Cut that out! We agreed to talk when we get back. And when we do, we can share another orange, okay."

He smiled. "Okay, deal."

Maykego and Azibo suddenly stepped from the meeting-house.

Azibo raised his arm and shouted. "Everyone—my people and New SUN people—come close." He motioned to Maykego. "She gonna be number-two leader with me 'cause she has informations 'bout where 'gades going. In few minutes we lead you together into battle, yes? And together, *we gonna win!*" The village warriors held weapons overhead and whooped.

Reya glanced at Kwada. "We are gonna win, Kwada, 'cause I still have to tell you my life story."

He smiled and, for the first time in years, she felt a warm flutter in her chest.

DAKU

"We humans do, when the cause is sufficient, spend our own lives. We throw ourselves onto the grenade to save our buddies in the foxhole. We rise out of the trenches and charge the entrenched enemy and die…We are, when the cause is sufficient, insane."

—*Orson Scott Card*

"*Shit!*" screamed Daku. He jerked the trigger of the shoulder launcher again and again. "It's a dud! Reload, Xian. Reload!"

"Oh God," muttered D'Shay. The lead rover would be around the hill and out of range in seconds. Daku was supposed to knock it out right below so the 'gades would be sitting ducks. But if the convoy got past, 'gades could come at them from any direction and the fire would be withering.

"Should we start shooting?" D'Shay shouted to Giambo.

"No! Hold fire. Gotta make missile work or whole plan gonna fail."

D'Shay watched Xian fumble with the lock-load mechanism. Finally the dud rocket slid out and Xian rammed in the second hornet. "It ready! Fire, Daku. Fire!"

The lead rover was nearly around the bend when the missile swooshed out with a blowback of flame.

A blinding explosion.

D'Shay held his breath. He waited for the smoke and dust to clear. The lead rover's right track unwound and flopped on the road. The armored hulk lurched to the edge of the cliff. Shouts from below. 'Gades leaped out of their vehicles, waving their rifles, looking for targets.

"Fire!" shouted Giambo.

Gunfire chattered around D'Shay. He squeezed off semiautomatic bursts. 'Gades shouted, some fell, but others took cover behind their trucks and rovers, all now at a standstill.

The disabled lead rover managed to lurch back onto the road with its single track. The cannon turret swiveled, then lifted toward them.

Shit oh shit, thought D'Shay as the rover's barrel pointed his direction.

A flash and explosion. Screams to his left. One of Giambo's men stood, dazed—his left arm and shoulder blasted away.

D'Shay looked to Giambo. "Do we retreat?" he shouted. "That cannon's gonna make hamburger of us all."

"No! Do not retreat," yelled Giambo over the gunfire. "Too much in open. They kill us all if we try and run. Try to shoot down cannon barrel. Maybe can hit a cannon shell before it fires."

Another boom. D'Shay felt the ground shift a bit. *Too close.*

"About every four seconds!" cried Jaym. "After their next shot, everyone open up two seconds later."

Another blast. A man to Jaym's right fell back, the top of his head gone. "One, two—now!" shouted Jaym.

Bullets sparked off the turret and cannon barrel.

The cannon fired again. More screams.

"Fuck this!" screamed Daku. "Cover me! Fire at the 'gades behind the lorries." He snatched up the dud rocket.

"Daku!" shouted Giambo. "What you—?"

"Now," screamed Daku. "At the lorries!"

Another blast. A boulder shattered.

Daku shouted at Giambo. "Tell Annja! I'm *not* a traitor." Before Giambo could answer, Daku jumped over the edge and slid down the gravelly cliff face.

D'Shay could only see 'gade shadows against the canvas tarps of the transports. *Good enough.* He fired bursts from truck to truck. Now he spotted Daku running. But halfway to the armored rover, he spun and fell.

"Cover him!" shouted Giambo.

Daku struggled to his feet, one arm dangling, bloody. He staggered on, now far enough that he was shielded by the rover askew on the road. He tucked the small rocket under his wounded arm. With the other, he grabbed hold of the metal turret ladder. 'Gade bullets pinged off the rover. The turret swiveled, trying to knock him off. Daku pulled himself on the armored deck as the turret swung toward him. The cannon fired again, this time randomly.

Blood now trickled from Daku's shattered eardrums.

Daku grabbed the dud rocket with his good hand and reached toward the mouth of the cannon. The barrel was now moving like the trunk of a blind elephant. Daku fumbled the rocket into the mouth of the barrel and slammed it home with his fist.

Nothing. Jaym and D'Shay exchanged glances.

Daku flopped onto the deck of the rover. He started to give a thumbs-up when the cannon fired again. The explosion within the turret blew rivets and shot flames. Daku and the rover vanished in a blast and fireball that blew the turret ten meters in the air.

For a moment all D'Shay could hear was the clatter of metal falling onto the road.

"What the hell?" said D'Shay. "That was a dud?"

Jaym shook his head. "The explosive head was still good."

The 'gades behind the lorries scrambled to run.

"Come!" yelled Giambo. "We now gonna be brave as Daku." He hopped over the edge and slid toward the road.

"Damn," said D'Shay. "Come on, Jaymo."

Together they jumped over the edge.

INTO THE SWAMP

A man lay dying in an African village. He was a very
poor man with a wife and two sons. He had nothing
to leave them except the hut he lay in, a small garden
plot some distance away, and a few words of wisdom.
To his wife, he left the hut and garden plot. He called
his sons to him for the words of wisdom. "My sons,
heed my words well and you will grow into fine men.
Always mind and respect your mother. Be kind to others.
Respect all elders. Do not be selfish. And above all
DO NOT GO NEAR THE SWAMP!"

—*Early Af-Am folktale*

In Ezondwei, Reya, Maykego, and the other archers heard
the distant barrage of cannon fire, followed by a brief
silence, then the echoing roar of an explosion.

Reya's jaw tightened. "Giambo's team. They've engaged
the 'gades."

Maykego turned to Azibo. "It is time for us to intercept
our 'gades."

"You sure they be coming through forest?" asked Azibo.
"They be crazy to cross that swamp."

"Xian got a solid intercept on that," said Reya. "These men

are coming through the forest to hit Ezondwei and do what 'gades do; loot, rape women, kill men, then torch what's left."

Azibo glanced at his men patiently awaiting orders. "Does the message say what path 'gade soldiers gonna take? They be two, sometimes three, paths through forest. Depends on how much water in the swamp now."

Reya shrugged. "The message only said the 'gades were taking the shortest route through the forest."

Azibo smiled and shook his head. "'Gades maybe see short forest path on map, but our Usiku forest gonna be hard for them to cross. They have to cut through many vines and much brush. It not be like open lowland forest."

"That is good for us," said Maykego. "A thick forest like that will give us cover—if we know where the 'gades will cross."

Azibo smiled. "They gonna be coming on the old hunting trail. That be the only high ground through swamp. I know that trail very good. Been hunting there since a boy."

"Then please lead us, Azibo," said Maykego. "Ready, Reya?"

"As I ever will be. Let's go."

———————

Azibo's men wielded machetes, slashing at vines as the overgrown trail became denser. Kwada, the archer who shared his orange with Reya, was just ahead of her, swinging his machete. She noticed he wore a tie-dyed tee shirt of green and brown as did the other village warriors. Perfect camouflage, thought Reya. Besides his bow and quiver of arrows, he had a .45 strapped to his hip. He glanced back and gave her a brief smile.

She returned the smile, then quickly looked away. She was surprised to feel her face flush.

She stopped for a moment to smear on more of the ointment the village women gave them. The stuff smelled like rotten garlic, but it helped keep the clouds of blood-sucking flies and mosquitoes at a distance.

Reya realized that without the village men, she and Maykego would lose the trail in half a kilometer. Every few hundred meters, she managed to spot a machete scar on a tree trunk, the only way a person knew they were still on the path.

Azibo turned to Nakhoza and Reya following close on his heels. "We coming to edge of swamp, so you gonna sink in a little."

Within fifty steps, Reya's boots sank to their tops. *Sink a little!* Her heart quickened as she sucked her feet from the muck with each step. Damn. Any worse and she'd go under. As she tried to pull her right foot from the ooze she started to lose her balance. She threw her arm out to recover, but a strong hand caught her by the waist to steady her. She stood there teetering, but finally got her balance. She looked over her shoulder. *Kwada?* "Thanks," she said. "Um, you can take your hand off my waist now. I'm okay."

He smiled and slowly removed his hand.

She wondered if he was behind her to check her out. Maybe looking at her ass? Well, what the hell. Guess it didn't hurt to get a little attention like that. His touch had been gentle. She smiled and slogged on.

Within a few minutes, Maykego stopped and pointed to the left. "Azibo!" she said. "What is that monster thing in the swamp?"

He paused and nodded toward the object. "Not a real monster. It is from the wars."

To Reya it looked like a huge creature on its back, half-sunk in the ooze. It had four legs, sort of, but they twisted in the air like those of a giant insect. The body and legs of the machine were so covered with moss and vines that it seemed like a malformed growth rising from the goo.

"Could that be a WarBot?" asked Maykego. "I hear the Northern forces used WarBots in the Pan-Af wars."

"Yes, I think that be the word. It was a big walking machine from days of those wars. My father told me that when he young he watched monster machines fighting tanks and crawlers on savannah. He say they look like a walking metal house. This be the only one we see. Father say when soldiers inside War-Bots know they be losing the savannah battle, they try to escape through this forest. He say all the others sink in swamp forever. Not even clever war machine can fight the swamp."

They slogged on for a few hundred meters before Azibo signaled to stop. "This be the best place to ambush 'gade soldiers."

"But I can hardly move," said Reya looking at her feet and fighting for balance in the swampy goop. "My boots suck in with every step."

Azibo grinned. "That be the idea. We going off trail into brush. When 'gades come to here they be walkin' slow and try-ing to keep balance, like you. When we make ambush, they try to run. Try to run in mud slop and person gonna fall."

"But we can't maneuver in this muck either," said Reya.

"I think you will. We show you. Come."

He led Reya, Maykego, and the others into the underbrush.

By now Reya's boots were waterlogged. It was hard not to lose her balance every time she sucked a boot free and moved forward—especially carrying a bow that seemed to tangle in every vine and branch in her path. Two or three times Kwada caught by her arm or steadied her with a hand on her waist when she lost balance.

Reya couldn't help but smile each time he touched her. It was nice having a guy touch her without the groping, she thought. He easily could have grabbed her ass or boobs by "mistake," but he didn't. Nobody had touched her that gently since Carlos back in the 'gee camp.

She hadn't thought about Carlos lately. She had known he was in one of the camp gangs—all the MexiCal boys had to join a gang to survive. She had cried most of the night when he was knifed for ration coupons, but the next day she set her chin and fought to show any emotion. Crying in 'gee camp showed weakness.

"Far 'nough," said Azibo. They were about ten meters off the trail, but in brush and the deep shade of the forest canopy. He shouted some orders in Chewan to his men. The men began work with their machetes—Kwada worked near Reya as he hacked branches.

"They are cutting mats for us to stand on," said Maykego. "Just enough brush to keep us from sinking in. It will allow us to maneuver a little—at least jump behind a tree when 'gades shoot at us."

When they shoot at us! This was it. The realization was like a punch in the gut.

PURSUIT

On difficult ground, keep steadily on the march. On
hemmed-in ground, resort to stratagem. On desperate
ground, fight.

—*Sun Tzu, The Art of War*

Jaym struggled to keep a grip on his rifle as he slid down
the gravelly slope. D'Shay and Giambo were ahead
of him; Xian and the others close behind. They hit the road
feet-first and ran after the 'gades. Jaym stumbled, but quickly
recovered. He and D'Shay scrambled after Giambo. The rest of
the team was quickly down, sprinting with them.

"Giambo!" shouted Jaym. But Giambo didn't respond, he
just kept running.

"What the hell's he doing?" asked D'Shay. "Was this part
of the plan?"

"Don't think so," panted Jaym. "But the 'gades are on
the run."

"Yeah, till they suck us into an ambush. Damn, maybe
Giambo's lost it," D'Shay said.

They ran past bullet-riddled trucks where dead 'gades littered the road.

"Giambo!" yelled Jaym. "We could be running into a trap."

Giambo slowed and turned.

When they caught up to him, Jaym recoiled from Giambo's wild-eyed stare. "Hey … Giambo. You okay?"

He blinked at Jaym and the others as if they were strangers. His panting slowed and he nodded. "Yes, I be okay. I just … want to kill them all." He glanced behind. "We must take cover and think. Come. Everyone behind lorries." He wiped sweat from his face. "How many we lose?"

"Besides Daku, two Chewan men," said D'Shay. "I don't know their names."

Xian spoke up. "Ngongo and his brother, Mitima. Good men."

"Who be wounded?"

"Bullet brush my ribs," said Xian. The right side of his tee shirt was blood soaked. "Not as bad as it look. Bleeding almost stop now."

Giambo grit his teeth. "I expect 'gades to fight, not run. DuShay, Jay-em, Xian—what you think they planning now?"

"Dunno," said D'Shay. "But we've messed up their convoy. They'll be on foot and either try to ambush us, or head to the outpost."

"I think they ignore us now and head for post," said Xian. "Annja and others cannot defend 'gainst so many by selves."

"He's right," said Jaym. "Taking the post is their main goal. We gotta catch them before they reach it."

Giambo nodded. "Then we must hurry."

Jaym ran with Giambo and the others down the rutted road, passing the line of stalled and bullet-riddled trucks. The only 'gades in sight were bodies in pools of drying blood. Jaym knew the ones who escaped were scrambling up the valley to beat them to the New SUN post, and if they did, the 'gades would not only wipe out Lingana and the other defenders, they'd have the high ground, too. They could pick off Giambo's force with no sweat. Jaym knew they couldn't let the 'gades get that far. If they kept sprinting at this pace they could catch them before—

A sudden chatter of machine gun erupted from a brushy hillside.

Bullets tore into truck metal and thudded into flesh.

Jaym leaped beneath the nearest truck as men cried out and fell. He crawled to the far side and crouched by the cab. *No, no, no!* he thought. We gotta keep moving. If they pin us down even for a few minutes, the advancing 'gades will take the post.

More bursts from the unseen machine gun. The cries and moans of fallen New SUN men were soon silenced by the constant raking of bullets pounding the road.

Shit! thought Jaym. Nobody was yelling commands. Was Giambo dead? And where was D'Shay? Okay, time to do something... now.

He eased high enough to peer through the truck's shattered window. There. A sputtered flashing from the brush. He shouted over the bursts of machine gun fire. "Everyone! We gotta take out the gun. Fire if you can—and don't hold back on your ammo!"

Within seconds, gunfire erupted from the survivors. A constant barrage tore into the brush for over a minute.

"Hold fire!" shouted Jaym. The machine gun was silent. He watched the brush. Nothing.

"Hell, yeah!" whooped D'Shay.

Jaym heard Giambo shouting from down the road. "Come! Must catch 'gades before they get to post. Gather this way and we—"

The machine gun opened up again.

"Goddamn it!" shouted D'Shay.

Two men fell, but Jaym and the rest made it back to cover. Again and again bullets kicked dust and tore into the trucks.

Hiding behind one of the troop trucks, Jaym felt a tug at his sleeve. With heart pounding, he glanced down to see a jagged bullet hole in the fabric. No blood.

The machine gun ceased firing again. Jaym knew the 'gades were trying to sucker them out in the open again. But maybe they stopped shooting because they were low on ammo. It might be suicide, but if they all charged the gun, some of them would make it. They had to take it out and get after the main body of 'gades before it was too late.

To his right, Jaym saw D'Shay crouched low as he dashed from truck to truck. He kneeled beside Jaym. "Look, Jaym, there's maybe a hundred 'gades heading to the outpost while we're hiding like rabbits." His eyes flashed. "Even if they don't kill Nakhoza and Lingana, you know what'll happen to 'em."

"You think I don't know that!" snapped Jaym. "Look, we're gonna have to rush the gun. Come at it from different directions. We get half a dozen to go at once and some of us will make it. You go right and get three others, and I'll go left and do the same. We'll rush when I shout the—"

Giambo's voice boomed. "All men start shooting at machine gun again when I give signal. This time we gonna take it out."

"Damn," said D'Shay. "That's his plan? Just shoot at bushes and waste more ammo?"

"If it doesn't work," said Jaym, "we're taking the hill. Just you and me." He white-knuckled his rifle. "One of us will make it."

"What about rushing it now?"

"Okay, good. We rush the gun when everyone opens up. The 'gades will be laying low during our fire." Jaym nodded. "When our guys open up, you go left, I'll go right. On the count of three."

"On three," said D'Shay. "For Lingana and Nakhoza."

"For Lingana and Nakhoza."

Up and down the line, the men reloaded clips and slammed them in place. It was quiet now. Just the *kreee* of a hawk soaring overhead. Jaym leaned across the hood of the truck and zeroed in on the brush patch. *Funny,* he thought. Minutes ago his heart was banging against his ribs, but now...some kind of weird calm. Was this the way you felt just before you die?

Giambo shouted. "Be ready. Okay, fire *now!*"

They opened up. The machine gun didn't return fire.

"On three, D'Shay!" Jaym shouted over the shooting. "One..."

A figure dashed across the road. The machine gun fired at the runner. Dirt spat around his legs, but he was across and in the lee of the roadcut.

"Giambo?" said D'Shay. "But, he's only got that damn machete with him."

"Keep firing!" shouted Jaym. "Gotta cover Giambo!"

Giambo pressed flat against the steep roadcut and moved a few meters to the right. The machine gun was about twenty meters above and to his right; silent now. Giambo moved a few steps further where tree roots dangled down the side of the cut. He clamped the machete in his teeth like a pirate and grabbed a root as thick as a heavy rope. He jerked the root, testing its strength, then began to pull himself up.

Jaym reloaded a clip as the firing continued. He watched Giambo shimmy hand-over-hand up the root. Damn, but he was strong—and gutsy. It only took seconds for him to reach the top of the cut and pull himself into the brush.

"Shee-it!" said D'Shay. "That's just impossible."

The machine gun opened fire again. This time in erratic bursts, firing randomly through underbrush where Giambo had to be.

Jesus, thought Jaym. Does he really have a chance with that .50 caliber mowing down bushes and making trees shudder under the impact?

Then—a spine-chilling cry was followed by a scream.

The machine gun was silent.

"Cease fire!" shouted Jaym.

Jaym and others watched the brush and waited. Moments later, Giambo stepped to the edge of the roadcut. He was collaring a wide-eyed 'gade spattered with blood. Giambo shoved the gade off the edge and watched him tumble to the roadway. "I think we keep this one alive," he said. "For now." He wiped his machete on dried grass then slid down the roadcut.

FIRST WAVE

"Dinna fire till ye can see the whites of their e' en ...
if ye dinna kill them they'll kill you."

—*Andrew Agnew, Scottish commander*
(Battle of Dettingen, 1743)

Nakhoza peered through her binoculars, scanning the valley below.

"Anything at all?" asked Lingana.

"Nothing yet. Just a few antelope grazing far down the hillside." Nakhoza let the binoculars rest on her chest. "All the mines buried?"

Lingana nodded. "I just did the last of the six. Do you think one of us should help Annja and the others in the tunnels?"

"No, she and Tarkin have enough help. They're double-checking the traps and will send a runner if she needs us. And she has the old and sick in the safe-room."

The "safe-room." Lingana had seen it once—a cavernous room off one of the mazes of tunnels. Even if the 'gades made it past this point into the interior, they'd likely never find the safe-room for days. Thank God. Her mother and sisters would be protected—for a time.

As if she could read Lingana's thoughts, Nakhoza said,

"Don't worry. Whatever happens to us, the 'gades will never find the safe-room in that tunnel maze. And they have plenty of food and water to hold out for weeks if they must."

Lingana nodded and tried to smile. "Why do you think the big guns went quiet? Those had to be 'gade guns, yes?"

Nakhoza shrugged. "I wish I knew. It sounded like cannons—then that explosion. They still could be fighting. We would not hear small arms fire from this distance."

Lingana hugged herself. "It is so hard to wait. To not know what is happening to our men."

Nakhoza kicked a stone down the hill. "The waiting makes for crazy thinking. I don't want to think of the bad, but it is hard not to. I would rather be out there fighting with D'Shay and Jaym. I feel so helpless here and not knowing if they are alive or dead."

"Yes, I…" Lingana looked downslope. "I saw a shape—in the bush there." She pointed to a brushy area a kilometer down slope. "It was definitely not an antelope."

Nakhoza trained her glasses. "All I see are bushes and—"

A flock of white-throated crows took flight just meters from where Lingana had pointed. Nakhoza crouched behind a limestone boulder. She grabbed Lingana's arm and jerked her down. "You are right. Not an antelope. I saw the shine of binoculars, maybe a riflescope. Stay low, but run to tell Annja and the others. The 'gades are here."

Annja, Tarkin, and ten other armed men and women crouched along the low defensive wall with Lingana and Nakhoza. "Only minutes ago we got a garbled communication from Xian," said Annja. "From what we can piece together, he and Giambo's group are pinned down by a rear guard. The rest of the 'gades are heading this way. Until Giambo's men break free, we are on our own."

"How many 'gades you think we will face?" asked Nakhoza.

"Xian's transmission was full of static. We only heard the word 'hundred.' Whether he meant one or two hundred is something we don't know. He mentioned their own dead and wounded, but again, the message was too choppy to hear a number."

Please God, thought Nakhoza, not D'Shay or Jaym. She glanced at Lingana, her chin trembling. Yes, she must be having the same terrible worry.

Annja's face looked older, tired. "We must hold the 'gade force until Giambo's fighters break through and reach us. We shall use the fallback plan only as a last resort." She looked up and down the line of defenders lying prone behind the wall of boulders. Annja's mouth was a tight line.

Lingana and Nakhoza exchanged glances. "I think most of the 'gade force is already below us," said Nakhoza. "They are gathering behind that thick brush at the edge of the forest."

"Then it is time for a test," said Annja. "Lingana, please get me a blanket and a camo cap."

Lingana scurried low behind the barrier of rock into the cavern. She returned with the blanket and cap.

"Roll the blanket tight. Yes, good. Now we give blanket-man his hat. Everyone stay low." Annja slowly lifted the dummy above the rock wall. In less than two seconds, the blanket was jerked from her hands. The gunshot thundered up the hillside and echoed off the cliffs.

Nakhoza looked at the blanket roll, nearly torn in two. She wondered what would happen to a person if that caliber of bullet hit them. Tear off a limb? Explode a person's head like a dropped melon?

Annja shouted. "Everyone keep to your defensive positions and do not rise up to fire. Also remember, it may be better to fight to the end than become a 'gade prisoner. Especially for you women."

Lingana, Nakhoza, and the others scuttled behind the protective rock wall with their rifles and took up their positions.

"Hold them off as long as you possibly can," said Annja. "Break and run for the tunnels *only* when the 'gades make it beyond the fifty-meter mark—the twin shrubs near the trail."

Nakhoza took up a prone position like the others along the defensive wall of boulders. The massive boulders they had rolled into place were about a meter across and rounded by weathering. Annja had them spaced so there was one for each defender. Between the boulders, smaller rocks filled in most of the gaps, leaving only enough space for a rifle barrel. Beneath the larger boulders, the defensive team had jammed two-meter-long tree limbs.

Nakhoza looked to her right and noticed Lingana was panting. "Lingana, you must slow your breathing or you could black out. Your heart will race too fast. Purse your lips and make tiny breaths. Yes, yes. Much better." Nakhoza saw that tears had streaked the dust on Lingana's cheeks, but as she gained control of her breathing, her expression became more rigid. Her fear was morphing to determination.

Nakhoza smiled to herself. Lingana had come so far in such a short time. She remembered the first time Jaym took her to the firing range and showed her how to properly hold a rifle. When Lingana had fired her first shot at the target, the stock slammed into her shoulder. "You need the stock tight like this," Jaym had said. Lingana later confessed to Nakhoza that she could handle a rifle pretty well, but she looked for any excuse for Jaym to be close to her; to touch her as he did. She described the warmth and smell of him as he stood behind her and moved her arms and hands to the proper firing position. "Don't jerk the trigger," he told her. "And don't close your eyes when you fire." Yes, thought Nakhoza. She had seen Lingana smile as Jaym hovered over her, his arms against hers, his cheek close to hers.

Nakhoza looked down the hillside again and wished D'Shay could be beside her. She knew that down below were 'gades with the newest guns, and they were used to killing. Was killing and death going to be the accepted way of life in Chewena? She could kill—had killed—but it haunted her. It haunted Lingana, too. Lingana once asked her if God would see the blood on their hands when they appeared for Judgment Day.

Nakhoza shifted her rifle and looked down the sights. At least this old gun had sights. Some didn't. D'Shay said it was a good weapon—for its age. He and the offensive team had newer weapons, but this had a worn wooden stock and held clips of only twelve rounds. It had no telescopic sights, but she'd finally figured out how to line up the manual sights and adjust for distance. At the one-hundred meter mark—the flamebush downslope—aim just above the head of the enemy.

At half that distance, target the neck. It had seemed like a game when she fired at paper cutouts of men. But the thought of putting bullets into living flesh and bone...

Thak, thak, thak.

Bullets slamming into rock jerked Nakhoza from her thoughts. Machine gun fire steadily raked their defensive rock wall and buzzed overhead like hornets.

"Keep low as possible!" Nakhoza shouted over the chatter of guns and twang of bullets. "This is their covering fire. They want us to fire back and waste ammo. 'Gades will rush us any time now. Remember—wait till they reach the hundred-meter mark, fire carefully. Don't panic. Breathe and squeeze."

Nakhoza glanced over to see Lingana lying flat, her eyes squeezed tight as the heavy gunfire shattered stones and showered her with rock fragments. Her entire body shook. "Lingana! Slow breaths. Pretend Jaym is helping you hold your arms steady. Breath, aim, and squeeze. Aim and squeeze."

Men rushed from the distant brush below. "Here comes the first wave!" shouted Nakhoza.

She trained her sights toward the twenty or more figures rushing up the hill. Nakhoza realized that her own rifle was now shaking. *Breathe, aim, and squeeze.* She looked down her sights and chose one of the men—a stocky white man with a shaggy red beard and shaved head. He bared his teeth as he ran. The 'gade and the other men began to yell—like drug-crazed warriors rushing into battle. Her gun barrel wavered. She fought to steady herself as the continuous covering fire from the tree line below rained fragments of stone around her.

The man in her sights was at the flamebush. She took aim

just above his head. Her gun boomed. The man spun. He staggered for a second, but recovered and kept coming.

"Body armor!" shouted Annja. "Aim for the head or legs."

The line of defenders on either side of Nakhoza opened up. She sighted in her 'gade, but before she could fire, the man's head sprayed red. His arms flew out as he was thrown backward. Then another fell, his leg torn and spurting blood.

She zeroed in on a 'gade toward the front. He was dark-skinned—more like an Af-Am than a native African. His heavy dreadlocks bounced behind as he ran. Nakhoza realized he had made it clear to the fifty-meter mark. Annja said to retreat when they reached that point—run into the cavern.

No. The machine gun was still raking their defensive wall. It would be suicide to run. She looked down the sights and aimed at the man's waist. She fired. The bullet caught him in the thigh and he went down; his leg bent at an impossible angle. Nakhoza swung her rifle barrel, looking for another target.

But there were none! All the 'gades were either dead or trying to crawl for some sort of cover. And the machine gun fire had stopped. Except for moans from the fallen 'gades, it was quiet. So quiet she could hear the whispering of defenders up and down the line.

Lingana looked at Nakhoza. "We did it, Nakhoza! We actually stopped them."

"Yes, but I think they were just testing us to see our strength. They will soon come again." She turned and shouted, "Annja, no casualties over here."

Annja called back. "One wounded here, but we've stopped the bleeding. She says she can continue fighting."

Tarkin shouted. "I see movement in the bushes. I think they are coming again!"

Nakhoza's expression hardened. She shouted to those nearby, "Reload your clips! You are now seasoned warriors and can do this." She licked her lips. "We have won round one of this. If many come next, again, do *not* leave your post until Annja or I give the command to fall back. Any questions?"

A Chewan girl on the other side of Lingana asked, "What if we are wounded so much we cannot run into safe part of the cave."

For a moment Nakhoza clamped her jaw, then said, "The truth is, we will not have time to carry you. Pretend you are dead. Lie still and do not move. Perhaps the 'gades will run past and into the cavern to chase the rest of us. But ... remember what Annja said about 'gade captives."

"Look down at the brush!" said Tarkin. "Over to the right."

Fear crawled up Nakhoza's spine like a swarm of insects. A swath of brush was smashed aside as a war machine lifted over brush and rock to crush into the open.

TAKING THE BAIT

It is the calm and silent water that drowns a man.

—*African proverb*

———————————

Reya tested the mat of branches and leaves Kwada had laid out for her. He crisscrossed the branches—almost like weaving a basket. When he finished, she had a barrier between the soles of her boots and the sucking mud of the swamp. The mat was about two meters long and lay behind the thick tree trunk she'd use for cover. The mat edges extended far enough that she could move to the left or right of the tree on firm footing.

"You think it is thick enough for you?" asked Kwada.

"Yeah, it's perfect." She stomped across the mat and grinned. "My magic swamp carpet. Bring on the 'gades."

He smiled. "Good, good. But don't be so anxious for 'gades. We can make a good ambush from here, but they gonna be many more than us." His expression became stern as he looked out to the boggy trail. "Every arrow must count. If we are lucky, this fight's gonna end good for us. But like hunting for game, sometimes the antelope does not cooperate as the hunter wishes. We must hope fate is in our favor."

"Yeah, but sometimes fate is what you make it. I gotta think we're gonna kick butt."

He nodded and looked up the trail. "Yes, kick butt. I must now check the others. Positions of archers must be just so to make best of battle. I think your friend Maykego gonna be on other side of trail, but a few meters to the right. Always must be careful so there is no death of friend."

"Yeah," said Reya. "We call that 'friendly fire'—the worst oxymoron ever."

"Yes, okay. Now I check Maykego's mat and see if it is solid 'nough. Then I'm gonna climb into my own position."

"Climb?"

He pointed up to a massive tree on Maykego's side of the trail. "Up 'bout ten meters. See that big fork in the trunk? Whenever I hunt, I find a solid, high platform. Up there I can brace 'gainst the trunk and there are enough leaves so it's gonna be hard to see where my arrows come from." He smiled. "To make it harder for 'gades to see me, I think the tree trunk and I are 'bout the same color of brown, yes?"

Reya grinned and nodded. *It's a nice color,* she thought. But she said nothing. Not a time to get dewy while death was marching their way.

"Okay," said Kwada. "I'm going across now and prepare. I think they gonna be coming in thirty minutes or less." He hesitated and looked Reya in the eye. "Be safe, yes?"

"Yeah ... sure. You too, Kwada. Thanks."

Reya leaned against her tree and shooed away mosquitoes. They hadn't been so bad when she was on the move with the others, but now, damn. Even though it was steaming hot, this was one time she wished she had long pants. She knelt over the edge of her mat and scooped up a handful of mud from beneath the algae-green water. The muck smelled of rot and death. She smeared her mosquito-chewed legs with the green-brown goop, and took another scoop to baste her bare arms.

She leaned back again and waited. The waiting was the hard part. During a fight there was no thinking. But now all she could do was imagine dozens of hopped-up 'gades charging them with semiautomatics.

Seemed she had stood for hours behind her tree while she was blood-sucked. After a while, Reya didn't even swipe at the bugs. The stinging and biting kept her from thinking too much of the fight to come. She took a swig from her canteen and peered around her tree. Up where Kwada would be positioned, she could only see leaves and shadows. And she didn't see any sign of Maykego either. *So silent,* she thought. It's like even the birds didn't want to be here. Only the buzz and whine of the damned bugs. She'd almost rather—

The *twee-twee-twee* of a bird call cut through the humid air. Far up the trail the same call echoed back.

Kwada's warning signal. This was it. He'd either spotted 'gades or heard their voices. Reya's entire body began to quake. *Easy, easy,* she thought. Gotta act like Maykego. Maykego wouldn't be shaking. Okay, just notch an arrow and get into a firing stance.

With trembling hands she drew an arrow from her quiver ... and dropped it. *Shit!* But at least it had fallen on her support mat. Good, the fletching wasn't damp. She picked it up and managed to notch the arrow onto the bowstring.

She told herself, *Get a grip girl.* Had to think about Lingana and Nakhoza up at the outpost. And about the Ezondwei villagers—just women and children who'll get slaughtered if we don't stop these 'gades.

As she took her archer's stance, she cocked her head. Yes, now she heard their voices down the trail. They couldn't be more than half-a-klick away. Reya took a deep breath and tried to exhale her fear. Had to remember that when 'gades got this far they'd be slogging through mud to the top of their boots. They'd be so mired down that this should be like target practice.

But, damn, the 'gades didn't sound like they were struggling through the mud. They were laughing at something. Bastards. Were they rehashing some recent battle? Maybe joking about who gets first choice of the village women before torching their homes?

She couldn't see them, but got a whiff of cigarette smoke. Then the first glimpse of faces. White men, striding along. Striding! But ... they should be struggling in the muck! Now she could see their boots. Oh crap! They had some kind of flat wicker things strapped to their soles. She'd heard there had been snowshoes before The Warming. Flat things to keep you from sinking in snow. These were swamp shoes. Somehow they knew about this muck.

A monkey chitter drifted through the swamp. That was Maykego's signal for the archers to draw their bows. Reya silently stepped to the right of her tree. She raised and drew the bowstring to her cheek. She sighted in on a tall man trying to light a cigarette as he walked. His shirt was open and she could see tattoos that looked like bands of barbed wire, like the deadly razor wire fence around her old 'gee camp.

Come on, Maykego, she thought. *Give the—*

The second monkey chitter was loud and clear.

At twenty meters Reya aimed just above his head. She released and watched her arrow fly across the reeds. It took him in the neck. His eyes went wide as he struggled for his shouldered rifle. His knees buckled, then splashed face-first into the muck. The 'gade beside him unleashed a barrage of bullets that slashed through underbrush and slammed into trees. Reya began to shake. God, she had just killed a man. She notched another arrow, but before she could loose it, a shaft hissed from the sky to pierce the top of the shooter's skull.

Had to be Kwada.

Reya shot at another 'gade firing wildly as he sprinted for cover. Her arrow lodged deep in his ribs, but he didn't go down. He looked at the arrow, staggered, then turned Reya's direction and raised his rifle. The man jerked and tried to turn, as if to look behind.

Two more arrows had sunk into his back. *Maykego,* thought Reya.

Three down.

"Here!" shouted a 'gade with a flat, NorthAm accent. "You men! Get to the trees and form defensive squares. *Move!*"

Reya still hadn't had a glimpse of Maykego, Kwada, or the other archers down the trail. She heard 'gades running. Retreating—at least for now. Then shouts and sporadic bursts of gunfire. Now they were out of sight, and here she was marooned on a couple of meters of matting. What was she supposed to do now? They had to be reassembling and they'd return in force with full firepower.

There, she saw a movement in the tree limbs. Kwada. He shimmied down his tree trunk and dropped to the ground. He crouched, and then trotted back into the underbrush, seeming to hop every few steps, then was gone. *But how?* wondered Reya. How could he move like a rabbit through this muck? She knew he didn't have swamp shoes. He hadn't signaled her, so what should she do now? Try to follow him? Whatever he was up to, he'd need backup.

"Reya."

Her heart leaped. "Maykego! You scared the crap out of me."

"Come, Reya. We are going with Kwada. I see how he can walk 'cross this. We must follow. I think I know what he's gonna do."

"But, how? And what's he—"

Semiautomatic fire chattered, just up the trail. The 'gades were trying to take out the other archers.

"Not time to talk," said Maykego. "Come, we must cross over and follow Kwada." Maykego waded out into the muck as Reya struggled to follow. A few times Reya thought she was going down, but she managed to slog across to Kwada's tree where Maykego waited; anxiously glancing up the trail. She reached for Reya's hand and pulled her up to the base of the tree.

"I see Kwada walk on these fat tree roots," said Maykego. She toed the massive roots anchoring the tree. The roots thrust out a meter or more before sinking their tendrils into the mud. "We can track Kwada's wet footsteps easy. Do what I do, but we must hurry."

Maykego hopped from one exposed root to the next, moving from tree to tree as nimble as a squirrel. Reya followed in her steps, but teetered as she struggled from root to root, expecting to fall into the swamp any second. But after twenty meters of stepping, teetering, and sweating, it came easier. Back on the so-called trail, all the trees had been cleared and they had to slog. Here where the trees were thick, root-hopping was so much faster.

They saw Kwada waiting for them. As they approached, he grinned. "I am glad that you both learn so fast."

"Kwada," said Reya. "What are we doing back here?" She waved her bow the direction from which they came. "The 'gades are *that* way, and they're going to get by us."

"No, I think we gonna bring them this way."

Another burst of gunfire and 'gades shouting across the steamy swamp. Good. That meant Azibo and his men were still harassing and putting up resistance.

"It is time for us to get the 'gade's attention," said Maykego. She nodded in the direction of gunfire and shouts. "They be there, 'bout hundred meters."

"But we can't see them," said Reya.

Neither Kwada nor Maykego replied, but were looking up at the forest canopy. Kwada pointed to an opening between two large trees. "I think we able to shoot clear of tree limbs through there."

"Yes, that be a clean path," said Maykego. She looked at Reya. "You do this also. Draw your arrow past cheek to ear. This shot take extra pull. Follow where we aim and make angle of your arrow same as ours. If we shoot together, I think we get 'gade's attention."

Kwada and Maykego notched their arrows. Reya quickly followed. She watched the two raise their bows and draw back to their ears. Reya raised her bow to their angle and drew back until she felt the fletching brush her ear. It felt like her bow would surely snap with this much pull. Her arms quaked from the strain.

"Ready?" asked Kwada.

Reya's voice was shaky. "Yeah ... ready."

"Then fire!"

They released at the same instant. Reya watched the three arrows arc together above the treetops. It only took three heartbeats.

A screamed curse was followed by bursts of gunfire. Now shouts. "They came from that way! They're deeper in the swamp. Follow me!"

Kwada nodded. "We have 'gade's attention. Come." He turned and started root hopping, moving further into the dark swamp. Maykego seemed to dance across the roots, while Reya did her best just to keep her footing.

"I see wet prints on the roots," shouted a 'gade. "This way."

The voice seemed much nearer. Reya moved faster, trying to keep up with Maykego. She was panting now. "Where's Kwada ... taking us?"

"No idea, but he know this forest and swamp."

Kwada looked back at Reya and Maykego. "We gonna spread out now. Want to make three trails for 'gades to follow. I will go straight, Maykego go to left 'bout twenty meters, and Reya to right. Whatever you do, do not fall from the roots. But you must keep going. 'Bout fifty more meters will be 'nough. Quick now."

Reya headed off to the right and moved forward. It was dimmer in this deeper canopy. Moss hung thick like beards of trolls. Steam hovering above the swamp drifted over many of the roots, making it harder to see where to step. *Don't fall here,* Kwada had said. *Was the water deeper? Were there crocs?* She looked to her left to see where Kwada was. There, waiting a few meters ahead. Further down Maykego waved and gave Reya a thumbs-up. Reya's stomach churned at the thought of the oncoming 'gades, but she forced a tight grin and returned her gesture.

"Now we just wait!" shouted Kwada.

Damn! thought Reya. *His shout's gonna let the 'gades know exactly where we are.*

Kwada must have read her expression. "It is okay, Reya. We *want* them to come."

Not me, she thought. Three archers against thirty or more 'gades?

"Is your tree wide enough to hide behind when the bullets come?" asked Kwada.

Oh God, she thought. But to Kwada she said, "Uh, yeah. Should be good enough, and there's a solid platform of roots too."

"Stay in the open till you see faces. We gonna make ourselves bait. Find all the courage you have inside you, and when we bait them in, shooting will start. Then get behind tree fast."

Reya and Maykego nodded.

"Hey! 'Gade men!" Kwada shouted. "You track like little girls. Cannot find us, eh?" He glanced at Reya and Maykego. "You shout also. Want them spread out."

Maykego hollered in Chewan. She sounded angry, maybe spitting cuss words.

Reya felt a hot fury rise in her throat. She shouted, "Hey

fuckers, come and get me!" She was stunned at the rage in her voice. She let the tears come and screamed like a panther.

At least thirty or forty 'gades splashed through swamp water toward her.

"There they are!" shouted one of the men. "Try to take the girls alive."

No way, thought Reya. *You'll never take us alive.*

"Now! Take cover," shouted Kwada.

But something had seized Reya in a grip of fury. It would not let her legs move. She stood there in the open and reached for an arrow. She was panting, her teeth bared.

"Reya, no!" shouted Maykego. "Hide now!"

Bullets sprayed Reya with swamp water and ripped into her tree. She blinked, then hopped behind the tree. *Get a grip,* she thought. Had to slow her breathing.

More shooting and shouting. Bullets hissed and hammered trees. Reya closed her eyes. *Please, God. Not here.* She couldn't die in this putrid swamp. Would Jaym or D'Shay ever know what happened to her? Whatever was going to happen, she was going to take out two or three 'gades first.

The angry shouts of the 'gades suddenly turned to something else. Their voices grew louder, alarmed. The shrill sounds of panic.

Their shooting had stopped. Reya had to see. She held onto the tree trunk and peered around the edge. She saw dozens of 'gades foundering in the thick slime water. Most already up to their waists. Wide-eyed, the men thrashed, grasping for floating limbs, even small branches. Only two had not been caught in the quicksand. They were up to their knees and waists, trying to pull themselves up by dangling vines.

Reya stepped around. One of the men saw her and tried to raise his gun. As he did, he sank faster. When he thrashed, his gun went into the water. "Help me!" he shouted. "Hey, girl! We're both white! We have to help each other. For god sake, throw me a vine!"

Reya reached down picked up a twig. She tossed it toward the man.

"I'll kill you bitch!"

"Sure, whatever." She watched him flail as he gulped air then disappeared. Reya drew an arrow and notched it. She looked at a 'gade trying to pull himself out with a vine. She was steady now. An icy calm fell over her and she felt no pity. Her bowstring twanged.

"Uhng!" groaned the 'gade. Reya's arrow had buried in his back up to the fletching. There was one more clutching a vine. She drew a second arrow, but the man lost his grip, floundered, and quickly went under. Reya leaned expressionless against the tree and watched. Maybe she should feel something for them, but she couldn't. Not after what 'gades had done. Raping, beating. Torching villages. Killing her friend Mai-Lin. And now Bettina was dead by the 'gades that overran New SUN Post-2.

Soon only the tops of a few heads and groping hands showed. Then it was silent. A few last bubbles and a couple of floating caps were all that were left to show anyone had been here.

"Reya," shouted Maykego. She and Kwada were root-hopping toward her. "You okay?"

Reya swallowed, trying to force back the bile. She nodded, but her entire body began to shake. The forest grew blurry and seemed to move—to whirl about her. She leaned over and vomited into the swamp.

ROADBLOCK

You cannot take hawks without climbing some cliffs.

—*Darkovan proverb*

———————

D'Shay watched Giambo circle the captive 'gade. The man lay on the rocky road, his nose askew and bloodied.

Giambo knelt and grabbed a fistful of the 'gade's hair and pulled him to his knees. "You kill many of my men with you big machine gun. You think that be honorable thing to do?"

The man winced, but said "Bugger off, ape."

"Tsk, tsk. We take you alive, and this be you thanks?"

The 'gade spat at Giambo's arm.

Giambo wiped off the spit. "What we gonna do with you, Mister 'Gade? I think we might be nice to you if you tell us some things, yes?" Giambo jerked the 'gade's head back and bared his teeth. "You better start saying things I wanna hear. Fast."

D'Shay leaned closer and whispered, "Better talk. I've seen what Giambo can do with a skinning knife. And with 'gades, he skins them alive."

The man looked wide-eyed at Giambo, but said nothing.

Giambo stood and drew his machete from his belt. "Before

you skin come off, I give my men souvenirs. Gonna start with fingers and ears."

The man glanced at the angry faces around him. D'Shay reached down and tore open his shirt. "Nice tattoos. Giambo, if we tanned this skin you'd have a classy ammo pouch."

"Hey," the 'gade sputtered. "I ... I'm just in this for the money. I mean, what else can a white man do in Africa?" He glanced at Jaym. "Can't be a blender like him. Too old. 'Sides, you gotta be connected to get sweet duty like that, yeh?"

"'Nough talk," said Giambo. "We must catch you friends quick. I think I gotta convince you more." He grabbed the 'gade's wrist and pinned the flat of his hand to the gravel. He raised his machete.

The 'gade tried to jerk away from Giambo's steel grip. "Okay, okay! Whaddya wanna know?"

"How many men," said Giambo. "And what trail they takin'."

The 'gade shrugged. "We started with a hundred and fifty, maybe two hundred, but you took some out."

"About thirty," said D'Shay.

The 'gade spat blood and wiped his nose. "We were gonna take some goat trail to a mountain cave in the foothills. Orders were to secure the cave."

"And kill all in cave, yes?"

The 'gade shrugged. "We had orders to take some alive."

"Yes," said Giambo. "The young women and girls. Okay, which goat trail your people gonna take. There be two."

"I just know it's up a ravine—on the west slope."

"Same as the one we came down," said Jaym.

Giambo nodded. "You doin' good, Mr. 'Gade. Now, where your people gonna ambush us on west-side trail, umm?"

The 'gade shook his head. "I don't know shit about any ambush."

"No ambush? That be very good news." Giambo jerked him to his feet. "Then there be no danger, so we let you go up trail first, yes?"

"No! Wait." He licked his lips. "Okay. They were talking about two ambush points. First one about a klick up. Second at klick two."

"Good, good. I think you keep your parts after all—even pretty tattoos."

"Lemme go, man. I gave you everything. I'll just leave and won't—"

Giambo tapped the man's cheek with his machete. "Shhh. We still need your valuable help. You still gonna lead us up trail and show us ambush places."

"But that's suicide. I don't know exactly where—"

"'Gades would not shoot other 'gade, yes? I think you all be loyal friends."

The man's eyes were wild with fear.

Giambo pushed him forward. He shouted to Jaym and the others, "We must hurry. 'Gades have big head start on us." He spoke softly to the 'gade, "You gonna walk fast 'cause my machete still be thirsty." He jabbed him in the back. "Move!"

———————

As they hurried up the trail D'Shay tried to remember details of the hike down—to think of the many places 'gades could set up an ambush. Not on this narrow section with its fifty-meter drop-off. But ahead there was a wide spot with boulders and brush. That would be about a klick from here, maybe less. He'd recognize it when they got close.

Within ten minutes the trail widened.

"Hey, Giambo," said D'Shay. "We're coming to a perfect place for an ambush. Bet they're in the brush ahead."

Giambo nodded and held up an arm to stop the column. He turned to D'Shay and Jaym, speaking softly. "Gun nest could be many places in the brush, and this is bad place to get caught. I think we need to find exact location." He glanced around. "We gonna spread out here and each man find cover."

D'Shay hand-signaled to the men behind. They each took cover behind slabs of gray basalt and boulders. D'Shay lay prone behind a rotted snag fallen from the cliff top. Not great protection, but he'd be hard to see and it would be a good position to fire from. Only Giambo and the 'gade remained standing in the open.

"Join you good friends," said Giambo, giving the 'gade a shove up the trail.

"No, man! I beg you, they'll—"

Giambo raised his machete. "Move or I take you head off in one swing. I count to three. One, two . . . "

The 'gade broke into a run. "It's me," he screamed. "It's Snake! Don't shoot. I can show you where they're hiding. Tell you how many there are!" He was panting now. "I was with—"

The 'gade was flung back down the trail by a burst of heavy machine gun fire.

"To the far right!" shouted Jaym. "Behind those red bushes."

"Do not fire yet," bellowed Giambo. He turned to D'Shay and Jaym. "Cannot waste more ammo like before."

"Yeah," said D'Shay. "But please don't play hero again and charge in with your machete. Too much open ground."

"How far you think that gun be?"

"About twenty meters," said D'Shay. "Funny; they could have shot us before we even got this far. What're they waiting for?"

"We were straggled out too much," said Jaym. "The closer we got, the easier it would be to get us all."

Giambo thought for a few moments. "You NorthAms be good at sports, yes?"

D'Shay shrugged. "I only shot hoops in my hood."

Jaym shook his head. "It was baseball in mine, but no bats. Only pitch and catch."

"That be good 'nough." Giambo motioned to one of his men.

A Chewan man ran forward in a crouch and knelt next to Giambo.

"You the one carrying those iron baseballs?"

The man swung his pack around and pulled out a grenade. Giambo took one and handed it to Jaym. "Here, Jay-em. Pitch this baseball. See if 'gades can catch."

They jogged beyond the remnants of the machine gun nest for several hundred meters. This time they had no bait to entice gunfire and expose the 'gades' next position. Again, Giambo signaled his men to halt. He pointed. "They gonna be on other side of bend."

The trail here rounded a rock abutment to the left. It would be single file across bare rock that had been blasted away for a pathway.

Jaym cocked his head. "Listen."

D'Shay and Giambo turned their heads. Above the whisper of warm wind they heard faint popping. "Oh God," muttered D'Shay. "The main force is already at the cavern."

"We gotta get past!" said Jaym. "Lingana and—"

Giambo waved him quiet. "Yes, yes. My sister and the others." He looked up the cliff. "Anybody climb cliff?" he shouted.

Jaym and D'Shay exchanged looks. "Back in the Corridor, I couldn't scale more than a couple of meters," said Jaym.

"Scale?" asked Giambo.

"Climb walls," said D'Shay. "Corridor dust storms sandblasted the project housing in our hoods. The mortar of the old buildings wore away and gave you fingerholds in the brick walls. Good purchase for climbing when rival hoodies cornered you." He looked up at the cliff wall and slipped off his pack. "Almost like old times in the Corridor."

The first few meters were easy, with solid footholds and finger grips—even better than edging up a brick wall back in the Corridor. But then his right foot slid and he gasped, feeling for a new toehold. *Damn sandals!* he thought. He shook one off and found footing. He kicked off the other. Yes. Now his toes could feel and grip crevasses almost as well as his fingers.

This is too weird, thought D'Shay. It was like what Reya had said about flashbacks. He could almost feel the Corridor fog that drifted in from the harbor at night. It brought the smells of rotting fish and seaweed, mixed with the smoke of the homeless making cooking fires in the alleys.

"You okay, man?" shouted Jaym from far below.

D'Shay blinked away the thoughts. "Yeah, fine."

"You're doing it! Go, D'Shay!"

Yeah, he thought. Just don't look down. He chanced a glance up. Good, only a couple more meters.

Sweat stung his eyes, but he pushed on and grabbed a root dangling from a gnarled tree. Brittle rock crumbled under his left foot. He fought for another toehold. There, a ledge. He caught his breath, and then pulled up and onto the cliff top. D'Shay lay on his back panting for a moment, then sat up and crawled through grass and brush to look over the far edge.

Three 'gades kneeled in a foxhole, one manning the machine gun, the other two laying out ammo belts. *Nasty gun,* he thought. An air-cooled .50 caliber. One bullet could tear off an arm. A burst would cut a person in half. D'Shay reached in his pack and lay the two grenades on the grass. He couldn't toss these things as good as Jaym, but it should be easy enough.

Damn! He forgot to ask how many seconds he had after pulling the pin. Was it seven seconds? Fifteen? Oh hell, just get on with it. He held one of the iron eggs in one hand, then jerked at the pin with the other. The pin didn't budge. He strained to give it all he had, and the pin suddenly flew behind him as he fell over backward.

He lay on his back staring at the thing, and realized he'd forgotten to count. How long already? Five seconds. Shit. He scrambled to his feet and lobbed the grenade in a hurried toss. It hit the road and rolled toward the 'gades, but stopped short. D'Shay dove back from the edge.

"Down, down!" shouted a 'gade.

Whoomp!

D'Shay eased back to look, his heart pounding. Damn, only dust and a crater in the road. Okay, one more chance. He yanked the pin on his second, and last, grenade. This time he stood and counted his heartbeats. At five he tossed it right into the nest. One of the 'gades yelled and scooped the grenade. He cocked back to toss it as D'Shay jumped for cover.

The explosion sounded different this time—more muffled. And now he didn't hear any yelling or screaming. He crawled back and looked over the edge of the cliff.

Uck, he thought. He stood and shouted to Giambo's team. "All clear. Move out!"

STICKS AND
STONES

Give me a lever long enough ... and I shall move the world.

—*Archimedes, ca. 250 BC*

Nakhoza watched the crawler lurch over boulders and brush as it began ascending the hill. Directly behind walked dozens of 'gades—at least a hundred. None had fired yet. The only sound was the whine of the engine and the grinding of its tracks over rock as the crawler moved closer.

"Do not fire yet!" called Annja. She and Tarkin were positioned at the far right of the defensive wall. Nakhoza and Lingana to the left. A dozen other New SUN defenders were between.

The crawler slewed its way up the rocky scree to stop about a hundred meters from their position. The 'gades on foot paused, their weapons at the ready. The crawler's turret was mounted with a cannon that slowly swiveled to point towards Nakhoza and the other defenders.

One of the 'gades near the crawler lifted a portable loud-speaker. "We mean you no harm, and only ask that you surrender peacefully. We come to liberate you from the tyranny of a corrupt global government that has brainwashed you. New SUN is a lie. It was created only to do the bidding of the Global Alliance." He paused. "And a message to you blenders: the Alliance doesn't care what happens to you. They sent you here only to get rid of you. You think you are going to help Africa, but only we have the means to organize and protect you and the Chewen people. What has the Alliance done for any of you? Nothing." The man paused.

One of the Chewan women near Lingana whispered to Nakhoza. "These are lies, yes?"

"All lies," said Nakhoza.

"We give you one minute," boomed the loudspeaker voice. "One minute to lay down your arms and come forward. You will be fed and treated with respect, then allowed to return to your villages and homes. If you do not, we have no choice but to apply force."

The crawler's cannon continued to move back and forth across the outpost's defensive line. From behind her boulder shield, Nakhoza watched the 'gades talking to one another. They were relaxed now, acting like this was a holiday. Some laughed, others lit up cigarettes.

"Twenty seconds left," boomed the loudspeaker. "Last warning."

Nakhoza crept back to her position. "Ready?" she asked Lingana and the others nearby. They all nodded.

Annja and Tarkin stood and raised their arms.

"Very wise," said the speaker voice. "Have the other defenders stand and move to—"

"*Now!*" shouted Annja as she and Tarkin dropped back behind the wall of boulders.

Nakhoza, Lingana, and all the others behind the wall took hold of the thick wood poles they had jammed beneath their defensive boulders. Nakhoza pressed down with all her strength. Her boulder tilted, slowly rolled forward, then toppled over the edge with the others. Within seconds the leaping, crashing boulders tore at the brittle cliff rock creating a roaring landslide. House-sized slabs of limestone bounded toward the men and the crawler. Panicked 'gades scrambled to the rear. The crawler tried to accelerate out of the way, but the booming tide of rock slammed into its side, flipping the thing like an enormous gray beetle.

The slide came to a rest, but Nakhoza could not see through the thick clouds of dust roiling below.

Tarkin shaded his eyes and squinted. "The crawler is done, but the rocks only took out a handful of 'gades. The rest are regrouping and moving this way." Annja turned the defenders and shouted, "Withdraw, withdraw! Into the cavern and down the tunnels. Tarkin and I will be right behind you!"

Nakhoza, Lingana, and the others scrambled through the mouth of the cavern, Nakhoza leading the way. They tread quickly but carefully across the vast floor. "Step only where I step." The dozens of tents had been collapsed by the defensive team into a litter of fabric strewn from wall to wall. Nakhoza looked at her feet as she threaded her steps between the piles of tents and headed for the tunnel in the cavern's deepest recess.

She should have been able to do this without thinking; she'd been in charge of choosing the location of each anti-personnel mine, but she was now so numb her steps were wobbly. Would they all be cut down from behind before they reached safety?

When she made it to the tunnel entrance, Nakhoza waited until everyone was through the minefield and into the tunnel opening. "Run!" she shouted. "Use your crank lights and watch out for the triggerstones."

Nakhoza turned back. Tarkin was weaving through the tents towards her. "Tarkin! Where's Annja?"

But Tarkin just elbowed her aside and sprinted into the tunnel.

"Annja!" screamed Nakhoza. "Hurry!"

"No, Nakhoza," shouted Annja. "Run and save yourself. They will need you." She was kneeling, firing bursts downhill.

"Annja! Please, come with us. We all can be safe if—"

"I said run! That is an order." She didn't turn, but kept firing. "The more 'gades I can stop now, the better your—"

Annja's arms lifted as she flew backward.

Nakhoza screamed. Now men were shouting below the rocky edge. They began to spray the cavern with bullets. Lead sparked against rocks. The ricochets buzzed like bees. Nakhoza fired off a long burst at the entrance, then turned and sprinted into the tunnel. Within seconds, she heard the first explosions and screams behind her. Some had hit the mines planted along the trail; then came blasts within the cavern as 'gades triggered booby traps inside.

But now she and the rest of the New SUN people were running deeper into the bowels of the mountain. As they ran, the sounds of gunfire faded, replaced by the slap of sandals against the stone floor.

Lingana flashed her crank light behind Nakhoza. "Where is Annja?"

"Annja...was killed," said Nakhoza. "She stayed to give us more time."

"No!" snapped one of the women.

"Her choice," said Tarkin. His voice was cool. "So, I'm in command now."

Yes, thought Nakhoza. *What you always wanted.*

"No time to brood about Annja," said Tarkin. "Those mines in the cavern will only stop a dozen or more 'gades. Keep running."

Nakhoza panted as she ran behind Tarkin. Ahead she saw the glow of the solar lighting to show the way—but that would also make it easier for the 'gades.

At a fork they took the tunnel to the right. Fifty meters later Tarkin stopped at a three-way split. "Nakhoza," he said. "Take your people into the left tunnel, and I'll go with my men to the right. The 'gades will split up and we'll have fewer to deal with."

Nakhoza glared. "'Your' people and 'my' people? Tarkin, we are all together. We must stay together. I know these tunnels and—"

Tarkin's face tightened. "Are you questioning my authority? I wasn't making a suggestion. That was—and still is—an order! Now get moving."

"No." Nakhoza's voice was firm. "The tunnel you want 'my people' to take is a maze of traps. I think you know that. We all go together."

Tarkin raised his weapon. "You've always been a troublemaker. That stops now. Get into that tunnel or I will shoot you for disobeying a direct order."

Nakhoza's voice was steady and firm. "You caused the death of Annja, didn't you? You told her to stay and fight with you, but then you ran to leave her alone to be killed. Now you are trying to have us die in the tunnel maze."

"Shut up! Annja was foolish to stay."

Nakhoza heard distant 'gade voices calling behind them.

"'Gades will be here in minutes," said Tarkin. "Last chance. Into the tunnel or take a bullet." He raised his rifle.

Nakhoza didn't move.

A single shot rang out. Tarkin looked down at his chest where blood began to soak his shirt. His rifle slid from his hands as he slumped to the floor.

All eyes turned to Lingana. She looked dazed as she lowered her gun. "I... had to."

Nakhoza squeezed her shoulder. She turned to the others and said. "Lingana, everyone; into the tunnel on the right. Quickly!"

Nakhoza waited until the last person was down the tunnel before she took a full ammo clip and tossed it into the mouth of the tunnel on the left. *Bait,* she thought to herself. She glanced at Tarkin. His eyes were glazed, but his lips moved slightly. She hesitated for an instant. Perhaps she should feel some pity for him, but she felt nothing. She stepped over him and raced after the others.

As she ran, she heard 'gade shouts and commands far behind. Then came screams. *They were triggering the mantraps,* she thought. 'Gades were falling onto the sharpened stakes—being skewered like fish on the tines of a trident.

Nakhoza saw the flash of crank lights ahead and soon caught up with the others. "They are still coming!" she yelled. "But they've hit the traps."

They came to another two-way split, then darted into the left tunnel. As she ran, Nakhoza wondered how many 'gades were left. Maybe twenty or more killed by the trail mines and the mines under the tents in the cavern mouth. Then the drop-traps would take one or two men each. They'd passed at least ten traps, so maybe twenty more down. Then at each tunnel split they'd divide their forces. Even if some managed to make it this far, they might be able to defeat any survivors.

Nakhoza stopped. "This is far enough," she said, panting. "I think most be in 'gade hell by now, or soon will be."

She looked at Lingana. "You better now?"

Lingana nodded. "But I am a killer. I will always see the expression on Tarkin's face."

"No," said Lingana. "You saved many of us. He was going to send several of us to our death. He was the killer. The tunnel he tried to make us enter was full of death. There were more drop-traps, rockfalls, and impossible mazes no one could survive."

"Yes, so much death," said Lingana. "Even now men are dying terrible deaths in those floor traps."

Nakhoza nodded. "As D'Shay has told me, 'War sucks.' But we are in a war that we did not choose. We must fight because they will kill us or enslave us."

Nakhoza leaned against the tunnel wall. "Everyone rest. I think we are finally safe. We'll wait ten minutes then return."

"When should we check the safe-room?" asked a woman.

"After we are certain all the 'gades are cleared from the tunnels. We cannot take even the slightest chance of them finding our elders and young people."

They waited in silence and darkness. Finally Lingana said, "I think our ten minutes is up."

"Yes, okay," said Nakhoza. "Crank lights back on, but let us go carefully. Do not assume the 'gades have been totally eliminated."

Poised and deliberate, they made their way out. After a few hundred meters, they saw the first gaping floor trap. As they edged past, Nakhoza glanced down to see three 'gades impaled on the sharp stakes. Further on, more traps had caught their prey. At least fifteen were dead or dying in these first few traps.

Within minutes, Nakhoza saw dim light from the cavern entrance. The muffled sounds of gunshots echoed up the tunnel.

"That's gunfire from the entrance," said Lingana. Her expression was grim. "'Gades are still here."

Nakhoza nodded. *Still here and shooting,* she thought, *but at what?* She turned and motioned with her rifle. They all crept forward, weapons at the ready. Stepping carefully into the cavern, Nakhoza tried to ignore the strewn remnants of bodies and the gore splattered across the walls.

Just outside the cavern mouth, where their defensive line had been, a dozen 'gades lay prone, firing downslope. The return fire from below was withering. *Giambo's team,* thought Nakhoza. *Please God, let D'Shay be alive.*

Nakhoza signaled to those behind her by raising her rifle toward the 'gades.

Lingana hesitated. When Nakhoza saw the look on Lingana's face, she mouthed, *Shoot!*

Lingana took a breath and raised her gun.

"Now," shouted Nakhoza. They all fired simultaneously. The 'gades slumped dead. Within minutes the firing from below became sporadic, then ceased altogether.

Lingana stepped past the bodies of the 'gades and waved toward the valley below.

"Stay back!" said Nakhoza. "Our men could mistake you for—"

"Jay-em!" shouted Lingana. She jumped up and down waving.

Jaym and D'Shay were the first to scramble up the trail. Lingana grinned and gave them a Chewan trilling cry of joy. When Jaym finally reached her and lifted her in a hug, she locked her arms around him and cried like a wounded animal.

REGROUPING

It is only the dead who have seen the end of war.

—*Plato*

After the tears of joy and sorrow during the reunion of the New SUN teams, the survivors carried Annja's body down the hillside. A Chewan woman laid her green-and-white *chitenge* over Annja as a shroud. Jaym and the others walked past the body, paying their silent respects. Some laid wildflowers on the shroud, others a cross of twined sticks, some a folded message.

Giambo motioned to Jaym and D'Shay. "Come," said Giambo. "Let us see what we can save from the cavern."

But once inside they were stunned at the carnage inflicted by the antipersonnel mines—the shattered flesh and blood spattered walls. They walked down the tunnel a few hundred meters to find every floor trap triggered. Impaled 'gades lay contorted with wood spikes piercing their bodies. Back in the cavern, they found a few small boxes of rations protected in a side room. The infirmary tent was flattened, but Jaym salvaged a few medical supplies that Reya and the other medtechs could use.

Jaym returned to where the survivors were gathered on

a plateau of grass and brush where a few trees grew along a trickling stream. He found Reya and another woman caring for the wounded. He handed her the few medical supplies he'd salvaged: gauze, a jar of ointment, and a roll of tape.

"Thanks," said Reya. "No morphine?"

"Sorry, this is it." She nodded. Jaym knew little about patching up wounds, but he could tell some of these wounded would not survive. Some had lost an arm or a leg, and only Reya's jury-rigged tourniquets were keeping them alive—for the moment.

He found Lingana with her mom and two sisters. Their eyes were still wide with the terror of being in the safe-room while explosions and gun battles echoed through the tunnel.

Lingana gripped Jaym's hand as if she'd never let go. He put his arm around her shoulder. "The 'gades are dead, Babe. We're safe." Jaym tried to make a reassuring smile, but they all knew that some of the 'gades could have escaped into the hills. Giambo had told him and others to keep watch for snipers. But more than likely, thought Jaym, 'gades wouldn't be hanging around Ezondwei. Any survivors probably would have headed for New SUN Post-2, the place Bettina and her people had been overrun, and was now in the hands of 'gades.

"Lingana," Jaym said. "How about you sit with your family for a while? I need to talk to Giambo, okay?" She nodded and moved closer to her older sister, Segelah. They held each other and spoke softly in Chewan.

By late afternoon, Giambo, Jaym, and D'Shay took a last survey of the cavern. It was now abuzz with clouds of flies. The heat had already created a gagging stench that quickly turned them back.

"Thought I was gonna puke," said D'Shay.

"There's no way we can move back in," said Jaym.

"That is true," said Giambo. "It gonna take a year till anybody live here again. Hyenas gonna come first, then vulture birds."

"Jay-em," said Giambo. "I think we must move our people to Ezondwei village if the chief allows. Can you find a runner to go to the village for help?"

Jaym trotted down the slope to Reya who was stitching up a man's scalp wound.

"Isn't war a goddamn rush?" she said. "Makes you wonder why everybody doesn't want to slaughter other fellow humans."

Jaym kneeled in the dry grass beside her. "As least we came out in one piece."

She nodded toward Annja's body. "We lost a lot of good people on each team. And I have a hunch some of us are going to be mental when this is over and done. If this will ever be done."

"Reya, Giambo needs a runner to the village. We need their help. How about that tall archer you're friends with?"

"Name's Kwada. I'll send him over to Giambo as soon as I'm through embroidering this man's scalp."

Kwada returned from the village an hour later. He nodded to Reya and smiled, then spoke to Giambo. Jaym walked over to listen. "The chief says the New SUN people and the Ezond-wei people are now brothers and sisters. You are all welcome at the village and he is sending villagers to help your wounded and the elders. He also says the New SUN and blender people fought like true warriors." He glanced at Reya bandaging up a woman's leg. "I was beside Reya and Maykego and saw that your women are as brave as the men."

"Your name's Kwada, right?" asked Jaym as he extended his hand. "I'm Jaym, and Lingana, over there with her family, is my blending partner."

Kwada smiled and returned a firm handshake. "I am glad to finally meet you, Jay-em. Reya says many good things about you and Giambo and D'Shay."

Jaym glanced at Reya. "Are you and Reya..." *No,* he thought. *That's too rude to ask.*

Kwada looked flustered. "No, Jay-em. I think we are friends only."

Nearby, Giambo cleared his throat and glared at Jaym

"It is okay, Giambo," said Kwada. "I think Jay-em and other NorthAms gonna learn Chewan customs someday."

"Sorry, Kwada. I don't know why I—"

"Jay-em, we will learn each other's ways in time."

"Please thank your chief for his welcome to us," said Giambo. "That be very generous for us. We gonna send down wounded and elders, but many of us gonna stay to bury our dead fighters. Tell chief we be very honored to come to Ezond-wei when we finish here."

———

The sun was brutal as Jaym, D'Shay, and a dozen others headed down to the road where they ambushed the convoy. "What about the 'gade bodies?" asked Jaym.

Giambo spat to one side. "Over the cliff. Let them now be something useful. They gonna give hyenas a feast."

Jaym and D'Shay exchanged glances.

"Um, how about we lay them in that trench?" asked Jaym.

"Yeah," said D'Shay. "It's ... closer."

Giambo glanced at the trench—an abandoned roadcut. He shrugged. "Do as you want. Makes no matter."

"Come on," said Jaym to D'Shay. "Let's start with this one. Drag him by his boots." The bodies already were beginning to bloat in the heat. One-by-one, Jaym, D'Shay, and other team members hauled the 'gades to the trench. Jaym and D'Shay shoveled a little dirt over the bodies.

"Why you be wasting time doing that?" snapped Giambo.

"Come on man," said D'Shay. "They're still human beings."

"Enough. We get our own people now. True human beings."

They managed to collect their own dead and pack them out in one trip—two bodies per stretcher. Jaym and D'Shay had to rest every few minutes and guzzled from their canteens. It took an hour to get back to the meadow below the cavern, a nice spot for their cemetery. By the time they arrived, the sweat-soaked burial crew had already dug the twenty-three graves.

Giambo walked by the stretchers, looking at each man and woman's body. "Brave warriors. They die a good death."

"Bullshit," muttered Reya. "There's no such thing as a 'good' death."

Jaym and D'Shay looked at Giambo, but he didn't respond to Reya. He just kicked at a dirt clod and said in a weary voice, "Let us put them in the earth now."

Reya leaned on a shovel, her tee shirt damp with sweat and

smeared with dirt. "I think they should all face the same way. Maybe toward the village."

"Yes," said Giambo. "That be good."

"What about Amai Annja?" asked Maykego, as sweaty and dirty as Reya. "Do we give her special place?"

Reya shook her head. "Yes, Annja was special, but she was a Quaker. She'd want to be with the rest. No special treatment."

"Yes," said Giambo. "She died with her people; she should be buried with them."

After all New SUN dead were buried, everyone stood in silence in the shade at the edge of the little cemetery. Their clothes were stained with dirt, sweat, and blood.

"Should we say special words?" asked Lingana.

"What would Annja say?" asked Giambo.

"I think she'd be happy with silence," said Jaym. "Quakers like silence. So give them a few minutes of silence and us thinking about each of them."

Giambo nodded. "Yes. Be best to have quiet time. I still have much shooting and death cries in my ears. So let us make silence."

———

By the time they had finished, it was too late in the day to join the elders and others in Ezondwei, so they made camp in the meadow near the cemetery. No one wanted to try to retrieve blankets from the filth of the cavern. Besides, the grassy meadow was soft and it was a warm enough evening.

As stars came out, they built a small bonfire. Jaym knew they didn't need the fire's warmth, but they wanted to talk.

After several minutes, Reya broke the silence. "I can't believe Annja's dead," she said. "I kind of thought she was more than flesh and blood."

Jaym poked the fire with a branch. "Annja was great, but wasn't perfect. Otherwise she would have seen through Tarkin. She had such faith in human goodness. Even in that bastard."

Xian, who had been so quite all day, nodded. "But there was goodness in Daku. Who would 'spect that Daku give up his life like that?"

"And Bettina going to help save Post-2," said Reya. "She was so gutsy. She knew she was gonna die. I bet she blasted plenty of 'gades before ... " Reya choked and turned her head.

Everyone stared at the fire crackling. Finally Giambo said, "It be good to think of our friends, but is time to think 'bout tomorrow. Must get sleep. We still have much to plan, and much to do."

Jaym was certain he couldn't sleep that night, but he barely remembered lying down beside Lingana and putting his arm around her.

Hours later he jerked awake, sweat-soaked and his heart pounding from a swirl of bloody nightmares. He stared to the east and tried to absorb the calm of the predawn glow. Behind him, Lingana lay curled against his back, warm and comforting. He reached back and rubbed her silky thigh.

Jaym watched the first rays of dawn strike the treetops. The Southern Cross and other constellations faded as the eastern horizon displayed a blood-red crack of light. The campfire was now dying embers. Giambo was already up, but Jaym just wanted to lock in this moment forever. Lingana safe and warm against him, birds singing, and the amazing African dawn.

He watched Giambo poke the embers back to life and lay on a few sticks of wood. The fire took hold and the sticks crackled. "Good morning, peoples," he said in his deep voice.

Jaym shut his eyes and pretended to sleep, but Lingana gave him a poke in the back. "Do you have lazy bones, Mister Jay-em?"

Jaym smiled to hear Lingana sound more like her old self. Maybe she was forcing herself, but she was trying. He elbowed himself up, cricked his neck, and sat up. He reached behind to give Lingana a little pat on the butt. "My bones are never lazy," he said. "A little sleepy at times, but never lazy, Miss Lingana."

Giambo shook D'Shay, still snoring softly. "Uh?" he wiped his mouth and sat up. He looked to Nakhoza who was already awake, watching him. "Morning, Princess Nakhoza." She smiled, stood and stretched, then squinted toward the horizon where the sun cast a pallet of reds, oranges, and yellows,

"Take toilet break, then we make morning meal," said Giambo.

"Do we even have anything for breakfast?" asked D'Shay.

"Cornmeal and water," said Giambo.

"Oh God," moaned D'Shay.

"What you expect?" asked Nakhoza.

"Bacon and eggs would be nice." He blinked as if surprised.

"What is the matter?" asked Nakhoza.

"Just had a flashback. I used to kid about having bacon and eggs with a little girl named Chirilie. She was the cook and bottle washer for my Wananelu family. It would be fun to see her again. Always wished I could do something to get her out of that trap of being nurse to Gramma, and house slave to Chaz, Gemmit, and MonstaGirl—the angry hippo I was assigned to."

Nakhoza wrapped a green bandanna around her head. "No more monster girl anymore. Unless I turn into one." She growled, then laughed.

Giambo clapped his hands. "Alright peoples, let us prepare ourself's to—"

"Wait," said Nakhoza. She turned. "I hear something."

At first Jaym heard nothing, just a squabble of birds in a nearby tree. But then … "Oh, shit," he muttered.

"Take cover," shouted Reya.

The subsonic hum grew more intense.

"There," shouted Reya pointing at the western horizon.

The three drones buzzed low, maybe a hundred meters overhead. Jaym grabbed Lingana and pulled her behind a tree. Lingana shivered against him as he tried to shield her.

But the drones passed over.

Barely.

Within seconds came the swoosh of rockets.

From the meadow, Jaym watched flames erupt from the cavern. Then the thunder of exploding rockets rumbled across the valley. The entire hillside lit up as a second volley slammed across the rock face.

The attack lasted thirty seconds at most, but the cavern entrance was now a pile of blackened rubble—sealed forever.

34

S.O.S.

The pillar of the world is hope.

—*Kanuri proverb, Nigeria*

———————————

Late in the afternoon, the New SUN survivors—dirty, some blood-spattered—straggled into Ezondwei. Kwada, Azibo, and the chief came out to greet them.

Reya and Kwada glanced at each other across the village square, but Kwada didn't smile. He looked anxious. *But why?* she wondered. Whatever it was, it gave her a shiver of fear. Something was going on.

The Ezondwei women led Reya and the others into the common house. Long tables were set up for the midday meal and servers brought in bowels of steaming yam and meat stew. Reya began wolfing down the spicy, hot food.

D'Shay, next to her, shook his head. "Where's your table manners, Girl? What're the Ezondwei ladies gonna think about us blenders? We have to project an image of civility."

Reya wiped her chin. "Bite me. I somehow lost my civility in the last couple of days of killing 'gades and having friends slaughtered." She wiped an eye with her sleeve. "Shit! My eyes won't quit leaking."

Lingana sat next to Reya and took her hand. "You cry all

you want. I think it get your grief out better, yes? You cannot hold hurt in or it will poison your insides."

Reya squeezed Lingana's hand and nodded.

"We will help each other through," said Lingana. She frowned at D'Shay.

"What?" said D'Shay.

"You cannot help anything by being wise-ass at this time."

Jaym choked on his stew. "Wise-ass? Where did you pick that up?"

"From DuShay. Who else talks like that all the time."

Lingana patted Reya's arm. "You eat like you want, cry like you want. Yes, Mr. DuShay?"

D'Shay raised his hands in submission. "I'll be a good boy, Miss Lingana." He whispered to Jaym, "You might have your hands full with your missus. For such a little gal she walks and talks pretty tall."

Jaym grinned as they finished their stews in silence.

————————

Back outside, Reya found Nakhoza sitting cross-legged in the shade of a fig tree. "Mind if I join you, Nakhoza?"

Nakhoza smiled and patted the earth beside her. Reya settled next to her.

"You alright Reya? Your face looks very tired."

"I'll be okay." She rubbed her face. "Nakhoza, do you have any idea why those drones blasted the cavern all to hell? I could understand if they hit the convoy trucks Giambo's team went after, but the New SUN outpost?"

"Xian is working with the radios right now and trying to

catch some chatter. We think other 'gades capture the drone control center. If they did, then drones maybe no longer are controlled by GlobeTran people."

"Crap," muttered Reya. "So that's why Kwada looked so anxious."

"One good thing is that 'gades gotta be working with old intel," said Nakhoza. "They hit cave, and must not know we are here in the village. Not yet."

"Don't they have vids on the drones to see us here? Those things are high-tech."

"Yes, high-tech many years ago. Cameras then could see a mouse in middle of the savannah. Once they even had night vision and I.R. to see body heat in dense forest. But computer and camera parts wear out and there be no replacements. What is that odd expression? They now must use chewing gum and string to keep drones repaired."

Reya smiled.

Nakhoza leaned back against the tree trunk. "Use to be dozens of super-tech drones before wars, now be down to eight or ten. Their guidance only be old GPS and bad video-stream. Controllers mostly have to punch in coordinates and let drones go off and hope they blast target."

Xian trotted over, grinning. "Good that I find you, Nakhoza and Reya. I have news for both. Nakhoza, I finally get some chatter from drone station. Message broken up, but from I catch, sounds like GlobeTran drone control truly captured by 'gades. They keep trying to contact 'gade convoy we attacked. When convoy did not respond, they send in drones to take out New SUN post."

Nakhoza stood. "Did you tell Giambo yet?"

"No, I see you first. 'Sides, you know about GlobeTran and 'gade intel best of all of us. Well, 'cept me," he grinned.

"We must tell Giambo and others. Good work, Xian."

As Xian turned to leave, Reya grabbed his sleeve. "Xian, you said you have news for both of us? Was that it?"

He looked at Reya. "Oh, yes Reya. While I scan frequencies, I also pick up something from near New SUN post number two. It is not from 'gades. It is very weak distress signal. Seems some New SUN people still alive."

Reya's eyes widened. "You're sure?"

Xian nodded. "Yes … pretty sure."

Reya jumped up. "Shit. We gotta save them!"

DECISION

Two people in a burning house must not stop to argue.

—*African proverb*

———————

Jaym squatted African style with the rest of the team leaders from New SUN and Ezondwei. For at least the last half hour they'd been wrestling with the issue of the Post-2 situation. Seemed like everyone had a different approach to rescuing any New SUN survivors. He'd already given his ideas, but they were soon lost in the murk of council bickering. Finally Jaym decided to tune out until Giambo or the chief called an end to the squabbling.

Funny, he thought, how he could now squat like this for an hour. Things once impossible for him—like this African squat—were now routine. He was becoming African—well, sort of. At least his ligaments and muscles had stretched enough that he didn't make a fool of himself when he squatted with others. He smiled to himself as he remembered the first time he met Lingana and her family. He'd tried to squat like the family members as he was grilled by this future father-in-law, Mr. Zingali. Jaym had lasted for maybe two minutes before falling on his butt. Lingana's sisters had tried to smother their giggles, but Mrs. Zingali just shook her head in disgust.

This endless meeting today was in the village's community house—a single vast room with flamingo-pink walls and a tin roof above twisted pine rafters. Jaym with Giambo's teams lined one side of the room; the Ezondwei leaders on the other—maybe twenty in all. The only furniture in the room was the chief's ebony throne that kept him half a meter above everyone else squatting or kneeling. The chief sat slouched, looking bored as he puffed on his cigar.

"Okay, okay, peoples," said Giambo. "Please let us hear *all* the information Xian has before we argue more, yes?"

Thank you, Giambo! thought Jaym.

Reya stood, her face red and tight with frustration. "Do we *really* need to waste time with this meeting? We know what we need to do. Rescue the survivors of Post-2! We have no idea how many are wounded and barely holding on at Two. There's gotta be some that need immediate treatment. And if there are still 'gades at the post then we'll have to—-"

Giambo waved his arm. "Yes, yes, Reya. You tell most of us that already. Please sit. We know your friend Bettina is at Post-2, but we have to look at big picture. Now, *sit down* and let us hear from Xian so we can make decisions." He turned to Xian, a head shorter and half the weight of Giambo. "Xian, please speak all you know so everyone hears same together. Already rumors causing wrong information in village."

Giambo squatted next to Jaym and whispered, "Your friend, Reya, need better manners."

Jaym nodded. "Yeah," he whispered. "She's worked up because of Bettina." Bettina might not even be alive, he thought, but she'd saved Reya's life after being shot by 'gades.

Reya was going after Bettina no matter what this council decided.

Xian stood and cleared his throat. "The information I get comes from 'gade chatter, sometimes in much slang and code words, so is hard to know exactly what is really happening."

Reya shot her arm in the air. "Can you please start with the information you have on Post-2? Those are our brothers and sisters out there."

Xian looked to Giambo who sighed, then nodded a yes. Xian continued. "Okay, like I tell you, signal from Post-2 is weak. I think New SUN survivors rig up solar transmitter. They send only one simple distress signal with Morse Code—it is just 'S.O.S.' They send no details, so there no information about number of survivors or wounded."

Jaym raised his arm. "Could that be a 'gade trap? Sending a distress signal might be a way for 'gades to lure us into a rescue, then ambush us."

Xian shrugged. "Don't know for certain, but I think signal is from our people. 'Gades would use stronger signal to be sure we hear, and I think they would give details to make us act more urgent. I lucky to find our people's weak signal cause it on very low frequency. Be very easy to miss."

"That be enough information about Post-2 message," said Giambo. "Now we need to hear about other chatter from 'gades—then we decide how we must act. Tell us other informations, Xian."

"Yes. The 'gade messages mostly coming from someplace near Wananelu city. I think from Alliance drone control."

"You mean GlobeTran," said Jaym.

"Yes, of course. Use to be run by Alliance before outsourced to GlobeTran, but message evidence now show 'gades have control center. They keep trying to send message to 'gade convoy that attack us. No answer, so I think is why they send in drones and missiles to blast our New SUN outpost."

"'Gades still sending messages?" asked Giambo.

Xian nodded. "They now asking 'gades at Post-2 if they know anything. But Post-2 'gades say they don't know anything about what is happening over here. They probably think only few of our people escape from drone attack, so we not so important to them."

Reya impatiently waved her arm for attention. Jaym shook his head, hoping she'd get the message to cool down. She wasn't doing her cause any good by mouthing off.

Giambo glared. "*What now, Reya?*" he snapped.

"Now that we have Xian's latest information, can I *finally* suggest some actual strategy?"

"Yes, but do not talk long. Others be waiting with ideas too."

Reya stood and looked at the faces around her. "We *have* to rescue our New SUN people first. We use any working 'gade vehicles from their convoy and drive at night to Post-2. Some of their convoy vehicles must have some shoulder-launching missiles, and probably mortars. We can blast out the 'gades holding Post-2, then rescue our people without interference. If Post-2 survivors are sending the signal, they're probably holed up near the base. If the brave warriors of Ezondwei join us, we'll have a strong enough force to finish those bastards once and for all."

Good job, Reya, thought Jaym. You kept your cool and buttered up the villagers.

"I think it be my turn to speak," boomed the chief from his throne. He tapped cigar ashes on the floor. "Tell me why my people must be part of this fight. I think this be between you New SUN peoples and 'gades, yes?"

Nakhoza stood. "Chief, I am a former SUN scout and know something about how 'gades think. Reya is correct that we should rescue our people, but we must also take control of the drone command center. If they can send drones to wherever they want, do you think your village is going to be safe?"

"Why would they attack Ezondwei? They be after New SUN peoples."

"Because your village is close to Post-1. They sent an attack convoy and many soldiers. When that failed, they blasted our post with drone missiles. If they even suspect New SUN has survived in Ezondwei, they'd blast your village to bits."

The chief puffed on the stub of his cigar and nodded. "Yes, I know. I just want her to tell it for my people to hear." He grinned. "Of course we will fight with your peoples. When you decide on final plan, we will be ready." He blew a smoke ring. "I am very sick of 'gades. It is time we squash them like termite bugs."

———

Outside the meetinghouse, Reya pulled Giambo aside. He crossed his arms and frowned as she waved her arms, nearly shouting. "We can't waste another minute talking, talking, talking!"

Jaym motioned to D'Shay and they walked over to Reya.

The chief's son, Azibo, noticed the commotion and joined them.

"Hey, Reya," said Jaym. "Look, we're on your side and wanna get Bettina and the others too. But we could get them *and* us slaughtered if we don't think this through."

"I've thought it through, damn it! We should be on the move. We know some of our people are still alive, but if we wait much—"

"It's not that simple!" said Jaym. "We still have the drones to worry about. When the 'gades at Post-2 discover that we've survived, they'll radio the drone center. Then we and Ezondwei will be toast."

Reya's face darkened. "Then we're damned if we do—and Bettina and the others are damned if we don't."

They were silent for a moment.

Jaym noticed that Xian was near them, quietly tracing a Chinese character in the dirt with a twig. "Xian, what you doing?"

"This is the Chinese character for 'hope.'" He looked up and grinned. "I have been thinking that maybe we not so damned if we do. May I tell my idea?"

36

TREASURE HUNT

Unmanned Combat Air Vehicle (UCAV), or "combat drone," is a class of unmanned aerial vehicle (UAV) designed to deliver missiles with a great degree of autonomy. The elimination of the need for an onboard human crew and onboard controls allows for a decrease in weight creating greater payloads, range, and maneuverability. Combat drones of the QH-37 series were successfully used during the Pan-African Wars and the Central Asian Conflict. The primary weapons carried by the QH-35 were Viper-XE missiles. As of this writing, only a few UCAVs are said to be operational and are in the control of The Global Alliance.

—*Global Alliance Factsheet-62//ucav.flitnet*

They formed two teams: a drone salvage team, and a Post-2 rescue team. The team to rescue the people at Post-2 would not proceed until the salvage team returned from its mission.

"Let us get move on, people!" shouted Xian.

D'Shay grinned. Xian was so pumped up to finally be in charge of something. *Little Big Man,* he thought. D'Shay glanced at the rest of the team—Giambo, Jaym, and Lingana.

"How long did it take you and women to get to savannah battle place?" Xian asked Lingana.

"Maybe five hours. We stayed the night to rest up for the journey back because we had to pack out the heavy guns and ammunition we found."

"Damn," said D'Shay. "We've gotta be out and back in the same day. Reya's rescue team can't leave till we return. If the Post-2 survivors don't have water, a lot of them might not make it if we take two entire days—especially if they have wounded."

Xian nodded. "We not gonna be carrying back so much as women did. We just want the one thing." He turned to Lingana. "You sure you can find same battle place again?"

"Yes. I remember the trail. The battle site is easy to find."

Xian eagerly rubbed his hands together. "You guys got tools you need?"

Giambo held up a heavy pry bar. "Village blacksmith say it is best steel in all Chewena. It be all I need."

Jaym leaned on a pick. "Giambo taught me how to handle a pick pretty well. It'll do the job."

"And as your mule," said D'Shay, "I'm packing ten liters of water and some luscious insect jerky. Oh, and a .45 on my hip."

"Lingana," asked Xian, "You ready?"

She thumbed the strap of the rifle slung over her shoulder. "Yes, I have five clips of 9mm hollow points." She grinned. "Any hyenas or 'gades better stay away."

Xian held up his canvas toolkit, "And this all I need." He looked at the sun just rising to the east. "So, five hours out, two hours getting the components, five hours return. Maybe one hour for resting times. Makes thirteen hours. Should be back before sunset." He bowed and gave a sweep of his arm. "Miss Lingana, please show the way."

———————

They approached the savannah battle site around noon. D'Shay pulled the bill of his cap lower. The sun blazed and the horizon wavered with heat. "Geez," he whispered as they walked toward the ruins of battle tanks, burnt helicopter gunships, and charred troop vehicles. He avoided looking at the bones and the charcoaled corpses forever trapped in their rigs. "They really went at it. Who was fighting who in the Pan-Af War?"

Lingana shrugged. "Lot of them were mercenaries from many countries. Not sure anybody knows who won. Maybe nobody. Mostly they just kill each other and anybody in the way."

"Lingana?" asked Xian. "Is that the one over there?" He pointed towards the ruins of a drone. It looked like it had hit nose first, but hadn't burned. Only the shattered tail section was recognizable.

"No," said Lingana. "That one is too destroyed." She scanned the area, squinting at the black shapes surrounding them. She pointed. "I think the one we are looking for is beyond those burned trucks. It was by itself, maybe a hundred meters out in the savannah."

D'Shay and the others walked carefully through the field of debris around the trucks. In the grassy scrub of the savannah, D'Shay spotted the forward half of the drone. "Hey," he shouted. "Over here."

Xian came running. The wings had been sheared off and it

was crumpled, but the nose jutted intact from the brush. "Yes!" shouted Xian, hopping like a child. "Is exactly what we need." He hugged Lingana.

"Let us go and do this now!" said Xian. He started toward the drone.

D'Shay grabbed Xian by the sleeve. "Come on boss, we need a lunch break before we tackle that thing. I know you're excited and all, but it's gonna be a lot of work."

"But we must—"

"Lunch!" bellowed Giambo. He turned and wandered toward the shade of a listing battle tank. Xian reluctantly followed the others.

———————

The drone panels were still riveted tight. Even the crash landing had not split any seams.

"Guidance system gonna be about here I think," said Xian, tapping one of the panels behind the nose. "Jaym, I think you start with the pickax. Go at bottom of panel crack, but not deep. Don't want to injure electronics. Panels probably titanium alloy. Lightweight but very tough."

Jaym climbed onto the drone and D'Shay handed him up his pick. He clunked the panel with the butt of the pick handle.

"What're you doing?" asked D'Shay.

"This is an art and a science," grinned Jaym. "From that thump I can calculate the amount of muscle I need for the swing. "Here goes," he said. The pick arced to bite into the sheeting. "Perfect," he said. "I've opened a seam."

Xian held his hands to his cheeks, his eyes wide. "Yes.

Good. I think is time for Giambo's pry bar. Work together. Pick and pry up the seam. Keep shallow and we gonna find treasure."

Thirty minutes later, Jaym and Giambo muscled the panel back like a can lid. "It be all yours," grinned Giambo. He and Jaym jumped off and dropped their tools. Jaym's tee shirt and cap were sweat-soaked. D'Shay handed them liters of water.

Xian climbed onto the drone and kneeled to peer inside. He looked up at Jaym and Giambo, his face beaming. "D'Shay! You bring champagne?"

"Absolutely. Chilled Chateau D'Shay, '57—a most excellent year."

"Pop cork, please, 'cause we strike gold!"

TOO SOON

The worst is death, and death will have its day.

—*William Shakespeare, from Richard II*

After three hours of trudging across the savannah, Jaym and Lingana finally walked back into the shade of the dry-river canyon. "I don't know how you stand the heat," he said to Lingana. "Look at you, you've hardly broken a sweat and I'm basted and roasted."

She smiled and squeezed his hand. "Two, maybe three years and I believe you will think nothing of it."

He took off his tee shirt and used it to wipe savannah dust and sweat from his face.

"Umm," said Lingana. She ran her hand against his chest. "You should take your shirt off more often. You getting muscles like Giambo."

"I will if you will," he grinned. "I think fair is fair, right?"

She blushed, but flashed a smile.

"I keep my shirt on in the sun because otherwise my skin would peel off like a cooked yam. Gotta thank my mom for that. She's half Swedish."

"Swedish? So maybe our baby girls are gonna have blonde pigtails?"

They laughed together. He hadn't heard Lingana laugh that often, but when she did, hers was a soft laughter, like the bubbling of a mountain stream.

As they made their way up the canyon, Jaym dragged the tip of his pick, leaving a thin furrow. It was something a kid might do in the sand, but the stars were just popping out and Lingana's warm hand was in his. He sort of felt like a kid. It was time to enjoy the moment. They'd all earned it.

Lingana shifted the rifle over her shoulder. "I think everything is gonna be very fine now that Xian has his little drone box."

"Hope so," said Jaym. *Yeah,* he thought. So much had been riding on the hope that Xian could find one of those boxes and jury-rig the electronics inside. If all went well, Reya and her team could—

Giambo, a few meters ahead, stopped and crouched. He waved his arm to the ground.

Jaym crouched and pulled Lingana low with him.

Giambo pointed to the cliff on the left of the canyon. There was still a twilight glow on the rock, but Jaym couldn't see anything on the jagged face of the cliff. He listened. Only a couple of crickets up the canyon. But then he heard the clicking of a rock tumbling down the cliff.

"I think maybe it is an animal," whispered Lingana. "Back in Nswibe, our goats would sometimes get loose and climb the cliffs behind—"

The silence was shattered by a burst of automatic fire. Rocks and dust pinged around Jaym and Lingana, ripping through brush.

"Shit!" hissed Jaym. He dropped his pick and grabbed Lingana's hand. They scurried low towards a large boulder.

Lingana stumbled, nearly pulling Jaym down.

When he turned to lift her up, he screamed. *"Noooo! Oh God no, please no."* He pressed fingers against her neck where her blood spurted to the rhythm of her heartbeat. "Please, please." he whispered. He pressed both hands against the wound.

Lingana's voice was weak and hoarse, her face a mask of sorrow. "I am sorry, Jay-em. This is too soon. We supposed … to make babies and live long life. It is not fair. I think … " But her whispered voice faded out.

The grip of her hand in his was weaker now. Her warm blood seeped steadily through his fingers. For the first time in his life he began to sob. He pressed his cheek against hers and shook as he wept. He felt her fingers touch his face, and then they slid away. Her arm dropped limp to the earth.

Jaym leaped to his feet and screamed like a wild animal. The sky turned blood red. He grabbed her rifle and howled as he started toward the cliff.

Then a white-lighting flash of pain exploded in his skull. He dropped into a well of darkness.

GOODBYE

I hold it true, whate'er befall;
I feel it, when I sorrow most;
'Tis better to have loved and lost
Than never to have loved at all.

—*Alfred Lord Tennyson*

Reya had been sitting at the trailhead for the last two hours. The waiting was so hard. She and her team were ready to head to Post-2 for the rescue, but where was Giambo's team? They should have been back an hour ago.

She heard the heavy crunch of footsteps. "Giambo?" No answer, but the footsteps were closer. It had to be Giambo. Maybe they were too exhausted to respond. She picked up her lantern and jogged down to meet them. "Hey, it's about time. I thought you'd—"

Her light caught the flash of Giambo's eyes. He carried Lingana as a father would a sleeping child.

"Oh, God! Giambo. Is Lingana hurt?"

He walked on towards the village, passing Reya without a word, without a look.

D'Shay and Xian trailed behind, helping Jaym stagger

between them. Jaym looked drained of life and emotion. He glanced at Reya, then back to the trail.

Reya was now shaking as she walked beside D'Shay. "What happened?"

D'Shay sighed. "Shit happened. Three 'gades ambushed us. Hit Lingana in the neck. She bled out fast. Didn't have a chance."

Reya's world tilted and spun. She thought she might throw up. It was that same panic and shock when her friend Mai-Lin was shot and Reya tried to carry her to safety. Reya grabbed D'Shay's arm for support. She took slow breaths. "What . . . happened to Jaym?"

"He went ballistic when they killed Lingana. Started to go after them like a crazy man, but Giambo knocked him out with a fist to the back of his skull. Giambo climbed the cliff and took the 'gades out with his machete. He took a bullet in the calf, but he plugged the wound with a piece of tee shirt. He picked up Lingana and carried her the entire way."

Reya heard the screams and wailing from Mrs. Zingali and Lingana's sisters.

"I need to see her again," droned Jaym. "Gotta talk to her family."

"Not now, buddy," said D'Shay. "The family needs time alone."

"Alone."

They sat him on the steps of the common house. He stared beyond Reya, his eyes red, his face drained of life. Reya touched his shoulder and felt his shaking. "He's going into shock," she said. "Get him to lay down and cover him with blankets." *Poor Jaym,* she thought. *His world shattered by a single piece of lead.*

She followed them inside, wiping tears as she headed for the community medicine chest. She grabbed a vial of powder and shook some into a cup of water.

The guys had already laid Jaym on a cot and covered him with blankets. "You're dehydrated," said Reya. "Drink this down." She held his head up as he sipped the liquid. It gave her a chill to see his eyes, dull as a dead man's. He lay back down and curled away from her in a fetal position. The sleeping powder had him snoring softly in minutes.

She walked over to D'Shay and Xian. "Jesus, where did those 'gades come from? I thought they were all wiped out."

"We did too," said Xian. "But Giambo warned us that some might have escaped from the convoy fight. We could not question them 'cause of Giambo machete work."

Reya looked at the box Xian cradled in his palms. "So at least you got it."

"Yeah," said D'Shay. "The goddamn thing only cost Lingana's life. I'm sure Jaym's gonna understand that, right?"

"Don't start a blame game, D'Shay," snapped Reya. "Lingana, or any of us, could have been killed a dozen times over in the fighting."

"She right, you know," said Xian. "She gave her life. But with box she help find, we gonna save many, many lifes."

D'Shay nodded. "Yeah, sorry. It's just that . . . " He looked away. "I'm gonna find Nakhoza."

The next morning they buried Lingana in the village cemetery. The Ezondwei women had wrapped her in colorful *chitenges*.

Giambo had carried her to the gravesite, his face stony. Lingana's mother knelt over the open grave, rocking back and forth and wailing. Lingana's two sisters stood quietly, tears streaking their cheeks.

Reya tried to read Jaym's face. He stared into the grave, swaying slightly like a drunk. His face was pale and blank—like his soul and spirit had deserted him.

The ceremony was brief because the time to rescue those at Post-2 was fleeting. Reya was surprised to see Kwada with a battered bible in his hands. He stood at the graveside and read the passage about "ashes to ashes, and dust to dust." Was he a part-time preacher too?

Then the village shaman chanted in Chewan and waved his hands over the opening, sprinkling a handful of earth. Lingana's sisters dropped flowers and handmade necklaces into the grave. Finally Jaym and Giambo shoveled dirt into the grave. As the *chitenges* disappeared under the shovels of dirt, Jaym started moaning, his face now twisted. He shoveled furiously, openly crying now in deep, gulping sobs.

After the villagers and New SUN people drifted away, Jaym stayed by the grave, kneeling with his arms across the mound of earth. Reya touched his shoulder. "Jaym? Come on. Let's go off and talk alone."

Jaym sat up, cocked his head, and blinked at her as if seeing her for the first time.

She took his hand and pulled him up. She lead him out to a meadow and they sat in the grass. He looked at the Blue Mountains and shook his head. His voice was flat. "When I first saw them I thought they were beautiful. Now I hate them. I hate Africa."

"Jaym, you've had the worse loss of your life. It's gonna take time. D'Shay and I will be with you through thick and thin."

"Gonna take time," said Jaym bitterly. "Funny. When Lingana and I first met in Nswibe, it was a disaster. We both just wanted out of the Blending arrangement. She thought I was a clueless mzungu—which I was—and I was still locked in culture shock having to marry an African girl with a bitchy mother." He shook his head. "Funny how … love can grow from that kind of beginning. Then, one day, poof; it's all gone." He stood and looked toward the savannah. "Once we take out Post-2, I'm going back."

"But you're not in the mission, Jaym. You need time—"

"I'm going with you. I need to kill some 'gades."

Reya had never seen Jaym's expression so cold; never seen this new cruel look in his eyes.

"Okay, you can go with us as long as you don't go suicidal on us. We need you, Jaym. And what're you talking about when you say you're 'going back?'"

"Back to the Corridor. I can't be here anymore. Lingana wouldn't be dead if it weren't for me. I should have protected her better. I *have* been a clueless mzungu and I don't belong here anymore."

"Get that guilt shit out of your head," said Reya. "Lingana's death was a terrible twist of fate. Nothing you could have done would have made a difference." She paused. "Yeah, you're right. You should be in on the Post-2 raid." She shook his shoulder and forced a smiled. "Come on, we're gonna be going soon. I'll help you get your gear together."

Nakhoza and Azibo rode up front, while D'Shay sat in the back of the truck with Jaym, Reya, Maykego, Xian, and Kwada. Reya wanted this to be a silent hit-and-run operation, so the best archers—Maykego, Azibo, Kwada, and Reya—all carried bows and quivers full of new arrows. He noticed that Kwada also packed a .45 on his hip. Smart move, thought D'Shay. A bow was great for some situations, but if you came face to face with a gade, you only had a useless stick in your hand.

Nakhoza drove the truck—lorry, as she called it—and had offered Reya a seat as shotgun. But when she started to climb in the passenger's side, she said it was like something had hit her in the gut. She couldn't breathe. "I can't sit up front," she said. "Oh God. This truck's too much like the one that picked me up in Wananelu for my Blender assignment. 'Gades ambushed the truck and I ended up as a 'gade slave. I was sitting up front when they shot the driver."

D'Shay looked at the blank faces of Reya and Jaym. She'd been through hell, now Jaym was trapped in his own hell. Did bad things come in threes? D'Shay hoped not, because he'd be number three. If something terrible had to happen, let it be to him, not Nakhoza. She was his miracle. If she hadn't picked him up in her SUN rig, he'd probably be rotting in a ditch outside Wananelu. When he first saw her in that SUN car, he was—for the first time in his life—tongue-tied. Nakhoza was gorgeous, gutsy, and for some reason she'd stuck with him. At first he thought her attraction to him was sort of a community-service thing. You know, try to mold the brown mzungu into a true believer. But even after she converted him to New SUN, she still was with him. Damn, if something ever happened to her... He glanced at Jaym, staring at the floorboards with no expression. D'Shay had a fleeting moment of the emptiness Jaym must be feeling. If Nakhoza went down, it'd be like someone opening his chest and sucking out all feelings, all hope.

It was hot as usual, but the canvas tarp at least cut the blazing sunlight. D'Shay looked out the back at passing foothills that looked all the same. He glanced at Kwada. "Any idea how much farther? I thought Post-2 was closer."

Kwada smiled. "I think it seem long 'cause of bad road. We not be driving on smooth tarmac. Besides, Nakhoza have to drive 'round mine fields from old wars. Nobody clean them up, so sometimes have go across savannah."

"No wonder I'm getting carsick," said D'Shay. "Worse than sailing the ocean blue in that Alliance transport ship. Remember how sick you were, Jaymo?"

Jaym only glanced up for a moment, then back to staring at the floorboards.

"A question, Kwada" said D'Shay. "You and Azibo aren't planning to drive us right up to the front door of Post-2—are you? I haven't heard the details of this mission."

"Oh, yes," grinned Kwada. "We go in polite and knock on door."

Maykego, who had been silent till now, tried to suppress a giggle.

D'Shay glared. "Come on, man. I'm kinda edgy about this operation."

Kwada nodded. "Yes, I know. That's why I make little joke. Here is the real thing. Azibo say we gonna pull off at a place about a half-hour hike to the post. Can't drive closer 'cause 'gades will see our dust. We hide the lorry and take old hunting trail that goes close behind Post-2. My father used to take me hunting out here for steenboks. I still remember the trail pretty well."

The truck lurched over a ditch, nearly throwing Reya and D'Shay off the bench. "Damn!" said D'Shay. He knocked on the cab window and shouted to Nakhoza. "Hey, driver! How 'bout trying to miss some of those potholes."

Fighting the steering wheel, Nakhoza shouted back. "That is not so funny, Mister DuShay. You are lucky this lorry still in one piece."

Within minutes, the truck slowed and stopped near a foothill ravine. Reya and the others hopped out and gathered around Azibo. "Good," said Azibo. He pointed up the ravine. "We gonna go up this cut in hillside and find trail, yes Kwada?"

Kwada nodded. "We come to the hunting trail in about two klicks. There is also a fork in three klicks. The one to the left leads to the outpost."

"But we're not going to the outpost," said Reya. "We're just looking for our New SUN survivors. They shouldn't be hiding too far off the trail—we hope."

Xian was busy with a small metal-and-plastic box that sprouted a mini-dish antenna. One side was open, exposing an array of colored wires. "I'm gonna triangulate S.O.S. signal from survivors," he said. "Is not perfect, but should work pretty good." In his other hand he waved a folded map. "We found this map of hills in one of the 'gade lorries." He lay the receiver on the ground and threw a switch. The solar-powered dish rotated slowly. The receiver crackled static, until suddenly there was a faint series of beeps.

"Is that them?" Reya asked excitedly.

"Yes. And I can get direction." He unfolded the map,

spread it out, and pointed to a topographical "V" amid the lines. "We here at the bottom of this canyon." He held a compass to orient the map with the terrain ahead. "Their signal coming from 68-degrees to southwest." He placed the compass on the map. "Reya, one arrow, please."

Reya drew one from the quiver on her hip.

Using the arrow as a straightedge, Xian traced a line across the map. He tapped the line. "People gonna be somewhere along this line."

Azibo nodded. "When we be up on trail we draw another line, yes?"

"Yes," said Xian. "Where lines cross should be our people."

Azibo pointed up the ravine. "We gonna go single file up canyon. Might be 'gade guards or scouts, so we gotta be silent. Archers go first. Then rest of us with guns follow. Only shoot guns if we be forced to. Don't wanna bring more 'gades. 'Member, we be here to rescue our peoples. Not want to get into big battle today. You hearing me, Jay-em?"

Jaym nodded. "Yeah, no battle today."

D'Shay was chilled by Jaym's tone of voice. Flat and without a trace of emotion.

LUGONO

If you know the enemy and know yourself,
you need not fear the results of a hundred battles.

—*Sun Tzu*

A klick up the trail, Kwada held up his arm and crouched. "Do you smell it?" he whispered.

Reya and Maykego knelt beside him. "Yes," said Maykego. "Cigarette smoke." She nodded to the left. "It comes from up there." She motioned to Azibo carrying his assault rifle. "No shooting unless necessary. We do not want to bring more 'gades. I think we archers can do this job, but stay with me, just in case."

Azibo signaled for the others to take cover. Jaym hesitated. D'Shay grabbed his sleeve and pulled him off the trail. "You'll get your chance," he whispered. They scurried into the shadow of the ravine. D'Shay clicked off his safety and waited.

Maykego, Kwada, and Reya headed up a side ravine, staying in the carbon black of its shadow, moving stealthily as cats.

"Shouldn't we be closer for backup?" asked D'Shay.

Azibo shook his head. "They know what they doing. One of them gonna return for us if they see many 'gades. But I think there will be only one or two this far out."

A man shouted in Chewan.

"Was that Kwada?" whispered D'Shay.

Then came a yelp like a kicked dog.

"Come," shouted Azibo. Jaym, D'Shay, Nakhoza, and Xian followed, jogging toward the cry, their weapons raised.

A silhouette appeared on the nearest ridge. Kwada. "Two guards," he shouted. "One dead, but we take one as prisoner." Reya and Maykego walked back down the small ravine with the 'gade—a Chewan, his eyes wild with fear. Maykego's bow was slung over her shoulder, but her sidearm was drawn and pressed against the man's back.

Jaym started to raise his rifle, but D'Shay grabbed the muzzle and forced it down. "Easy, Jaym. Easy."

"Kwada ordered them to surrender," said Maykego, "but the white 'gade went for his weapon. He is dead. This one was not armed and threw up his hands."

"You speak English?" asked D'Shay.

The man nodded, his eyes down. He was shaking.

Azibo grabbed the man by his throat and shouted, "Look at me! What kind of Chewan man are you that work with 'gades? Why do you turn 'gainst your own peoples?"

"I...do not be a 'gade," the man choked out. "I must work for them because they have my sister and her family. Mzungu 'gade men make sister a prisoner slave. They tell me if I don't work for them, they gonna cut off sister's nose before they kill me."

Azibo took his hand from the man's throat. "You gonna cooperate with us?"

The man rubbed his throat. "You gonna help my sister?"

"Maybe we can free you sister. Now, how many 'gades be at post?"

"'Bout forty, maybe fifty."

"How many New SUN people did the 'gades kill?" asked Azibo.

"Me and the three other Chewan men bury nine of your people. 'Gades call them blenders. We also bury many 'gade soldiers. Blender people put up strong battle. We put maybe thirty 'gades in earth."

Azibo nodded. "Why are you out here with a white 'gade?"

"He be posted on guard duty. Is my job to bring him water and meal. They know I gonna go back to post because they got my sister."

Azibo turned to the others. "You think he's telling truth?"

Nakhoza stepped closer and smiled at the Chewan man. "You are not in danger from us. You are not our prisoner. What is your name?"

"Is Lugono."

"Lugono, I am Nakhoza, a Chewan like you, and I have a nephew with name of Lugono. Now, I have important question for you. We think the New SUN people—the blenders—who escaped the 'gade battle are hiding somewhere close to here. Do you know any places they—"

"Oh yes, Amai Nakhoza." He pointed down the trail behind him. "They be back there hiding in small canyon. I bring them little bit of food only half-hour ago."

———

Twenty minutes up the trail, Lugono pointed at a scrubby oasis at the base of a cliff. D'Shay spotted a trickle of spring water that oozed from a crack in the granite, just enough to sustain a few struggling thorn trees and a thick tangle of brush.

"Here?" asked Reya, her expression was a mixture of anxiety and doubt.

"Yes, I show you, amai," said Lugono. "Come," he said. "There be open place here."

He edged between the rock and brush and vanished.

"Can I go next?" asked Reya, her voice tight, eyes pleading with Azibo. "I need to know if Bettina…"

Azibo nodded.

"Thanks."

"I'm gonna back you up," said D'Shay. Reya nodded, then quickly pushed through the brush then through the gap in the cliffside. D'Shay stepped in behind her. Lugono was waiting on the other side. D'Shay scanned the box canyon, maybe a hundred meters wide, and a few hundred deep. Much of the canyon floor was covered with weathered boulders washed down the hillside during flash floods in the monsoon season. In this harsh light, the rocks were stark white, and the shadows ink-black.

"I can't see anybody," said Reya. "You sure this is the place?"

Lugono cupped his mouth with his hands and cried a *skreeee*—the cry of a soaring fish-eagle. Within seconds the cry was returned from the far end of the canyon.

Reya began to sprint toward the sound. D'Shay ran with her. "Don't shoot!" she shouted. "We're friendlies." As they stumbled through the field of boulders and brush, D'Shay heard her say, "Please God, let Bettina be alive."

Half a dozen figures materialized from a cliff shadow.

"Reya?" came a rasping voice.

Reya ran into the group and grabbed Bettina in a hug that almost knocked her over. "Thank you, God!" said Reya, laughing and crying at the same time.

"Yes," said Bettina. Her face was sunburned, her lips cracked and bleeding. "Please, do you have water?"

Reya flipped the lid of her canteen. Bettina's hands shook as she drank. D'Shay and the others shared their canteens with survivors. "Not too much so fast," said Reya, taking the canteen from Bettina's hands. "You'll get cramps and puke it all up."

Bettina wiped her mouth and smiled. "Lugono brings us water every day, but it only a little because he does not want the 'gades to be suspicious of carrying so much. He is a brave man to take such a risk. He saved our lives."

"Thank God we found him. He was with a 'gade we had to kill." Reya's eyes watered up again. "It's so good to see you alive, *chica*. We'll get you and the others back to our village and—"

Bettina shook her head. "No, Reya. Not without Lugono's family and the other Chewena captives. You know what will happen to them when the 'gades discover the dead guard and Lugono has gone missing."

Reya said over her shoulder, "Azibo! Time for planning."

"We cannot stay longer," said Azibo. "When the 'gade people discover Lugono has not returned on schedule, they will send scouts looking for him."

"Let 'em come," said Jaym. "We can ambush them."

"No!" said Lugono. "They will kill my sister and the other Chewans."

"He's right," said D'Shay. "He has to go back, alone. And there's no way we could take down a cave full of 'gades."

Xian turned to Bettina. "I have question. How you get away from 'gades?"

"We fought the 'gades off as long as we could," said Bettina. "When we knew we were going to be overrun, we escaped through the back of the cave. An abandoned mine tunnel cuts clear through the hillside. The attack was at night, so it was easy enough to slip away into the darkness. And since we had scouted this area previously, we knew about this hidden canyon."

"Maybe we get Lugono's people out the same way," said Xian. "Lugono, how many guards they have in nighttime?"

"One in front opening and one in back. They be on watch all night."

Maykego spoke up. "Lugono, think you can get you peoples out the back exit at midnight?"

"But there's the guard at the rear exit," said D'Shay.

Maykego smiled. "If Azibo and others agree, I think archers will give guard quick surprise at midnight." She looked at Reya, Azibo, and Kwada. "I think we do some night hunting, yes?"

"I must go back now," said Lugono. "But what do I tell 'gades when guard does not return in evening?"

"Tell them a black mamba strike him in the leg," said Azibo. "You tried to cut out the poison, but guard died in a few minutes." He glanced at his watch. It will be dark in 'bout two hours. They will not come for his body until morning. Okay, Lugono. You understand?"

"Yes, and I will tell them I am late because I try to help the guard with snakebite."

Azibo nodded. "And remember, exactly at midnight you take your people out the back way." Azibo took off his wrist-watch and handed it to Lugono. "You know the numbers for midnight?"

Lugono nodded.

"Then run like gazelle. We see you at midnight."

As Lugono jogged away, Jaym said, "Don't leave me out of this."

"Your gun make too much noise," said Xian. "Maykego and archers can do the job quick and quiet. Don't want angry hive of 'gades after us."

"Okay then," said Jaym. When it's past midnight the cap-tives will be out. Then the 'gades are fair game. I'll give you all thirty minutes to get down the trail and out of here before I go in. And don't try to stop me from this."

"Damn it, Jaym," said Reya. "Getting yourself slaugh-tered isn't—"

Xian waved his arms. "You wanna kill 'gades, Jaym? Okay, I have a way you can kill many 'gades. But you must wait till tomorrow."

"Bullshit."

Xian laid his hand on Jaym's shoulder. "Is no bullshit. I promise."

PAYBACK

ju·ry-rig
Transitive verb: **ju·ry-rigged, ju·ry-rig·ging, ju·ry-rigs:**
To rig or assemble for temporary emergency use;
improvise. Jury rigging refers to makeshift repairs
or temporary contrivances, using only the tools and
materials on hand.

—*Englishdefs.eur.satfeed*

They took Bettina and the other New SUN survivors
back to Ezondwei where med-techs and hot meals were
waiting.

Then, at 1030 hours the archers climbed into the truck
and headed back toward Post-2. The moon was so bright
Nakhoza didn't need headlights.

As they drove, Reya watched the passing landscape of foothills and savannah. It looked like the surface of another planet
in this moonlight. No color, just stark black and white boulders, cliffs, and ravines.

She glanced at the silhouettes of Maykego, Azibo, and
Kwada. Kwada was staring at her. "What are you thinking
about, Reya," he asked softly.

She smiled. "I was just thinking, here I am joining with

three Chewan archers toward a dangerous mission. Hard to believe that six months ago I was back in the Corridor 'gee camp where I was no one, and I thought I had no future. Now I'm an archer about to save some lives. After we do, then all of us are going on to clean up Chewena, then save the rest of Africa, right?" Her laugh was anxious.

Kwada didn't laugh. He moved to sit beside her. "Reya, I think we can do more for Africa than you can imagine. We must, yes?"

He sounded so positive, so certain. She didn't want to disappoint him, so she said, "Yes, Kwada. Of course."

In the dark of the truck, he brushed a lock of hair from her face. His fingers lingered on her cheek.

Reya shivered. *Such a gentle touch.*

Nakhoza shouted from up front, "We're here … I think. But everything looks so different in this moonlight. Kwada, is this the place?"

"Yes. The ravine to the trail is maybe a hundred meters from here."

Within minutes they were heading up the ravine with their bows and quivers; Nakhoza with her assault rifle—just in case things went wrong.

After thirty minutes of hiking, Kwada held up his arm. "The Post's back entrance gonna be just around these boulders. Reya, Maykego, go 'round to right. I go left, Nakhoza, you stay with me. Okay?"

Reya and the others nodded. She hadn't been nervous till now. Taking out the guard should be easy, but it would have to be a quick, clean kill. A scream or a cry would bring on a pack of 'gades and they'd be finished.

Maykego motioned Reya to follow. Maykego moved soft as a night cat. Her dark skin let her vanish when she passed into the shadows toward the cliffs and rockfalls. Maykego reached back and touched Reya's arm.

"What?" whispered Reya.

Maykego pointed. There, the glow of a cigarette. But Reya couldn't make out the guard in the dark. Damn, he had to be out in the moonlight so they'd have a target. You just couldn't shoot at a cigarette glow and hope for a quick kill.

"Remember signal," whispered Maykego. Reya nodded.

The *tweee* of a nighthawk cut through the silence. *Kwada.* The cigarette glow fell to the ground, and a figure stepped into the moonlight, his AK at the ready. He glanced into the shadows as he paced in an arc just a few meters from the opening.

"Ready your arrow and draw to shoot on signal," whispered Maykego. Together they drew their bowstrings to their cheeks.

Reya was sweating and her arm shook a little. *Give the signal, Kwada!* Reya would take the heart shot. Kwada the man's skull, and Azibo the throat.

Tweee, tweee.

Three arrows hissed. The 'gade crumpled to the earth. When he hit the ground, his arms twitched in his death throe.

Shit, thought Reya. That jerking hand is gonna pull the trigger.

But Maykego had already drawn another arrow and fired. It pinned the man's hand to the ground. The hand still twitched, but could not reach the trigger.

A group of figures emerged from the cave and huddled beyond the guard.

Tweee, twee, twee.

Lugono and the other captives hurried from the opening. Reya and Maykego scrambled down to join them. Some were hobbling elders, a few older children, and a half-dozen men and women. Reya and Maykego helped a limping woman down the trail, while Kwada carried one of the elders. Nakhoza trailed behind, constantly glancing back and ready to hold off any 'gades with her AK.

———

By the time they returned to Ezondwei, the predawn glow shone in the eastern sky. The freed captives hugged each other and their rescuers. Jaym stood aside, watching the jubilation of the freed Chewans. Would he ever have that joyous feeling again? How could he? He was an empty shell. Just what was the point of living if the only good thing in your life had been stripped away in an instant? Lingana had been a good churchgoer before the 'gades pillaged her village and killed her father. That still didn't stop her faith. Hell, he was even willing to join her at church when they settled down. Not now. Wasn't God supposed to be loving? Forgiving? So, what kind of God kills a sweet girl like Lingana and destroys all of his own hopes?

"Hey, Jaym," said Reya. "You see the sunrise? Gold and every kind of red possible."

Yeah, he thought, *Red. Blood red.* Jaym just nodded and avoided her eyes.

Reya squeezed his shoulder. "Come on, Jaymo. Xian says he wants to carry out his promise to you."

Jaym looked up, puzzled.

"To kill 'gades," she said.

"Is this a game he's playing? Like 'Shoot-a-'gade' and win a stuffed giraffe? Tell him to take his carnival act and shove it."

Reya knelt beside him and laid her hand on his knee. "I know you're going through hell, but you're strong, Jaym."

He shook his head. "I'm empty." His voice cracked. "There's nothing left."

She stood and held out her hand. "Xian's not bullshitting you. Come on, I'll show you."

He took her hand, stood, and followed her to the edge of the village. Xian and a few others were huddled outside the community house. The rising sun cast their shadows halfway across the village square.

"Mister Jaym," said Xian. He sat cross-legged with the others standing around him—Giambo, Azibo, Kwada, Maykego, and D'Shay. "I glad you come, Jaym. You ready to kill 'gades?"

Jaym glared. "If this is some sort of sick joke—"

"No," said Giambo. "Is not a joke. Xian wants this to be a gift. Thinks it might help a little. So sit with Xian and kill 'gades. Do it for Lingana and me."

Jaym moved next to Xian. "What's the box? Is that the thing we pried out of the wrecked drone?"

"Yes. This a drone guidance mechanism. I make reverse wiring. Here, you hold."

The box was open at one end. Jaym could see a tangle of newly soldered wiring. The box fit easily in both hands. "What's the keypad for?"

"No, no. Do not push keys. I tell you what to push when is time."

Xian looked to Reya. "You check GPS coordinates with 'gade map?"

"Yes. The Post-2 coordinates are the same as on the map. X-163 by Y-370."

"Is that what LED reads to you, Jaym?"

He tilted the box to see the faint readout. "Yes, X-163 and Y-370."

"It is good to double- and triple-check."

Jaym gave Reya a puzzled look. Her face was serious, squinting towards the east with others.

"Are other people watching for them?" asked Xian.

"We have six scouts with binoculars," said Azibo.

Reya squatted next to Jaym and spoke softly. "This is real, Jaym. By now the Post-2 'gades will have figured out what happened last night. They'll know we must have come from Ezondwei. They've surely ordered a drone strike on the Ezondwei."

"Then why hasn't the village been evacuated?"

Azibo overheard them. He shook his head. "My father be a good chief, but believes in old ways. Thinks that prayers and offerings to right gods gonna make drones miss village."

"They wouldn't miss," said D'Shay.

Azibo shrugged. "Chief say it be for gods to decide. Say it be insult to gods to send peoples away. Doesn't wanna get gods angry if we don't trust them."

Yeah, thought Jaym. Wouldn't want to get the gods angry. They might smite some innocents just for the hell of it.

Shouts hollered out from the other side of the village. A runner raced over to Azibo. He pointed to the horizon. "Scouts see drone planes! There be three coming."

Despite the chief's order, Nakhoza and Lingana's sisters were helping the village women herd children into root cellars. Men scrambled to ready rifles and machine guns as they scanned the sky. So, thought Jaym. If Xian's box failed, the drones would at least encounter a hail of bullets and rocket-propelled grenades. As if they could ever knock out a drone.

Jaym stood and finally saw the three drones come into sight. If the box failed, he was glad Lingana wasn't here to see the village blown to pieces.

Nearby D'Shay and Nakhoza held hands and watched the approaching drones. Kwada stood near Reya, but Jaym stood alone with this metal box.

Reya looked to Xian. "When does Jaym trigger that thing?" Her voice was tense.

"Need to be less than klick away."

Reya nodded and began to finger her rosary of berries.

Jaym could now make out the wings of the drones. The deep thrum of the engines grew louder.

"I think about thirty seconds," said Xian. He rechecked the coordinate readout. "Jaym, point antenna at the drones." Jaym could now sense the engine rumble like a vibration in his gut. Jesus, they had to be less than a klick.

Village men raised their weapons.

"Now!" shouted Xian. "Push red switch forward."

Jaym snapped the switch. Nothing changed. The drones did not deviate from their course.

Azibo shouted, "All armed men fire when they be in range!"

But then, with Jaym still pointing the antenna at the

drones, the lead drone slowly began to lift. It banked and turned. The other two did the same.

"Is working!" shouted Xian, jumping up and down like a child.

"I'll be damned," whispered Jaym.

Village men shouted, whistled, and fired their guns at the sky in celebration.

Nakhoza laughed and squeezed D'Shay. Reya grinned, then turned to Kwada and grabbed him in a crushing hug.

Giambo shouted. "Everyone be quiet for moment. Xian trying to say something."

Xian pointed. "Show is not over. Watch the drones."

The three drones were heading south, in the direction of Post-2. "It gonna take maybe a minute more," said Xian.

Everyone waited in silence. First, they saw the missile flashes, then within seconds came the thundering roll of rocket explosions.

"Jaym, I think you put those 'gades in hell now," said Xian.

"But what about the drones?" asked Giambo. "They gonna maybe come again someday?"

Xian smiled. "I also make small program change so drones fly into mountain after firing rockets." He smiled. "Three drones are no more."

Giambo turned to Jaym. "For Lingana, yes?"

"For Lingana." He walked to Xian and gave him back his drone controller. "Sorry I doubted you, Xian." He had to clear his throat. "Thank you."

DEAR JAYM

For everything there is a season,
And a time for every matter under heaven:
A time to be born, and a time to die…
A time to weep, and a time to laugh;
A time to mourn, and a time to dance…

—*Ecclesiastes 3:1–8*

———————

Two days after the rescue and drone destruction, Jaym still walked in a hopeless daze. A black pit had replaced his soul. Maybe he should just wander off into the savannah as far as he could go, lie in a ravine, then use his .45. Poof, the pain and emptiness would be gone. And no mess, no fuss for anyone.

This evening he'd wandered to the outskirts of Ezondwei to sit beside Lingana's grave. The sun was beginning to set and the sky was cast in warm pastels of orange and yellow.

"You should see this, Lingana," he said softly. "Maybe you can. Remember when we used to go out alone and watch sunsets and stay till the stars came out? You taught me how your people used to believe stars were the eyes of your ancestors watching over you."

He reached over to straighten the little wood cross at the

head of her grave. "You can probably read my mind, so you know I have no clue what to do now. You probably wouldn't want me to head out to a ravine like I've been thinking. But, damn. It hurts so much. Blasting the 'gades didn't help bring you back, did it?" He fussed with a tangle of wildflowers someone laid on her grave. "I think I'm gonna have to leave Africa. You probably wouldn't want me to, but—"

Giambo appeared from nowhere. He squatted beside Jaym and laid his hand on the soft earth of Lingana's grave. "What you be thinking, Jay-em?"

"Just sharing the sunset with Lingana. Back in the Corridor we never had sunsets. Just gray and dirty skies during the day, then in the evening it just dimmed till it was dark. Couldn't even see the stars. But here…" Jaym choked. "But here Lingana taught me your stars. Showed me the Southern Cross."

Giambo nodded. "When Lingana killed, part of my inside die."

"Yeah, I feel gutted." Jaym picked up a stone and tossed it at a bush. "I can't stay here any longer. It hurts too much."

"Can't stay in Ezondwei?"

"Not in Ezondwei, not anywhere in Africa. Africa gave me Lingana, a purpose—then it snatched her away. I'll try to catch a freighter back to NorthAm."

"You think Lingana want you to leave?"

"Lingana's gone. What I do or where I go doesn't matter anymore."

Giambo pulled a folded paper from his tee shirt pocket. "This be from Lingana. She made me promise to give to you if she be killed."

Jaym hesitated, then reached for the paper. He tried to say something to Giambo, but words tangled in his throat.

"I have not read it," said Giambo. "I gonna leave now. You read it when you ready."

Jaym's chin trembled as he unfolded the paper. The letter was in pencil, her handwriting small and neat. He fought the urge to rush through the letter, so just stared at the "D" in the "Dear Jaym." He imagined her touching this paper and holding the pencil; weighing her words in the light of a kerosene lantern. It was undated, but he guessed she had written it just before they faced the 'gade attacks.

The midsummer sky was still light enough that he was able to read her words.

He read it three times. Each time he read the penciled words they brought to life the lilt of her sweet voice. He folded the paper and lay on the warm earth to watch the stars. He held the letter to his chest. There, beside Lingana, he drifted in and out of sleep as she spoke to him.

————

The next morning, Jaym opened his eyes and looked up to see Giambo standing beside him. Jaym still clutched Lingana's letter to his chest.

"Morning, Jay-em," said Giambo.

Jaym sat up and folded the letter. He slipped it in his tee shirt pocket. "Morning," he replied. He wiped his mouth and stood.

"You still wanna go back to NorthAm."

"Why should I stay?"

Giambo tapped Jaym's tee-shirt pocket. "You think Lingana want you to leave?"

"I thought you didn't read her letter."

"I did not. But I know my sister. Our hearts beat to same rhythm, so I think I know what she gonna say to you, and what she want for you."

Jaym held up his hands and shook his head. "Giambo, even if it's what Lingana wanted, I just can't. It's too soon."

"There be plenty of time to decide. You think on it, Jay-em. Pray, if that help you." Giambo hesitated. "Come see us this afternoon, 'bout 1600 hours. It just be for a visit. It gonna be cooler then and we be waiting under that oak tree." He nodded to a gnarled oak at the edge of the village. "I think you owe Lingana that much, yes?"

Jaym looked at his feet for a moment then nodded. "Yeah, I do."

———

That afternoon Jaym wandered back toward Ezondwei after a walk in the foothills. He sat on a boulder in the shade of a ravine as he tried to sort out his jumbled emotions. Yeah, in his gut he just wanted to run—to get out of Africa and head home. If he couldn't make it to the Corridor, he'd settle for one of the other Sectors. But some part of him fought to stay. He remembered Annja saying how he and all the Blenders were Africans now. At the time that sounded like bull, but he had given so much of himself to this land. Besides, he had friends here. Reya, D'Shay, Giambo, and many more. Each of them had been through a lot of shit and they hadn't fled Chewena. And they were as close as he'd ever have to sisters and brothers.

Walking back to the village, the cooler air from the mountains drifted down the ravines to wash over Ezondwei. Up ahead, he spotted Lingana's family clustered in the shade of the great oak tree. He took a deep breath and walked toward them.

Mrs. Zingali and her two daughters sat beneath the tree. Giambo stood, his arms crossed, his face sober. Jaym thought how little real contact he'd had with Lingana's mother and sisters. For the most part, they stayed within the tight circle of Chewan women at the New SUN post, and the same here in Ezondwei. He remembered the younger girl, Nabanda. She was about twelve, born just before the Great Flare. In his first days of working in Giambo's quarry, when he'd blistered his hands to bloody ribbons, Nabanda had helped Lingana salve and bandage his hands. But he'd forgotten the name of the older girl— until he read Lingana's letter. Her name was Segela.

Jaym squatted before the family. *"Moni, Amai,"* he said to the mother. Mrs. Lingana nodded, *"Moni, Jay-em."* The girls each said a soft *"Moni,"* their eyes down.

Jaym looked to Giambo. "Please tell your mother I am very sorry for the loss of … her daughter."

"I gonna have Segela translate for you, yes?"

The older girl, Segela, blushed and nodded, but kept her gaze to the ground. As she spoke in Chewan to her mother, Jaym studied Segela's face. So much like Lingana's. High forehead, strong cheekbones, and those same dark, soft eyes. Segela could have passed as Lingana's taller twin. She couldn't be much younger than Lingana; maybe sixteen.

Segela finally looked up at Jaym. "Mother say thank you for your sorrow. She also say, she is sorrowed for your loss."

Jaym nodded. "Did she say more, Segela? I heard the word, *mzungu*."

"Yes, a little more. She say … even though you are a NorthAm mzungu, she think Africa is now in you."

Jaym looked at Segela and wondered if she knew what Lingana wrote in the letter. Yes, he thought, of course she would know. They were sisters, and Segela was probably of age by Chewan standards.

The mother spoke to Giambo, pointing to Jaym, then Segela.

Jaym needed no translation.

MOVING ON

Tsalani bwino.

—*Chewan "goodbye" to the person staying.*

Fikani bwino.

—*Chewan "goodbye" to the person leaving.*

———————

"Come on, Jaym. Please come with us," said Reya. "Just a hike with D'Shay and me."

Jaym was spading one end of the village garden. "Thanks, but I'll pass. I have to finish this patch for Mrs. Zingali's squash seedlings."

Reya put her fists on her hips and glared. "I know how hard it must hurt, but it's been nearly a month. You need to get out of the village, and we three should talk alone."

Jaym shoved the spade into the soil and rubbed his hands on his shorts. "What's the point? You two gonna lecture me on the 'five stages of grief'?"

Reya's mouth tightened. Right now she wanted to slap the shit out of him. "Knock off the sarcasm. You know we wouldn't do that. We just want the three of us to talk before we leave. When we separate, we might not get another chance for a long time."

"Yeah," said Jaym. "Sorry. I'll join you." He picked up his tee shirt and pulled it on. "Where we going?"

"The 'Lions Head.'" She pointed to the plateau a kilometer south. "We'll see if we can absorb some of the magic energy of 'The Great Stone Lion.' Give us powers for our mission."

"Mission," Jaym muttered. "Haven't we given enough?"

"Yeah," said Reya, "but GlobeTran's gotta be stopped before they send 'gades to wipe Enzondwei off the map. They know all our New SUN people are here."

After a steep hike, they sat on the plateau's edge and dangled their legs over the sheer drop. Reya watched cliff swallows swoop and dart after mosquitoes in the warm evening breeze.

"Nice for us three musketeers to get a little time alone," said Reya. "Don't know how much we'll see of each other when we go off to the big city."

D'Shay tossed a pebble and watched it fall out of sight. He looked at Jaym. "If we come back from Wananelu in one piece, what're you gonna do with yourself, Jaymo?"

Jaym shrugged. "Not sure. I was thinking about catching a transport ship back to NorthAm, but now I don't know. Getting out of Africa's not gonna bring Lingana back. Besides, NorthAm is a mess. You guys must know about Lingana's note she wrote to me."

"We do," said Reya. "Even though her sister isn't Lingana, Segela seems like a sweet girl."

"Yeah, she is," said Jaym. "Did I tell you Giambo arranged for us to have a long walk together? We were both so uptight and nervous. I really felt sorry for the poor girl. It was a get-to-know-you sort of 'date,' but she was so quiet, and I couldn't think of a damn thing to say. Finally she started talking about

Lingana. Somewhere along the trail we both started bawling. That kinda broke the ice. Turns out she's really bright and talkative, once you get her going."

"She sounds like a catch," said Reya. "Does she have plans?"

Jaym smiled. "I figured she was content taking care of her mom, and doing whatever Giambo and the rest of the family wanted her to do. But get this; she wants to go to Johannesburg and work at a biotech lab. She says her goal is to help find a genetic fix to reverse the effects of the Chomosome-11 damage. She's been reading a 400-page genetics textbook she salvaged from a library, and has the information down cold. Says she has a 'camera' memory."

"Beautiful, black, and brilliant." said D'Shay. "So marry her when we get back."

Jaym shook his head. "I think she'd only do it because Lingana wanted her to."

"I don't think so, Jaymo," said Reya. "I've seen her watching you."

Jaym looked aside. "Let's talk about you guys. How about you, Reya?"

"Well, once we do our part to get New SUN a solid foothold in the city, I'd like to come back to Ezondwei. It's nice here. You both probably know Kwada's got a crush on me, but I'm too superstitious to commit to anyone right now. As soon as I did, one of us would get killed." She put her hands to her face. "Oh, shit. I'm so sorry Jaym."

"It's okay. Every day I hear things that remind me of her."

"D'Shay," said Reya, "How about you and Nakhoza? Any plans after the mission?"

D'Shay tossed a rock toward a vulture circling below the cliff face. "If we actually succeed in Wananelu, Nakhoza wants to stay and live in the city. I'm a city boy, so that's good by me. Hell, we might even find a place with a flush toilet."

"So, I guess you miss the street gangs and dirty air of city life?" asked Jaym.

"Hey, buddy. The air is so much better in Wananelu than back in the Corridor. And after dealing with 'gades, I think gangs of punk kids are gonna seem pretty tame."

Reya stood up and stretched. "Off your butts, gentlemen. Tonight we feast and make merry, for tomorrow we may—"

"Don't say it!" said D'Shay.

"Okay guys," said Reya, her arms outstretched. "Group hug."

They hugged with their heads against each other's. Reya fiercely clutched Jaym and D'Shay until it was time to let go. She bit her lip to keep from crying. D'Shay turned away and wiped his nose. She saw that even Jaym's eyes had watered up.

Reya made a shaky smile. "Okay," she said, "Let's do it."

THE END

GLOSSARY OF TERMS

Blender: A SUN Colonist assigned to a C-11 African. Mission: to repopulate Africa.

'Gades: Short for **Renegades.** The 'gades arose from the power vacuums created by the Pan-Af Wars. Most 'gade factions are independent groups headed by a warlord. A majority of 'gades are former soldiers and mercenaries who remained in Africa after the wars.

Global Alliance (or, **Alliance**): An alliance of global powers charged with restoring order caused by the chaos following the massive climate changes in the 2030s. The Alliance headquarters is in Geneva, Switzerland.

GlobeTran, Ltd.: An international conglomerate that provides outsourcing of services to governments, armed services, and intelligence agencies. Due to financial shortfalls, the Alliance in 2067 contracted with GlobeTran to take charge of SUN's Blending Program.

New SUN: An underground army of former SUN personnel, Blenders, and Chewan natives fighting to rid the country of 'gades and GlobeTran corruption.

Chromosome-11 Syndrome: A genetic defect caused by exposure to the **Great Solar Flare of 2058.** The continent of Africa took the brunt of the Flare. C-11 presents as sterility within the affected populations. Because it is a recessive trait, a person with C-11 matched with an unaffected person could produce offspring.

Pan-African Wars: A series of violent conflicts between African nations in the 2050s. Outside powers supplied weapons and "advisors" in exchange for diminishing natural resources. The Pan-Af Wars decimated much of Africa.

About the Author

Michael Kinch (Corvallis, Oregon) is a freelance writer and the author of *Warts*, an educational book for middle-grade students. While working as a science librarian at Oregon State University, he taught a workshop in Malawi, Africa, and *The Blending Time*, his debut novel, arose from the experience.